Brute

Brute

Lauren Rose

MIDNIGHT
ATELIER
PRESS

ISBN: 978-0-6457344-3-0 (eBook)

ISBN: 978-0-6457344-2-3 (Paperback)

Book Cover by Kostya at Get Covers

1st edition 2023

Published by Midnight Atelier Press

To my husband, Sean, for being my one true love.
And to anyone who picks up this little book.

The course of true love never did run smooth.
William Shakespeare (MSND 1.1.136.)

Chapter One

T HE PATH FROM HIS cottage was slick with mud but his large, brown boots made light work of the treacherous ground as Narcisse sauntered toward town. It had been pelting down all night, the pitter-patter of rain hitting his tiled roof lulling him to sleep far earlier than most nights. Narcisse had waited all morning at the window, frowning up at the sky until the weather finally settled enough for him to reach for his burgundy hunting jacket and push out into the frigid autumn air. On days like this, he preferred to be bundled up before the fireplace, cleaning his rifle, but he had somewhere he needed to be.

The sky remained gray. The threat of rain never abated, but he frowned up at the dispersing clouds once more as he continued along the muddy path until it evened out into hard cobblestones.

Laughter and bartering replaced the roaring of wind long before the town square came into view. Narcisse's brows lifted as he walked through the streets and was swallowed by the masses. The weather hadn't kept anyone away; everyone seemed content to enjoy the week's end despite the chill that hung in the air.

The noise only intensified as he approached the town square. Each person he passed stopped him in his place, tugging at his jacket or slapping him on the shoulder. They interrupted his mission, all to say their greetings and ask him about his day. Narcisse had the sudden urge to chastise them all, like children, for speaking to him when he did not want to hear their praise. Ever since taking over his father's carpentry business the townspeople had thrown themselves at him. He couldn't help the smirk that played over his lips at how they feared and admired him. As much as he gloated over the attention, he found it amusing that they did everything they could to please him. Like lowly servants groveling at the feet of their leader. Narcisse chuckled.

"You're late." Louis leaned against a pillar; his arms crossed as he waited for him to arrive. "You said noon."

Narcisse cocked a brow at his friend, taking in his damp clothing. "It was pouring, Louis."

Louis gestured to the people milling about. "A little rain never hurt anyone."

Most of the people wore clothes in varying stages of dampness, and the women's hair had come loose, clinging to their faces. Narcisse cringed. "It took me longer than I care to admit to get my hair exactly how I wanted it. I wasn't going to have it ruined the moment I stepped outside."

"You're worse than the women!" Louis' shoulders shook with laughter. "Their hair came out of their plaits and buns hours ago and they care for nothing but the music and shopping."

Narcisse's face fell. "I'm nothing like them. All the women do here is nag and spend money."

Louis flashed his teeth at Narcisse, an evil glint in his eyes. "The hair products speak for themselves," he said, disappearing amongst the shoppers.

Narcisse touched his hair, his fingers coming away black and oily. "I don't use *that* much product," he called, chasing after his friend.

Vendors called out to Narcisse as he passed, but he managed to avoid them all. All except one.

"Narcisse!" A man pushed a shot of mead in front of his face, sloshing the measly contents around haphazardly. "Care for a try? I've sourced new ingredients and it's now the best in town."

He had every intention of turning him down, whatever the quality the vendor claimed it to be, but then he saw her. Her chestnut hair was curled loosely around her shoulders and the little sun that broke through the clouds painted her milky skin with color.

"Yes, I'll try it." Narcisse took the shot from the vendor and tilted his head back; the amber liquid warmed his throat on the way down and pooled heavily in his stomach. "I'll take a bottle."

The vendor barely had a chance to hand him his change before Narcisse snatched the glass decanter and popped the cork. His eyes never left *her* as he tipped his head back and swigged straight from the bottle. Wiping his mouth on the back of his hand, he continued through the crowded streets, once again ignoring anyone else who sought to gain his attention. Most saw the hardness in his eyes and the determination in his stride and were wise enough not to get in his way. But then there were some who were not so wise.

"Narcisse!" He refused to look. "Narcisse, wait."

He growled in annoyance when two women darted in front of him, stopping him in his tracks. One of them had the audacity to place a hand on his bicep, rubbing it nonchalantly.

He plastered the biggest smile he could muster, but cringed inwardly at the way they giggled back. "Ladies," he said, "I don't have time for this." In the time that they had stopped him he had lost sight of her, his towering form no match for the tiny women. "If you'd excuse me."

They didn't budge.

"But, Narcisse, don't you want to hear our joke?"

"What about my dress? Don't you think it's pretty?"

His head ached with how hard he rolled his eyes. Since the moment he was old enough to attract the ladies, he had. He could cause eyelids to flutter and cheeks to color without a single word. He had enjoyed the attention — there was no doubt about that, but today it was an irritating distraction.

"Another time, perhaps." He pushed passed the women, their cries and whines of disappointment dissolving into the wind. Turning back once, he found them standing where he had left them, their faces a mix of annoyance and sadness, as people parted around them.

"Such a terrible life you lead." Louis fell into step beside him once more. "So many girls fall at your feet, and yet you refuse them all."

"Not all," Narcisse's breathing hitched. "*She* doesn't want to know me. . ." *Does she even know I exist?*

Louis paused, tilting his head back as far as it would go to look up at Narcisse. "Who?"

Narcisse ignored the little man, marching on and forcing Louis to jog after him.

The force he used to push through the crowds was unnecessary, shouts and grunts following in his wake. He navigated his way through the town square until he stood where he had last seen her.

"Where is she?" His eyes scanned the crowd.

"*Who?*" Louis repeated.

"The inventor's daughter."

Louis's eyebrows lifted in question. "Why on earth would you want to know where *she* is?"

"Any sane man would want her. . ." Narcisse's voice trailed off as he spotted her waltzing out of the library, a stack of books in her arms. He should have guessed. Narcisse could travel into town every single day and he could find her in the library, her face buried in a book, lost in some far-off world. *It wasn't appropriate for women to read*, he thought. People stared, moving away from her as if she were diseased. Most muttered under their breaths, but some had the nerve to utter their disgust loud enough for her to hear. She ignored them all.

"There she is." His heart fluttered uncontrollably. "That's her."

"Who?" Louis said once more, as if he could think of nothing else to say. His head swiveled around.

"There." Narcisse pointed across the street. "She's the one. She's the girl I'm going to marry."

"*Bluebell*? Really?" Louis' face fell.

Narcisse nodded slowly. He could never understand why her parents had named her Bluebell; such a fanciful name didn't help settle the town's already bad opinion of her. But she was as beautiful as a flower, more so even. He almost thought the name fitting, somehow.

"But she's so strange, and well read. Besides, you don't even know her. Have you even spoken to her before?"

Narcisse bit his lip. "Once or twice." *She was always so distracted when I tried.* "But she's the most beautiful girl in town. So, I must have her."

Louis nodded slowly. "She is quite the beauty. But is beauty the only reason to marry? You don't seek any other quality? *Like sanity.*" His friend whispered the last part under his breath.

"Of course not. I deserve the best, don't I?" Louis didn't answer him. "And no one in town is as perfect as her."

"But. . ."

"I *must* have her."' Narcisse grabbed his friend by the scruff of his shirt and pushed him aside. He straightened the collar of his hunting jacket, then breathed in his hand, testing his breath before trudging up to Bluebell.

The sounds of the busy street melted away. All he could see was her. Bluebell had paused in the library doorway, her eyes flicking over pages of her book, as if she couldn't help herself before she got home. But then she suddenly frowned up at the reforming clouds. Was she fearful that the books would get wet? Narcisse smiled fondly when she lifted her shawl and tucked the books underneath, hugging them against her chest. But that smile faded as he noticed that his were not the only eyes that followed her as she passed. Harsh whispers from passersby only grew with each step she took. The town had noticed long ago that she lived a distracted life, spent mostly helping her father build his strange contraptions or with a book in her hands. Narcisse would be quick to fix this problem when they married. No one would be talking about *his* wife that way. He'd stop the unnecessary reading and have her participate in more womanly duties. *Perhaps the piano forte would be a more appropriate hobby.*

Louis followed close behind Narcisse as he weaved amidst the crowd, his breath loud as he rushed to keep up with his long strides. Narcisse intended to tell his friend to wait for him at the tavern for him, when she stepped in front of him. Bluebell usually walked through the crowd confidently, even with her eyes scanning her book, but today she seemed more distracted than usual. This meant when Narcisse stepped directly into her path, she could do nothing but walk straight into him.

"Oof." She fell back a step and would have ended up sprawled beside her book in the mud if Narcisse hadn't reached out a hand to steady her.

"My apologies." He snatched the book from the ground, opening to a random page and frowning distastefully at what he found. "Romance?"

Narcisse flicked through more pages, taken aback to find she was reading a novel about dark magic and an unrealistic romance, instead of the educational material he had expected her to read.

Bluebell snatched it from him without hesitation, scanning the pages for any damage. "Anything to escape this place," she whispered, almost to herself.

He had shared the same thoughts at one time or another but knew better. Sometimes life came down to dreams and reality, but to succeed in life it was unrealistic to dream. "Why on earth would you need an escape?"

Her lips pursed. "Life here can be great for people who fit in." She gestured at Narcisse. "But for the ones who don't. . ."

She began to walk away, and Narcisse realized belatedly that she meant herself — that she didn't feel like she belonged here. *I can fix that.* All he had to do was marry her and her life would become far easier.

"Have you thought about doing something other than reading?"

She paused, looking at Narcisse over her shoulder. "Like what?"

"I don't know. But reasonable women don't read. Men don't like when women have their own ideas. Books give them thoughts and feelings that aren't becoming."

"And what thoughts and feelings should a woman have then, hm?" She held her novels in a white knuckled grip with one hand, the other coming to rest on her hip in defiance.

"Well, for one, pleasing her husband—"

"Pleasing her husband?" Bluebell interrupted, shaking her head in disbelief. The clouds overhead darkened, seeming to deepen the color of her pale blue dress to midnight blue. "A woman's role isn't to please her husband, Narcisse. She has just as much a right as a man to enjoy her life and do as she pleases, *without* the ridicule of others!"

Narcisse stared at her, unsure of what to say. "I didn't mean that she couldn't do things that pleased her."

Bluebell's eyes bore into his and he ducked his head, rubbing at the back of his neck as she continued. "Yes, women can please their husbands and society by behaving in a particular way. But they can do so while still enjoying their lives. This means they don't have to be confined to the kitchen — they can read or paint or write poetry and still provide for their husband's needs. They're more than a cook, scullery maid or a broodmare." She closed her eyes and sighed heavily as if realizing she was fighting a losing battle, loose strands of hair billowing away from her face. When she opened her eyes, her face softened. "You would do well to learn that," she said, before turning and disappearing into the crowd.

"That went as well as I imagined," Louis snickered.

Narcisse glared down at his chubby friend, balling his fist, but refrained from hitting him like he had done many times before. "I don't know what her problem is."

"You basically told her that she shouldn't read because it gives the wrong impression, and that if she expected to marry, she needed to learn her place." Louis backed away when Narcisse threw his arms up in exasperation.

"Am I wrong to think that?" He stared out at the throng of people, as if he could still see her retreating form. "The whole town thinks her strange; I was merely trying to help her see the bigger picture. If she wants to fit in here and stop being treated so poorly, then she needs to start behaving more like a lady."

"And ladies. . . *don't* read?"

"Certainly not. You should know that." Narcisse recalled the ridicule Louis' mother received for volunteering in the library.

"If I were you, I wouldn't push her."

"And here I thought you were against this. Did you not call her strange yourself earlier?" Narcisse cocked a brow.

"She is strange, but it has nothing to do with books. Some might think a woman refined and intelligent for such a trait." Louis rubbed his little hands together in such a way that Narcisse grimaced.

Narcisse mulled it over while watching the men, women and children scuttling about, shopping, laughing, and gossiping. He tried to imagine them reading around the water fountain together and browsing for books at the small library. He scoffed over the thought. "Not in this small, provincial town."

Thunder roared loudly above them, echoing in the wide streets and everyone stopped what they were doing to gaze up at the sky. A thick blanket of gray clouds had rolled back in as they talked, covering the sun completely.

"I'm going home," Narcisse declared, worried the oil from his hair would start to run down his face.

"What do you plan to do?" Louis ran to keep up with his friend's long strides.

"Eat dinner and enjoy the warmth of the fire before I go to sleep. What do you think?" His words dripped with sarcasm as his headache compounded. Louis glared up at him, puffing as he struggled to keep up. "I didn't mean tonight; I mean about Bluebell. What are your plans to woo and marry her?"

Narcisse had known exactly what Louis meant. He stopped, clapping his friend on the shoulder. "Exactly that. I will use my charm and good looks to woo her. It won't be long and she will want nothing more than to marry me." Narcisse smirked. "Perhaps soon she will be the one chasing me."

"If today is any indication, I don't see *that* going to plan at all."

He wasn't stupid. Narcisse knew that it was wishful thinking. Bluebell was too strong-headed, and after what he said to her earlier, he wasn't sure he could do anything to convince her. Narcisse's stomach roiled at the thought that he wouldn't get his way. How was that even a possibility? *I simply won't allow it.* He turned to Louis, flashing his teeth in a frightfully arrogant grin. "Perhaps it would be more likely if I were to approach Jacques."

"You're going to confront the crazy inventor? What will *that* achieve?"

"I will ask him for his daughter's hand. He'd be an idiot to refuse." *Money is the key to all problems, after all.*

"And if he does refuse?"

"He won't." Narcisse clapped his friend on the arm and stomped back home through the mud.

Tomorrow everything will change.

Chapter Two

NARCISSE AWOKE TO THE sounds of birds outside his window and the kiss of a soft breeze on his face, much different from the roaring winds of the day before. *A good omen*, he thought as he steeped a pot of tea on his stovetop. He needed all the luck he could get today.

He had never felt anxious before, but there was a tightness in his chest that only got worse the closer he got to finishing his tea. His thoughts spiraled in his head. One moment he was picturing his future with Bluebell, and the next he could see Jacques laughing in his face.

"You're being ridiculous." He swallowed the last of his tea in a large gulp, scalding the back of his throat, and then dumped his cup in the kitchen trough. "I'm *Narcisse*, for goodness sake! I'm the most eligible bachelor in this damn town, and there is no way that crazy old man is going to turn me, *Narcisse*, down!" He growled the last part, nodding at his own words.

Without another thought, Narcisse buckled his leather boots, slung his hunting jacket over his shoulders and stomped outside. The streets of their small town were much quieter than they had been the day before, even though the weather was more welcoming. A few people milled about, preparing for the week ahead, but there were no desperate women or men who tried to cling to him as he passed. But that also meant no distractions. As much as he had given himself the pep-talk he needed, he was still anxious. It was another very important day, after all.

Jacques' and Bluebell's cottage was all the way on the other side of town, past most of the residential buildings, up on a large grassy hill. Once upon a time, before Bluebell's mother had passed and Jacques had lost his mind, their cottage used to be large and prosperous. But it had since fallen into disrepair. The wooden stairs creaked ominously as Narcisse took them two at a time, up to their chipped front door. The deck creaked even worse under his booted feet, alerting them of his arrival long before he had the chance to knock.

Jacques cracked the door and stared out at him warily. Surprise flashed on his face before it settled into a practiced indifference. "Narcisse, what can I do for you?"

Narcisse ignored the urge to rub anxiously at his hands. "May I come inside? I would like to speak with you."

"Of course." Jacques swung the door open, stepping aside to allow Narcisse to enter. "I don't see any reason why you would need to speak to me, though."

Narcisse ignored the implied question — *Why are you here* — and walked past Jacques to hang his coat on the rack by the door. Leisurely, as if he belonged there. He had never seen inside, had rarely been to this side of town before, and he couldn't help the slight spark of disgust. It wasn't a tiny home, by any means, but it was dark and dingy, with old, decrepit furniture. It was divided into two halves. One half had the kitchen and living room, with the other half being divided by a door that Narcisse assumed opened into the sleeping quarters. He hadn't known what to expect, but he thought it would be better maintained with a daughter still at home.

Choosing not to comment, Narcisse strolled into the parlor, taking up a seat by the fireplace. He couldn't help but notice the pile of books on the table before him, one still lying open on a dog-eared page. Without thinking he leaned forward and picked up the book, turning it over to admire the cover. It was an older book, made of worn cowhide, stamped with a pattern Narcisse had not seen before. *A family book, perhaps?* He turned it back over, looking at the page that had been open, surprised to see the couplets, stanzas and odes that decorated the page. Narcisse knew very little about poetry, but there was a time that his own father would recite poetry to him and his mother, as they reclined in the parlor after supper.

Jacques joined Narcisse, sitting on the chair across from him.

"My daughter has good taste," he said as he gestured at the book.

Placing the book gently on the table, Narcisse merely replied, "indeed."

"What can I help you with?" Jacques examined him with curiosity, as if Narcisse were one of his wretched inventions, and he could see his inner workings.

Narcisse gave the old man a tight smile. *Where to begin?* Narcisse was suddenly a ball of nerves, struggling to look anything *but* anxious as Jacques looked across at him, his eyes assessing. He had figured this would be simple, but now he found he could not begin to broach the subject. Would it be better to butter up the old man first?

"It has been an age since you have spoken to me. You have never been to my home before." Jacques said, staring off into the distance as if recalling Narcisse's poor behavior.

Narcisse rubbed at the stubble of his jaw, recalling the times he had made fun of the old man, or outright ignored him. "I've been meaning to," he lied. "You have a lovely home. And I've been interested in your inventions." *Don't push it.*

Jacques' lip twitched as if holding back a smirk. "I'm sure you have. But I'm going to assume that you're not here to talk to me about my inventions."

There was no easy way to ask. "I want to marry Bluebell."

Jacques watched Narcisse, his stare harsh and assessing. Narcisse resisted the urge to squirm, keeping silent. He opened his mouth, ready to plead his case, when the old man finally spoke.

"You?" Narcisse flinched. "Why on earth would the *Narcisse* want to marry *my* daughter?" Jacques shook his head in disbelief, his ludicrous mustache rustling with the movement.

Narcisse hesitated. "Why *wouldn't* I want to marry her? She is the most beautiful woman I have ever seen."

"Ah," Jacques nodded slowly. "I see. You wish to marry my precious daughter because she is beautiful. You wish to treat her like an accessory, rather than a woman."

"There are other reasons." *I think.*

"And what are those reasons?"

"She's. . . Bluebell," Narcisse surprised himself. "She intrigues me."

Jacques' brows lifted so high they almost became part of his receding hairline. Narcisse continued. "I'm intrigued by her, and I find myself wanting to know more about her. I want to get to know the real Bluebell." Narcisse glanced at Jacques, smiling wickedly. "There is no other in town who has fascinated me so much. Women throw themselves at me. They beg me to want them. And yet Bluebell is immune to my charms. Now I find myself wanting to be around her more often."

He waited for the old man to question him, to yell, to reproach him for even thinking of his daughter in such a way. Instead, Jacques watched Narcisse, his eyes softening.

"She *is* beautiful, and she has a brilliant mind, like her mother. But she is her own woman, Narcisse." There was no stern reproach in his voice, just a simple statement of facts.

"I know." *And I will change that.*

"She does not like you." Jacques scratched his stubbled cheek. "It wouldn't be right for me to agree to this without her consent."

Narcisse's face fell. His hands clenched where they sat on his thighs. His mind whirled as he thought of a way to argue, to compel the old man.

"I'm sorry, Narcisse, but I just can't—"

Narcisse narrowed his eyes at the foolish man, flashing his teeth in an unsettling grin. The chair scraped against the wooden floor as he stood, stalking to the fireplace, and staring down into the dancing flames. "I have a feeling you won't be able to refuse."

Jacques crossed his arms, as if in challenge. "Are you threatening me?"

"No. In fact, I'm making you an offer."

"A bribe, then?"

"I wouldn't call it a bribe. It's more of an incentive."

Jacques remained silent.

"Tell me, Jacques, have you made enough income from your inventions to support yourself lately? Have you made enough to eat? To feed your daughter and your livestock?"

"That's none of your concern," The old man's eyes narrowed.

"It will be once I marry Bluebell."

"You do *not* have my permission to marry her!"

"Ah, but I *do* have an offer for you. One you won't want to turn down. If you give me permission to marry your daughter, I will ensure you never go hungry. I will pay for your rent and your food for the remainder of our marriage. You can spend the rest of your life working on your inventions. You can travel and sell them and do whatever you wish. Just give me Bluebell."

Narcisse held his breath as the old man's eyes widened, sure he had won. That warm feeling brimming within him, his rising ego, quickly burst as the door slammed open.

"Pardon?!" Bluebell stormed into the room; the door swinging shut behind her. "You are discussing me while I'm not even here? I am no one's to give."

She must have been listening through the door. Wiley girl.

Narcisse pushed out his shoulders and grinned at her. "It is impolite for a woman to interrupt the negotiations of men."

Bluebell's nose wrinkled as she glowered at Narcisse. "You will soon learn that father will let me decide. Father wouldn't wish me to marry such a *brute*."

For a moment he was lost for words, and he shot a distressed glance at Jacques. *Surely I have given him what he wants?*

"BluebellBluebell, dear, it would be best if you took a seat."

"I'm fine where I am," she stood in the middle of the room with her arms crossed defensively against her chest.

"Well, Narcisse, he uh, he has come to ask for your hand."

"I heard." Her head snapped towards Narcisse, her eyes seeming to pierce into his very soul. He gulped.

"I've said yes."

"You have?" Narcisse and Bluebell said in unison.

"How could I refuse? You clearly want what's best for my daughter."

I do? Of course *I do!* Narcisse feigned a cough to cover his smirk. "A wise decision. I can give Bluebell what she needs."

"Don't talk about me as if I'm not here," she snarled, turning to her father and adding, "how could you think this is what is best for me?" She gestured at Narcisse viciously.

"My dear, please try to understand. Narcisse has offered me security and a chance to work on my inventions without disruption. I won't need to worry about where the money for the rent will come from. I won't have the livestock to worry about. And I will not go to bed every night fearful that I won't be able to feed my daughter. I won't have to worry about you starving."

"You offered him *money*?" Bluebell turned on Narcisse, her face twisted with hatred as she flung her arms around.

His smile faded. "It seemed only right to ensure my future wife's father is cared for." He felt himself stumbling over the words, deflating at the look on her face. The contempt she held for him, *because* of him.

She whirled on her father, "Have you taken it?"

"I need it, Bell," Jacques sighed. "I'm really struggling. Since your mother died, creating these machines has given me something to work on. It brings me happiness. It just doesn't bring much of an income." He leaned forward his chair, reaching for his daughter's hands. Her shoulders slumped and she shuffled toward him, letting Jacques take her hands in his. "This town doesn't get that. They don't care for a foolish old man and his happiness. But I need this. Besides you, it's all I have."

Her eyes softened. *Was it sadness or pity she felt for the old coot?* Narcisse wondered. She smiled at her father, but it didn't reach her eyes. "I get it. I do. My books bring me that same happiness. But there must be another way."

Her father released her hands, returning his attention to Narcisse. "I can't accept. Her happiness means more than my own."

Narcisse's face fell as his heart swelled with white-hot anger. They dare reject *him*? "No, father, it's okay. I will do it." Bluebell crossed her arms once more, as if holding herself together. "I. . .I will marry Narcisse. For you, Papa."

"No!" Jacques groaned, putting his face in his hands. "I will find work. I'm sorry I ever considered it."

Bluebell shook her head sadly, turning to face Narcisse. She glowered at Narcisse as he leaned against the fireplace mantle. "I will marry you, if it is true that you will ensure my father is cared for."

The heat in his heart began to fade. The hopeful flutter returned. "He will never go hungry. I can promise you that."

"And," she added, furrowing her brow, "you will provide my father with the materials he needs to continue his work, and you will gift him with a wagon he can use to transport his inventions to and from fairs."

Narcisse regarded her carefully, his eyes narrowing. "You want to negotiate with me?"

"It's only fair, is it not? Given that as a woman, I don't get much of a choice."

Narcisse contemplated her words for a long moment as the small, resolute woman stood her ground. There was a fire to her that he'd never seen. A passion and calculation to her. They both wanted it their way. Narcisse couldn't concede to a woman's demands though. He still needed to *win*.

"Consider it done," he nodded. "But you must agree to marry on Wednesday, no later."

A few days from today meant that she had little time to back out. But that also meant there was barely enough time to plan. Narcisse couldn't risk her changing her mind.

"Fine," she hissed, her ears reddening. "But I get to decide where it is and who is there."

"Fine," he grinned. She was pushing her luck already and he liked the challenge.

"I don't want the town there. They have done nothing but ridicule me, and I do not wish for them to bear witness to our marriage and be given the chance to judge me for marrying *you.*"

Harsh. "Fine," he repeated, resisting the urge to snap back at her. "Where do you wish it to be held, then? If you don't want anyone there?"

"Here," she grinned.

He lifted a brow, glancing about at the dull, rundown cottage.

"Out in the flowering field, by the large oak tree." She clarified, glancing about too as if she had just noticed the clutter and disrepair.

"Where your mother and I were married," Jacques whispered. Narcisse startled — he'd almost forgotten about the old man in their heated discussion.

She nodded at her father and then spoke once more. "I will have Papa as my only guest."

"Only your father? What of the other women?" Bluebell's eyes flashed at his suggestion.

"I don't have any friends. He is all I need."

He nodded slowly. "In that case, I will have one in attendance. Louis, my closest friend will come as my guest, your father will hold witness and the pastor will marry us."

"Perfect." But everything was far from perfect. Bluebell's face was drained of all color, the brown of her eyes dark against her pallor. "If you'll excuse me," she said and then disappeared to the back of the house.

Narcisse watched her retreat and then turned toward the front door.

"What have I done?" Jacques moaned "I am a terrible father."

Narcisse paused before commenting. "On the contrary, you're a good father for giving her a chance at life." He glanced around the neglected cottage once more before shutting the door behind him.

Narcisse had just sat down at his table when a knock interrupted his dinner. He sighed, nostrils flaring. He wasn't surprised when he found Louis at the front door.

"How did it go?" his friend asked, pushing past Narcisse to occupy the newly vacant seat.

Narcisse flashed his teeth in a grin.

Louis' jaw fell. "You're serious?"

Narcisse leaned against the closed door, crossing his arms smugly. "I am to marry Bluebell on Wednesday in a small ceremony at her father's property."

Louis merely stared at him, unable or unwilling to speak.

"I didn't think it would work myself," Narcisse confessed with a wry smile. 'When she interrupted and her father sided with her, I had lost all hope."

"What happened?" Louis sat forward in his seat.

"She couldn't turn down my offer to ensure her father's security with my coin. He turned it down, but she insisted."

"That's. . . surprising."

"I need you to spread the news. Tell them all we're getting married on Wednesday, but none will be in attendance. You'll be there, of course." His ego swelled as he sighed dramatically. "All the poor, broken hearts."

Louis sank further into his chair, splaying his fingers on the table. "They won't like that. The whole town has done nothing but sing your praise, and will no doubt be upset that they escaped your mind."

"They haven't escaped my mind. Tell them there is to be an after-party at the tavern and that I expect everyone there." *Everyone will see that Narcisse has snagged the most beautiful girl in town.*

"Right away." Louis raced out the front door faster than Narcisse had hoped.

The house suddenly felt quiet, and he was left to think about the disasters that could occur on Wednesday. Groaning, he dropped down next to the unlit fire and began shining his rifles.

Chapter Three

NARCISSE HAD NOT EXPECTED to have zero time for himself after becoming engaged. Although he had demanded the wedding happen in a few days, he hadn't expected to plan it all *himself*. Not only was he too busy to get any carpentry work done, but he was also far too busy to see Bluebell, who had no desire to help him plan. *My future wife*. He just hoped she hadn't changed her mind since seeing her last. His heart had begun an incessant uncontrollably loud pounding in his chest since he asked her, and it only seemed to worsen the closer the day came.

Finally, the day had come, and he could do nothing to ease his nerves.

"Smile." Louis pushed Narcisse into a chair at his dining table and rubbed at the knots in his shoulders. "One would think it was the end of the world with the way you've been moping around all morning. You're getting married, Narcisse! To the woman of your dreams, nonetheless! Surely that's cause for happiness."

"You're right." Narcisse shook him off and stood. "Let's go."

With a tight-lipped smile he shrugged on his soft midnight blue hunting jacket and paused at the window to admire his reflection. Narcisse owned hunting jackets and simple shirts, all in varying shades of red, but he had gone to the seamstress and had this jacket made especially for his big day. The seamstress had informed Narcisse that the shade of blue brought out the gold in his eyes. He'd shrugged slightly, instead admiring the way his muscles were defined underneath the tight fabric.

Louis scoffed at the way Narcisse winked at his reflection, shouldering past him and disappearing outside. Narcisse simply grinned, stepping out into the brilliant sunshine and catching up with his friend. Together, they began the short trek to the inventor's house.

Though much shorter than him Louis kept up with his long strides, his friend's breath hitching beside him.

"Ready?"

Narcisse was sure Louis was talking about the ceremony until his eyes found the town square. *Why wasn't there another way there?* He had never seen the streets as busy as they were at this very moment. Narcisse faltered, realizing that nearly the whole town had come out to wish him well, before squaring his shoulders and adding a slight pep to his step.

"No," he ground out through his clenched teeth, nodding at the first group of people who approached him. It seemed he would never get used to such attention.

Each and every villager who had come out followed him, chattering and cheering at his side, only stopping when he reached the gated yard of Bluebell's cottage.

Louis stopped when they were finally out of earshot peering behind them at the crowd that still gathered at the gate. "That was. . .overwhelming," he grimaced.

Narcisse nodded slowly. "It was definitely something." A hard laugh rumbled in his chest, and he clasped his friend's shoulder.

"Narcisse?" Louis cocked a brow, gazing up quizzically at his friend.

"Who would have thought the town were going to be so supportive of a marriage to a woman they criticize so!" Shaking his head, Narcisse marched toward the back of the farm to the large oak that loomed in the distance. Louis jogged after him, puffing between his words.

"It's because they admire you. You could marry a horse and they would celebrate for days."

"Even so! She will become an honored member of society in no time." *No more books. No more libraries. There will be no reason for others to ridicule her. Cooking and cleaning. A wife.*

Pastor Dorian was waiting by the base of the tree when they arrived, his hands clasped loosely before him. "Narcisse," he nodded, his smile not reaching his eyes.

"Pastor Dorian," he nodded in return, ignoring the disapproval on the older man's face. It seemed not *everyone* in this town wanted to kiss Narcisse's boots.

The day was quite warm, without a single cloud in the sky. Minutes passed in awkward silence. Narcisse stood below low-hanging branches, Louis fidgeting at his side. He scanned the space around them, trying in vain to keep his eyes from the house, waiting impatiently for Bluebell and Jacques to emerge. Candlelit lanterns of various colors hung from the branches and wildflowers were scattered along the base of the oak. They stood on a dark cowhide rug, the pastor in front of him with a bible in his hands. It wasn't the extravagant wedding he had hoped for, in the aged church on the other side of the village, but it was elegant besides its simplicity. Despite Bluebell being so against planning, she had insisted that no one touch the tree. He was impressed at what she had done.

He heard the back door click; the sound as intense as a round fired from his rifle. He straightened, stiff as a rod as he clasped his hands behind his back, fighting the urge to wipe his clammy palms on his breeches. With her arm tucked securely in the crook of his elbow, Jacques lead Bluebell from the house in a slow, agonizing walk. Narcisse's heart thundered, echoing loudly in his ears, and drowning out all other noise. He held his breath, counting each step Bluebell took toward him, releasing it only when she stood before him.

"Whoa," Louis whispered beside him.

Whoa, indeed. Narcisse could do nothing but stare. She wore a simple silk gown, soft and white as freshly fallen snow, that flowed over her body like water and pooled at her feet. The detailed lace veil obscured her face and draped down the back of her dress, trailing behind her over the leaf speckled ground.

Perfection. The world around him disappeared, and he could see nothing but the woman who came to a stop before him. The glow of her snow-white gown in the morning sun blinded him to all else, like a pair of glittering angel wings.

Narcisse could do nothing but stare. He gulped as he found her eyes behind the veil.

"Hold hands, if you please." Pastor Dorian's request snapped Narcisse from his reverie.

He held his hands before him, palms up, thankful though surprised when she placed hers in his. Narcisse's breath caught as he felt her soft skin against the calluses on his fingers. Her grip was strong and steady, much more so than Narcisse's. He cringed at the sweat that pooled on his palms but was grateful that Bluebell was either too nervous or polite to react.

Their ceremony was much shorter than most ceremonies, but Narcisse had designed it that way. Although Bluebell was here, although she had agreed to this, there was that small voice in the back of his head that told him she would run. He tightened his hands slightly, as if that would keep her from changing her mind.

He was so lost in thoughts of her leaving that he barely registered her words.

"I do." Her voice was hollow, as if she no longer remained in her body.

Narcisse's heart was loud in his ears when the pastor proclaimed, "I now pronounce you husband and wife—"

He had barely given the man time to finish before Narcisse greedily lifted Bluebell's veil. He had expected to find her glowering at him. Instead, he found her wide-eyed, her mouth open in a soft 'oh' of surprise. Her milky skin was flushed, her breathing labored. He reached out to touch her cheek and she flinched. He smiled at her softly and gave her one small peck on her temple when the pastor deemed it time to kiss his fiery bride.

"That wasn't so bad, was it?" His smile vanished when her eyes turned icy once more and she narrowed them at him.

Bluebell made to leave the moment the ceremony was over, but Narcisse moved in front of her path. "Going somewhere?" he asked.

"I have a headache. I'd like to lie down for a bit." Her words were clipped, her eyes flashing as she watched him, waiting for him to step aside.

"How terrible," Narcisse frowned. "Allow me to have the horse and cart prepared."

Bluebell halted. "Is that not father's cart?"

He had indeed had a newly acquired cart brought to his new father-in-law's home yesterday evening, a part of the deal he had struck with Bluebell.

"It is, but I don't want my *wife* to walk so far when she has a headache. I will return his horse tomorrow."

"And the cart?" Her eyes narrowed.

Narcisse shook his head in wonder. "It is his, after all. And I do have a cart of my own, I don't need two."

Bluebell stalked off toward her father without another word. Narcisse watched her as she threw her arms around Jacques and buried her face in the crook of his neck.

"I don't get women." Louis appeared beside him.

"Does anyone?" Narcisse crossed his arms, the muscles straining against his jacket.

They watched Bluebell in silence, until she stomped back toward them. They both dropped their gaze, neither one wanting to brave the hardness in her eyes.

Bluebell walked right by them, not even pausing to stop when she spoke. "Let's go," she called over her shoulder.

Narcisse didn't move. "The horse is not ready."

Bluebell huffed and spun to face him. "I can walk."

"What of your headache?"

"I'm fine." She continued down the hill, glancing back once to see if he followed.

"Wish me luck," Narcisse muttered to Louis before rushing after his bride.

"Slow down," he called. His long legs struggled to keep up with her persistent gait.

Bluebell tipped her head back, sighing dramatically, as she slowed to match his pace. But then she stopped completely, and he was all but ready to chastise her for playing games with him until he saw *why* she didn't want to go any further. The town's people were still gathered outside the gate, waiting for Narcisse and his new bride to make an appearance. He came forward, leaving Bluebell behind, giving her the time she needed to gather some courage. He stopped before the gate, giving a feral grin to all who had gathered. They cheered loudly, throwing their hands in the air.

"Narcisse! Did she run?" a man called out.

Narcisse glared at the man, and he shrunk back into the crowd. Suddenly the voices died down, leaving a thick silence. Bluebell came from behind the house, sidling up beside Narcisse. The smile she gave them was strained, and it looked as though she would be sick. He grinned triumphantly as he watched her assess the crowd. *She's mine now.*

"Thank you," he yelled over the din. "My wife and I are humbled that you have all gathered here to wish us well." The crowd hooted and cheered once more, their voices ringing out around him. "If you would excuse us, we would like to go home and calm ourselves after such a wonderful ceremony. We will ready ourselves and join you all at the tavern for dinner."

Narcisse could feel his wife seething beside him. He refused to look, refused to acknowledge the fury that simmered in her eyes. Instead, he grabbed Bluebell's hand and said his farewells to the townsfolk, pushing through them toward his cottage. He grimaced as he waited for her to tear her hand away but breathed a sigh of relief when her hand tightened in his. Most people left quickly, running ahead to the tavern, but some followed the couple, chattering away with Narcisse as far as the town center, until finally leaving them to join the others in early celebrations.

When they were finally alone Bluebell released his hand so she could cross her arms. "The tavern?" she hissed.

"Yes. The townies weren't permitted to come to our wedding, so I planned a celebration with them later at the tavern."

She halted but Narcisse continued toward his cottage, not bothering to see if she would follow. After a few moments she ran after him, appearing at his side once more. "The town has snubbed me since I was a girl, why would I want to celebrate anything with them?"

"Nonsense," Narcisse held his front gate open for her. "They didn't snub you; they were just afraid."

"Afraid of *what*? A girl?"

"Your intelligence and independence, I would say. Most women know to obey and follow orders."

"I'm not most women." She glared.

"Oh, I know," Narcisse grinned. "But that may change."

Bluebell bared her teeth in a terrifying grin. "We'll see."

Narcisse paused, watching her, and the way she watched him right back had his heart leaping into his throat. He pulled the rusted iron key from his front pocket, unlocking the heavy front door before he replied. "Is that a challenge?"

Bluebell gave Narcisse no further reply, pushing past him and stopped in the kitchen. She looked around, and Narcisse suddenly felt stripped bare as she scrutinized all that he had. Her eyes wandered from the kitchen to the parlor, where she frowned at the thick wooden pillars that held his roof up and acted as a dividing wall between the two rooms. Her eyes stopped at the unlit fireplace in the parlor.

Finally she spoke, her voice soft, her eyes trained on the hearth. "You find marrying me some sort of challenge?" She didn't move, as if afraid to step any further inside. "How do you plan on "winning" this challenge? Do you plan on changing me, making me into the perfect wife by forcing me to act and behave in a certain way?"

Narcisse shucked off his hunting jacket, hanging it on a hook by the front door. "I don't see anything wrong with helping you better fit into society." He shrugged. "This town is very small-minded and only accepts people who act as they deem fit. Do you not wish to fit in? To find companionship with the other women?"

Bluebell finally turned to face Narcisse, her eyes softer than before. "No, Narcisse, I don't wish to become friends with anyone who doesn't like me the way I am. So what if I like to read, or like to be my own independent human and not follow men around like a lost puppy? I won't change for anyone."

Narcisse narrowed his eyes slightly. *How was he going to rein in his strong-headed wife?* It was going to be a hell of a lot harder than he first thought.

"Will you punish me if I don't conform?" Her words were an angry whisper.

Narcisse blinked slowly, not quite certain how she got *that* idea. In fact, he was even a little offended by her accusation.

"No." His words were clipped. "I witnessed too much of that from my father to ever think of treating a woman like that, let alone my own wife." In the twenty-nine years he had been alive the thought had never even crossed his mind. The way his father had spoken to his mother, belittled her time and time again, was burned into the back of his mind. As a child he would cry at the yelling, at the hollowness in his mother's eyes.

Sure, he got angry often and had the urge to fight other men, often entertaining tavern-goers with the brawls he initiated. But he was far from the brute most thought him to be. He furrowed his brows as he moved her aside and filled a pot with water. He sucked in a deep breath, clearing the weight from his chest.

He looked over his shoulder at his wife. She hadn't moved, hadn't spoken.

"Tea?" he asked gruffly as he lit the stove and placed the pot over the flame.

She inclined her head, sliding into a chair at the table, eyes downcast. She eyed the bowl of apples that sat in the center and then reached for one. "I'm sorry." She breathed on the apple, wiping it on her silk dress before taking a tentative bite. "I didn't . . . I didn't mean to suggest you would hurt me, or any other woman. I was angry. and I spoke without thinking. Please forgive me."

He sat across from her and watched her take another bite, a drop of juice spilling from the apple and dripping down her chin. "You don't need to fear me, or this marriage."

She remained silent as she wiped her hand across her chin, her eyes focused on some spot on the table.

"Give it time," he reached across the table and grabbed her free hand, squeezing it tentatively. "You'll see I'm not the worst husband."

Bluebell finally looked up at Narcisse, her eyes filled with a sadness that had his breath catching painfully in his throat. *Surely I'm not that bad?*

"We'll see," she repeated her earlier statement before releasing his hand and gesturing to the pot of water that was near to boiling over on the stove.

Narcisse could feel her eyes on him as he busied himself with the tea.

He placed a steaming mug in front of her before she finally spoke again. "I'm not going."

He had beside her with his own tea steeping in his hands. "Hmm?" He took a tentative sip, watching her over the rim of the mug.

"To the tavern," she clarified. "I'm not going to the tavern with you."

Narcisse sat his mug on the battered wood table before answering. "Yes, you are."

"No" she crossed her arms, the silk of her dress rustling. "I'm not."

"Why not?" Narcisse's grip on his mug tightened, the scalding heat a calming pressure on his palms.

"I can think of *far* better things than being stuck in a room full of people that do nothing but whisper and call me names behind my back. I'd rather stay here and read by the fire."

Narcisse wrinkled his nose slightly. He was annoyed by her refusal to join him. But could he truly blame her? She was right about them, after all. And forcing her to go with him would only make it more difficult to win her over. "Fair enough," he exhaled through his teeth. "I'll tell them you fell ill from the excitement of today, but thank them for their well wishes."

"They've never wished me well, so why does it matter? Tell them what you wish." He watched as she pursed her lips to blow on the hot tea, before taking a sip.

"I haven't prepared anything for dinner. I had planned for us to eat there."

She lifted a single shoulder. "I'm not hungry."

"You will be in a few hours." Perhaps his first task to win her heart was to bring her back some hot food from the tavern?

"Just light the fire, bring me a blanket and a book, and I'll be happy."

So, he did just that. When he set out for the tavern his new wife was curled up on his favorite chair beside the fire, with a blanket draped over her lap and a book in her hands.

He could hear the music before he reached the steps up to the tavern; the organ and violins filtered through the open windows, followed by the loud voices of his neighbors.

Their voices were a mix of various stages of drunk, and they belted out words to a song he had heard inside this tavern many a time before. The lyrics were almost unintelligible thanks to the hours of drinking they had entertained themselves with before he had arrived. Narcisse pushed through the door, the cacophony simmering to a quiet din as everyone turned to stare at him.

"Narcisse!" the crowd cheered.

He faltered just inside the door, looking around. Then a brilliant smile, one that wasn't forced, spread across his face. So many people had come out to celebrate *his* new marriage, and they cheered further when he continued inside. The room was a buzz with mixed conversation and shouted excitement that grew the further into the room he swaggered. The alcohol had been flowing for some time apparently and each person who approached him slurred as they spoke, the breath that washed over his face reeking of whiskey and gin.

"About time," Louis shouted above the din, gesturing for Narcisse to join him.

He grinned and nodded at each person who stopped him, prying their hands from his coat. "It's been quite eventful," Louis spoke as Narcisse reached his friend's side.

"It didn't take long for them to consume all the alcohol in the tavern." Narcisse arched a thick brow.

"Well, when I told them you were going to pick up the tab, they went a little overboard."

Narcisse paused, crossing his arms over his chest as he stared down at his friend, who sat at their usual table. "You *what?*"

Louis's grin faltered at the anger that no doubt flashed momentarily in Narcisse's eyes, but then the smile returned. "You said you wanted the town to know you were still thinking of them after your wife refused to have them at the ceremony."

Narcisse inwardly applauded the way his friend thought sometimes, but by the way people yelled and swayed and the number of empty tankards strewn all over the tavern he already would have to front a lot of gold. By the time the night was over he was going to have an empty coin pouch.

"I don't like the way you speak about my new wife, Louis. She had every right to refuse their attendance when they've treated her so poorly all these years."

"You said it yourself that they treated her that way because of her strange habit with books—" Louis started, quickly closing his mouth as a dark look crossed Narcisse's handsome face.

"Even so, she *is* my wife, and I will not have anyone criticizing her anymore." *Even if I have done so myself on many occasions. . .*

"If you say so," Louis huffed, lifting a tankard to his mouth and cocking his eyebrows before taking a deep drink. "Thanks for the beer."

Narcisse suddenly felt the need to throttle his friend, but his mouth tugged up and a deep laugh rumbled from his chest before he could stop it. "Enough of this, let's drink and be merry."

As if on cue, the barmaid dropped three large tankards on the table before them with a wink before disappearing into the crowd once more.

"Three?" Narcisse cocked a brow.

"Everyone is basically on the floor already. I'm even starting to feel the effects. You need to catch up, friend."

"Is that a challenge?" Narcisse shrugged his jacket off and draped it across the back of his chair. Louis was given no time to reply as Narcisse lifted two of the large tankards to his lips and tipped his head back. Brown liquid poured from the corners of his mouth and cascaded down his chin, soaking into the collar of his red shirt. The alcohol brought a welcome heat to his chest.

All eyes were on him, the crowd silent as they watched him slam the mugs onto the table with excessive force. It wasn't until he wiped the beer from his face with the back of his hand and gestured to the barmaid for another round that the crowd broke out in raucous cheers,

"Narcisse," one of his many female admirers crooned from behind his chair, her shrill voice causing the hairs on the back of his neck to stand on end. He shifted uncomfortably as she slid her hands up his biceps onto his shoulders. "How impressive," she drawled, rubbing at his bulging muscles.

"Yes, so manly," another woman, who seemed to have materialized out of thin air, gazed at him hungrily, her head as she watched him, her eyes trailing over the dampness the alcohol left on his shirt.

He couldn't help the way the women treated him, but he cringed slightly at their touch, feeling almost guilty that he had left Bluebell at home. "Thank you, ladies."

"We didn't have a chance to congratulate you on your wedding." The elder of the two fluttered her eyelashes. "My sister and I can't help but feel disappointed that the most eligible man in town is no longer single."

Narcisse raised his brows, glancing over them condescendingly. "There are others, I'm sure, who would be glad to have such. . .loyal and abiding wives like you." He smirked.

They giggled and fled, as if the backhanded compliment he had given them was exactly what they wanted to hear.

"Isn't that what you want in a wife?" Louis wiggled his brows at him from across the table. "You want to change Bluebell into exactly that, and yet you make fun of those girls for wanting to be *that*."

Narcisse hesitated. "You're right. That is what I wanted — what I want." *But was it?* He did want a loving and obeying wife, but now that he had married Bluebell — the complete opposite, someone who wouldn't grovel at his boots like all the other women here —he realized he wanted something much more. Someone who would argue with him, chastise him, and refuse to love him because of who he was. He would convince Bluebell to love him for other reasons.

Narcisse shook his head. The alcohol must have gotten to him already, the warmth in his chest spreading throughout his body like the blood in his veins. He looked down at Louis to find his friend flashing his teeth at him like a wild animal. "Whatcha thinking about?" the smaller man crooned.

"Shut up." Narcisse glared at his friend before chugging another beer. "I was thinking about beer and roasted potatoes."

"How many have you had?" Louis laughed. "You've well and truly caught up with the rest of the drunkards to be thinking about roasted potatoes with such longing in your eyes."

Narcisse had lost count of the number of tankards he had drunk; the barmaid had not stopped bringing them to him the moment he walked into the tavern. He could feel it though, his body sinking into the soft fabric of the chair as he lifted his boots to rest on the table.

"I think I'll go soon," he spoke to no one in particular, "at this rate I won't make it home."

"Already?" Louis frowned, "You've barely been here an hour."

It felt longer to Narcisse. His eyes blurring, he looked down at the empty mugs on the table in front of him, spread out like trophies. "I can't keep my new wife waiting now, can I?" he slurred in response.

"You can't leave just yet." Louis whined as he looked around at the people who'd begun to surround the table. "We've all prepared something for you."

Narcisse's brows knitted together, his mind fuzzy from drink as he took in the crowd gathered around him. He pushed up from the chair to make his escape and almost fell into the table.

"Sit down," Louis cooed as he guided him back into the chair. "Please," he added when Narcisse's eyes narrowed.

Narcisse hissed through his teeth but didn't move to leave again.

"Enjoy!" Louis chortled, motioning to the musicians.

The loud, raucous music stopped abruptly, leaving the tavern in a expectant silence. Louis took a step forward from the crowd. "From childhood, you have always been my closest friend, and as we grew older our friendship only became stronger." Narcisse was silent, watching his friend curiously. "And today I was honored to witness the most important day of a man's life."

Speeches. He groaned inwardly. Narcisse hated speeches, particularly if they involved him. As much as he loved the attention, he hated how formal they were. But he couldn't deny Louis his chance in the spotlight.

Then other notable townsfolk joined in. Narcisse watched them as they stepped forward one by one. He had the thought to stop them before they got out of hand, his cheeks heating considerably, but he also couldn't help the sense of satisfaction he felt. They really liked him — to the point that they could have continued with the speeches all night if he had let them. He reveled in the attention, but after Louis moved to take the floor for the third time Narcisse grabbed his friend and pulled him into a quick, firm embrace. The unexpected tenderness he showed was even a surprise to himself, but it did the trick. The speeches trailed off and he was able to rein in his embarrassment.

"Now I must truly go," he frowned at the old wooden clock that hung above the fireplace.

He had been there longer than he intended to, the speeches and the conversation that came thereafter had kept him there for hours. If Bluebell wasn't asleep when he got home, then she wouldn't be far off. His face fell when he realized he hadn't even shown her around his cottage before he left. He was sure she wouldn't be against looking around and going through his things herself, but it seemed like something he should have done.

"Why the long face?" Louis bumped his shoulder.

"I have been married for a day and I'm already a terrible husband," he sighed.

His friend led him through the dispersing crowd. "Don't be so harsh on yourself. Give it some time to sink in before you rule yourself out."

"Wait!" Narcisse's eyes bugged. "I almost forgot." He really was a terrible husband.

"Forgot what?"

"Is the cook here? I need to bring Bluebell home some dinner."

Louis motioned the barmaid over and requested some food be wrapped up for Narcisse. There was nothing in his house besides old stale bread and the apples that sat on his dining table, which meant if Narcisse went back to his wife empty handed, she would be going hungry until tomorrow morning when he could get some eggs and fresh bread.

The barmaid nodded and held out a large bundle. "Mutton and roasted potatoes."

His stomach rumbled as she walked off. He hadn't eaten either. "Hopefully there's enough in here for me," he licked his lips.

"Away with you," Louis pushed Narcisse toward the door and swatted his behind before he shut the door in his face.

Narcisse glared at the closed door as he turned and stumbled down the stairs.

With his mind clouded from alcohol and euphoria from the day, it seemed as if only seconds had gone by when he found himself at the end of town. Looking up from the bottom of the hill his eyes struggled to focus, causing his stomach to roil. The alcohol clawed at the base of his throat. He doubled over, clutching his stomach. He had made a mistake by not eating before he celebrated.

Narcisse grinned at himself as he straightened again and looked at the bundle of food that he still clung to his chest. He had managed to keep a hold of it as the beer he had consumed projected from his mouth and splashed up his boots. He wiped lazily at his mouth and continued trudging toward his home. As he approached the property line, he could see the soft glow of the fire shining through the windows. Was she still awake or had she kept it alight for him? He smiled as he decided it was the latter. *She does think of me.*

But he was disappointed when he almost fell through the door and saw that she was bundled up in the same spot she had been when he left. Narcisse straightened, playing off his stumble as nothing. Her eyes lifted from her book to glare at him. The glow of the fire washed over her face, and he could see nothing but her. Maybe it was the alcohol, but he was once again struck by her beauty. Why had he wasted time at the tavern when this magnificent creature was lying in wait for him?

Narcisse could see that slight disappointment reflected in her eyes when she looked up at him. "You're back early," she pouted.

Narcisse squinted at his towering pendulum clock. "It is after midnight." He rubbed at the back of his neck, realizing just how long he had left his new wife alone.

"So it is," Bluebell frowned. "I must have lost track of time." She proceeded to fold the corner of the page she was reading and placed her book on the arm of the chair.

"I brought food," Narcisse thrust the bundle toward her.

Bluebell unfurled from the armchair like a cat and stretched. "I'm starving."

Narcisse's eyes roamed over her body as she stretched her arms above her head and yawned. She had changed from her dress into a loose-fitting shirt that swam on her petite frame.

"Is that mine?" His brows knitted together.

Bluebell looked down at her attire and blushed slightly. "Yes, I uh, couldn't find any of my night clothes in my trunk."

Narcisse made to move toward her, not even sure of what he would do when he reached her, but instead caught his foot on a fold in the carpet and stumbled into a dining chair.

"I see you had fun." Bluebell stalked up to him and took the bundle of food from his outstretched hand. "Let me."

He remained seated at the table, leaning slightly to the side as the world moved around him. "Is there enough for the both of us?" he asked.

Bluebell turned to face him. "You didn't eat?"

"I forgot to eat."

She watched him for a moment. "Who forgets to eat?"

"Drunk men," Narcisse smiled wryly, shrugging.

Bluebell bit at her lower lip, but Narcisse noticed the amusement that danced in her eyes. She watched him under her soft brows, studying him. "It's still warm," she said when she opened the wrapping.

"I had it prepared just before I left."

"How could someone so drunk remember food on their way out, when he himself couldn't remember to eat?"

"My wife needed food and I delivered," he winked, withholding the fact he had almost forgotten to bring anything back.

Narcisse watched her as she dished up the food. He couldn't help but notice the way she watched him back, sneaking shy glances at him as she poked and peered into cabinets. There was a slight blush on her cheeks, and a sparkle in her eye, as if she enjoyed the attention he couldn't help giving her. But that couldn't be the case, as she still hated him. Surely half a day of marriage and a drunken husband hadn't changed her mind about him just yet.

But she continued to eye him as he ate, shoveling in spoonful after spoonful of warm, thick jus covered mutton. Her bites were slow and tentative, meticulous even. He watched the way she ran her mouth over the silver spoon, the way her throat moved slowly as she swallowed. He couldn't help picturing her mouth on his, and the way she would taste.

But those thoughts were interrupted. Suddenly his stomach lurched, and his hand flew to his mouth. Bluebell's eyes sparkled as he ran from the house. He had eaten too fast and the alcohol he had consumed would not have any part of it.

"Are you okay?" Bluebell's soft voice flitted out through the door he had left ajar.

"Fine," he growled. "Just fine."

"You don't *sound* fine," she called dubiously, her voice closer now.

"If you have had alcohol before then you know I am fine. It is normal." *If you drink too much.*

She was silent. "I've had alcohol before." Suddenly she was beside him, handing him a damp cloth. "But after making this mistake the first time, I learned *my* limits."

Narcisse groaned, accepting the cloth. "And here I was thinking you were too proper."

"Ha!" Her laughter stayed with him as she retreated inside.

Narcisse rubbed his face with the cloth as he stood and followed her inside. "I need to sober up if we are to consummate the marriage."

Bluebell's steps faltered. "Consummate?"

He moved toward her warily, his voice soft, calming, as if approaching a startled deer. "Yes, you know full well that for our marriage to be legally binding it must be consummated, before God will accept it."

She was so quiet, so still, that Narcisse didn't know what to do. "Are you alright?" He placed his hand on her shoulder and she flinched under his touch, as if his skin had seared her.

"No one would know." Her voice was barely a whisper. "If we don't" consummate our marriage, no one has to know."

Narcisse said nothing — what was he to say to someone as innocent as Bluebell? She looked so fearful. What had happened to the strong-willed woman she had been only moments before?

"I suppose you're right." She sounded almost defeated. A soft pink blush spread over her cheeks and down her neck. "It must be done," she nodded as if convincing herself.

He almost felt bad for her, but the tightening in his pants was enough for him to ignore the guilt. His lust overcame his muddled mind and he stalked toward her. "I've wanted this for such a long time it almost doesn't seem real."

Bluebell took a step back with each step Narcisse took, but then the door was behind her, and she had nowhere further to go. Her eyes were wide, her mouth open slightly as he dropped to his knees before her. "Bluebell," he crooned. "My Bluebell." He ran his callused hands up her legs, stopping at her inner thighs when she gasped slightly and pushed into the door behind her back.

"I will be gentle," he rasped, his hands still splayed on her supple thighs.

"Right here?" she questioned, looking around at the living room. "Don't you want to go to the bedroom?"

"Of course!" The room tilted slightly as Narcisse stood, but he ignored sudden nausea that popped back up, instead sweeping Bluebell from her feet, and carrying her into their now shared bedroom.

It was a large room, filled with dark, hardwood furniture that he had made himself. The mirrored vanity he had put in the room for his new wife sat across from the bed he deposited her onto, and he couldn't help the sudden need to flex before it, his muscles bulging as he pulled his shirt over his head.

Narcisse bit his lip as he looked down at Bluebell lying stiff on the bed. "You are a masterpiece," he breathed.

Bluebell said nothing, though her thighs shook as she held them closed. Narcisse crawled clumsily over the bed, only stopping when he held himself over her. She still looked so fearful, so uneasy, so unwilling, and Narcisse didn't know how to approach her, just like a spooked mare. With a swift kiss to the check, he rolled onto the bed beside Bluebell, pulling her to him. Perhaps if she were in control, it would help ease her nerves.

However, the moment his head hit the pillows he succumbed to sleep.

Chapter Four

THERE WERE FEW THINGS in the world that annoyed Narcisse, but as he woke up in the morning to the overly enthusiastic sounds of birds outside his window, he added one more thing to that list.

Blasted birds. He groaned louder than was necessary. His head was pounding more than he had experienced in some time. As he got older, he had learned to control his drinking and usually stopped right before it got too bad, but last night he had had enough alcohol to rival his younger self. He expected to wake up on the couch, like he had so many other times when he had enjoyed himself too much, but waking up on the bed, with the covers over him was not what he was expecting.

It took a lot of effort to pry his eyes open and lift his head, but when he did the night before rushed back at him hard enough to knock him back against the mattress.

Fuck. "Fuck!"

Narcisse mashed his palms against his eyes, trying to work up the courage to roll over and face his wife.

Hopefully she doesn't remember. But Narcisse knew full well she would remember, as he was the one drunk and not her. Thankfully, when he rolled over, he found her side of the bed empty, the sheets icy from the morning chill.

Had I truly fallen asleep right before Bluebell and I. . . Narcisse coughed, fumbling with the covers.

Gulping down the nausea that threatened to unleash itself, he slipped his feet into his slippers and reached foSr his robe. His hand found nothing but air. The hook that his robe hung from was bare.

He flung on the first hunting jacket he could find, the morning air too crisp to go without *something*. With his chest bare, the hunting jacket hanging open, he pushed open the door, only to find his wife fast asleep before the unlit fire. He paused in front of her, smirking slightly at how she was curled like a lump, bundled up on the couch in his maroon robe.

She stirred as if she could sense his presence. She opened a single eye, peering up at him, her face smooshed against the couch cushion. "Narcisse," she rasped, still half asleep.

A sudden urge to fall before her and run his hands over her face overcame him but he swallowed it back. "You slept out here." It wasn't a question, but more of an observation. He couldn't help the disappointment that laced his voice.

"You took up all the bed," she smiled softly.

Narcisse looked away, rubbing at the back of his neck. "About last night. That's never happened to me before."

The robe fell from Bluebell as she sat up and Narcisse stopped short when he saw her bare legs, the way the shirt moved dangerously close to the curves of her backside. He should have looked away, as even a husband should be a gentleman, but he couldn't help himself. He moved to stand by the dining table, admiring his wife's leg from afar.

Bluebell nodded slowly, as if she'd rather forget it happened in the first place. *That makes two of us.* Her cheeks had turned a soft shade of pink, her throat bobbing as she swallowed. It was then that Narcisse decided he would wait until he tried to be intimate with her again, at least until she was ready. But that didn't mean he couldn't continue admiring her legs.

"What's for breakfast?" she asked, narrowing her eyes as he stared.

"What would you like for breakfast?" He couldn't tear his eyes from her.

"What's here?"

Narcisse looked around the kitchen, frowning at the loaf of stale bread. "Not a lot, I'm afraid."

Bluebell rolled her eyes, as if to say "typical."

"'I'll go down to the market later this afternoon and stock up, but until then what about some eggs?"

"I thought you said there was nothing here?"

Narcisse rarely kept food at his house. He hunted for his meat, sometimes bought it from the grocer, but he mostly ate at the tavern. So he did the next best thing. Narcisse went to his closest neighbor and used his charm to persuade them to give up some of their eggs, bread, and cheese. He returned home to find Bluebell exactly where he had left her, but when he revealed his winnings, she jumped up and took charge.

"Here, let me." Bluebell found a mixing bowl by the window, humming as she cracked eggs.

"I was just going to boil them," Narcisse rubbed the back of his neck.

Her hand stilled. "Boiled eggs and cheese?"

"What's wrong with boiled eggs and cheese?" His brows furrowed as she stared at him, exasperated, as if he were a child. Choosing to ignore him, Bluebell gestured at the cheese she had placed on the bench, "cut that up finely."

"What will you be doing with it?"

"What would you expect me to do with it?" With a hand on her hip, she added, "how do you serve cheese with your boiled eggs?"

"I usually just eat it." He pushed the shredded cheese toward her.

Bluebell watched him under her lashes while she mixed in the cheese, but she flashed a crooked smile at him.

Narcisse's brows knitted together. "What's so funny?" He folded his arms across his chest.

"What do you do, bite into it like an apple? No bread, no nothing?"

The corner of his mouth twitched. "I am utterly offended."

"Set the table, please." The eggs sizzled as she poured them into a pan, and she began pushing them around with a fork.

He opened his mouth to argue, not expecting his wife to be so stern with him, but the way she fussed over the food and teased him for his eating habits had him grinning inwardly.

"What are you staring at?" Bluebell barked.

His smile faltered, only to return when she placed her hand on her hip. "A woman has never cooked for me before, save for my mother."

"What? All those women that come and go in your life never once made you breakfast before you kicked them out?"

Narcisse's smile fell completely, his eyes downcast. "The idea you have of me is very wrong."

He wasn't going to deny the attention he received or the fact that he enjoyed it, but did she think that he actually took *advantage* of everyone who pined after him?

But he *did* take advantage of them, didn't he?

"Did I go too far?" she asked, placing the leftover eggs in the middle of the table, and taking the seat beside him.

Dragging his eyes from the eggs, he finally met hers. "The whole town sees me that way. Is it so wrong to wish my own wife to see me differently? To treat me differently?"

She shifted uncomfortably, stabbing at her eggs aimlessly with her fork. "I thought you wanted to be seen that way?"

Narcisse sighed. "I enjoy the town looking up to me. Admiring me." He rubbed the back of his neck again with his free hand. "I'll even admit that their envy is appreciated. But this?" Narcisse gestured between them. "This is different. I didn't marry you so you could treat me as they do."

Bluebell's hand stilled, the fork poised in the air before her mouth. "Didn't you marry me for appearances? 'Because there is no other as beautiful as you?'" she mocked, deepening her voice to mimic Narcisse. Narcisse watched her as she chewed, speaking around a mouthful of egg. "I am nothing but a piece of jewelry to you. Something you can parade around town."

"That's not true." A pang shot through his chest.

"You didn't marry me because of appearances? Of course." She rolled her eyes again.

A lump had begun forming in the back of Narcisse's throat and he had to swallow more than once to dislodge it. "Not at all," he lied.

Bluebell smiled at him, though it never reached her eyes. "If you say so," she said, returning to her eggs.

Narcisse watched her for a moment then frowned down at his own eggs. Of course he had married her for appearances, but did it have to remain that way? He shrugged, digging into his eggs. Only time would tell.

"Perhaps I could show you around?"

"Show me around?" Bluebell finished washing up and then turned toward him. "You left me alone for hours after our wedding. Don't you think I would've taken it upon myself to snoop?"

Narcisse thought as much. He felt slightly bad about dumping her alone at his cabin on their wedding night. "Right." He rubbed at his stubble sheepishly.

Bluebell watched him for a moment before shaking her head. "I didn't leave the couch," she admitted, "you may show me around."

"Let's change that, shall we?" Narcisse spread his arms out before him in a dramatic gesture. "As you are aware, this is the kitchen. I built almost everything in here, besides the oven, of course."

She nodded slowly, her brows lifting as she took in the handcrafted furniture.

"The parlor," he extended his arms out once more, causing Bluebell to snort. "This is where I imagine us growing old together," he smirked. "Our dogs and sons playing and growing in front of the fire."

"Sons?" Bluebell balked.

"Of course!" Narcisse dropped down in front of the fire, stoking the flames. "Our lives will be quite full, with six or seven of them."

"Six or seven *dogs*?" she breathed.

"Sons, woman! We will have six or seven strapping young lads, like me."

"God forbid we have a daughter," she shrilled.

"Don't be silly," he chuckled as he rose to his feet. "We haven't had a female born into our family for generations."

Narcisse pushed past her and opened a door to the left of the room. "This is the spare room, where guests will stay when they visit."

"It'll be a tight squeeze when it's filled with six or seven boys." She stood on her tippy toes to look over his shoulder at the small space.

"I plan on extending the cottage."

Bluebell simply nodded, waiting for Narcisse to continue. He watched her from under his brow, wishing he could see into her brain.

"Let's go for a walk around town," he said, pulling her in the direction of the front door.

Bluebell resisted, but it wasn't long before they were strolling through town. And he wouldn't admit that he did enjoy having her on his arm, just like the beautiful jewel she was.

They spent hours wandering through the streets and enjoying the tame weather, and more importantly enjoying one another's company.

It didn't last long.

Chapter Five

"**E**MELIA!"

The hysterical scream of a woman cut through the market square. Narcisse had been browsing the stalls for grocery items to fill his pantry, his ears pricking at the scream. The coin had only just been dropped into the of a butcher's palm when the scream cut through the hustling crowd. Every single person there paused in their tracks, some even dropping whatever they had in their hands, startled from the distraction.

"Who...?" The butcher's voice was harsh, but he knew just as much as Narcisse did.

But then a woman burst through the throng, her arms flailing in the air as she cried. Her words were almost unintelligible, her distress clearly affecting her sanity.

"What is it?" a man asked, approaching her slowly, as if trying to calm a startled horse.

"Emelia!" She grabbed the man, clenching his shirt in a white-knuckled grip. "My Emelia is missing."

"Oh, dear," Bluebell clutched Narcisse's arm.

"She isn't at home. My daughter has been gone since I woke up yesterday. I thought maybe she was just behaving poorly because of her age, but when I went to bed last night, she was still gone." She released the man just to start wringing her hands, the skin reddening in an instant.

"I know Emelia!" a young man called from behind a group. He pushed his way forward until he was face to face with the girl's mother.

"You do?" she turned her attention to him, reaching out to grab him, just as she had the other man. "Have you seen her" There was true hysteria in her voice now, and Narcisse was sure they would have to call for the lunatic asylum proprietor.

"Oh, I do, as do many of the boys." His eyes were harsh as he shucked her off. "She has thrown herself at everyone I know, begging them to marry her."

The woman gasped at the accusation, shrinking away from him. "She would never."

"I bet she has run off with one of them." The youth snickered, disappearing into the crowd once more.

"She would never," the woman repeated, but her words fell short, staring into nothingness as if she were starting to question her own daughter.

"My husband," someone called from the gathered crowd. "My husband is also missing." An older woman stepped forward, causing the crowd to murmur.

"He went to visit his brother and should have arrived back home days ago." There were dark circles under her eyes as if she had not slept since.

Some of those gathered became restless, hushed whispers and outcries spreading through the masses.

"Perhaps it was he who ran off with the girl." Many voices echoed the accusation, but it didn't sound like anyone truly believed it. Two people in town were missing, and no one knew why.

A young man appeared beside the hysterical mother, his arm going around her shoulder. He leant toward her, muttering something that Narcisse could not make out. He narrowed his eyes as the crowd before escorting her away, his face twisting with concern.

Narcisse could feel the sadness Bluebell felt for those women, for the people they loved. She had been the center of the townspeople's ridicule for such a long time and yet she still held some compassion for those around her.

He smiled softly at his wife, watching the way her eyes scanned the crowd, as if looking for the people who had been lost.

"Let's go home." He placed a gentle hand on the small of her back, steering her away.

The news of the missing people spread as more and more villagers came forward to declare that their family members or friends were also nowhere to be found. More people went missing as more days went by. There had never been a murderer in the town's history before. What other explanation could there be?

They had been married for a week and Narcisse's head ached with worry for his wife, scared to let her out of his sight. And yet he found himself going hunting more and more simply to clear his troubling thoughts.

"What is that?" Bluebell pointed at the trophy he dragged in from his recent hunt.

"It's a trophy."

Bluebell nodded slowly. "Do we have to have them in here?"

"Why not?" he frowned. "I use these in most of my decorating." He motioned at the various antlers, some still attached to the skulls lining his walls.

"It's barbaric."

"And killing simply to eat them isn't?"

She puckered her mouth in thought, the pout transforming her soft lips into something so sensual he ached.

"I hunt deer to put food on the table, and I will have to hunt more often because I'm no longer only fending for myself. When we have children, I will have to hunt even *more*. I am killing them for food, and their antlers would be going to waste. Why not take them and make use of them?" When she remained silent, he continued. "I use them in furniture, too."

The furniture he made for others contained wood and nothing more, unless they paid extra. But the furniture he had crafted for his cottage made use of the antlers and furs he collected with each kill. The couches by the fire had been created with oak and the cushions were upholstered in deer pelt. The candle holders and side tables stood on antler bases.

Bluebell's pout fell as she took notice of each item Narcisse had handcrafted. There was a hint of admiration when her stare moved to his hands. Her throat bobbed, as if she were thinking, *imagine what else those hands could do.* Narcisse coughed at the sudden images that filled his mind, willing a change in subject to distract him from the throbbing in his trousers. He dropped to the couch, draping his legs over the arms of the chair. "What shall we do with the remainder of our day?"

"Will you walk with me?" Bluebell asked. "I would like to explore more of our land."

"You haven't taken it upon yourself to explore any further?"

She shrugged nonchalantly. "I was sulking."

Narcisse couldn't help but smirk at her admission.

He spent the remainder of the morning and long into the afternoon taking Bluebell over the lands that surrounded his home. It wasn't much, but he did own a few acres, which was just enough to keep some horses and some goats. The goats gave him milk, which he sold in between carpentry sales. He rode a few of the horses, while the others helped work the land.

It was almost mid-afternoon when they returned home, and Narcisse left Bluebell at the cottage once more and ventured back into town to meet with Louis.

Louis was his same old charming, yet annoying self, pestering Narcisse for details on the marriage and whether they had intercourse regularly. He didn't have the heart to share that they were yet to consummate their marriage.

Two beers later, and with a plucked duck over one shoulder, and a large loaf of bread, carrots and beets in a sack over the other, he pushed in through the front door of his cabin, expecting to find his wife inside.

Only the house was empty.

Had Bluebell disappeared, like one of the missing villagers? His heart beat rapidly at the thought and he frantically searched the cottage for any sign of trouble.

Narcisse breathed a sigh of relief when he found a delicate, handwritten note. Bluebell had gone to visit her father and assured him that she would return before dinner.

But dinner time came and went.

Dinner had grown cold long ago and the sun had set, yet Narcisse still waited. Bluebell had not returned.

Perhaps she had decided today would be as good a day as any to run away.

Although they had been married for a week, he enjoyed having her around, and he was sure Bluebell had also begun to enjoy his company.

Perhaps he had been wrong to assume that.

He pushed the dishes aside, standing from his chair. If she really didn't want to stay here any longer, then he had no right to drag her back. But what if she had gotten lost along the way? Perhaps she had gotten sidetracked and didn't notice the time? It wouldn't be very husband-like to allow her to walk home alone in the dark.

What if she was wherever all the others had disappeared off to. . .?

He shrugged his hunting jacket on and trudged to the stables to ready a horse.

"Ophie," he greeted his favorite mare. "Sorry to disturb your rest."

Running a quick hand over her nose, he saddled her up and took off toward Jacques'.

Narcisse had an ominous feeling when he arrived at Jacques'. There was no light coming from inside the house and a small older woman was sitting on the porch, cast completely in shadow.

"Thank goodness," she jumped up as he approached, startling his chestnut mare.

"Who are you?" He watched her cautiously as he calmed Ophie. He had seen her around town, and nodded to her each time he came to Jacques' cottage to spy on Bluebell — but he had never spoken to her, never been polite enough to care to ask her name.

"One of Jacques' neighbors." Her voice was withered, her words soft yet gravelly as she spoke. "No need worrying who I am, dear." Her small arm shook as she pointed toward the forest. "She's gone in there."

"Who?"

"Your wife."

Narcisse squinted into the dark thicket of trees. "What on earth are you talking about?"

"Jacques left this morning to take one of his inventions to the fair. Horse came back without him or the cart."

"No," he whispered in horror.

"Bluebell went after him. Took the horse and ran into the woods like lighting."

"No!" Narcisse bellowed, kicking his heels into Ophie's side, and taking off recklessly toward the trees.

Narcisse's heart hammered in his chest as they bolted blindly past trees and bushes. These woods were far from safe during daylight, but at night? The darkness seemed to sap any sort of safety from them, leaving any who entered prey to the wolves and other creatures who called the forest home.

He felt no fear for himself as he tore through the woods, his mind fixed on finding Bluebell alive. He hoped desperately that she was not so far in the woods that he couldn't find her at all. Perhaps she had found her father and they were already on the way back? In his mind's eye he could see the hunting rifles he kept on his dresser– what good they were now? All he had was a small hunting knife he kept strapped to his belt; it would be little use if he had to protect them.

Ophie nickered, pulling against the reigns until they were forced to slow to a trot. Narcisse suddenly noticed the silence that surrounded him. Ophie nickered again and he hushed her, rubbing idle circles on her neck as he listened. His ears pricked at every small noise, until he could hear the screams. They started off small, almost too quiet to hear. The screams became louder and more panicked. Kicking hard at Ophie's sides, they picked up speed, dangerously weaving in and out of trees.

But then the mare stopped abruptly, and he was almost flung over her head. He was skilled enough to stay in the saddle, but only just. She whinnied, pawing at the dirt and backing away. Narcisse tried to calm her, but then he saw them.

Three large, grey wolves faced away from him, hackles raised. Their growls were like thunder in the quiet woods, but they didn't entirely drown out the sound of a soft whimpering.

There, in the harsh darkness, he saw her. She was backed up against a tree, her father cowering beside her.

"Bluebell," he cried.

Her eyes widened as they fell upon him. The wolves noticed his presence about the same time, and they turned toward him, their growls becoming frenzied, thick drool hanging from their maws.

In one swift motion he jumped from Ophie, tied her reins around a low hanging branch and pulled the knife from his belt. He had just prepared his battle stance when they leapt at him. Bluebell's startled screams reached him when the first wolf struck. With no time to defend himself, its teeth sunk into the flesh of his forearm. Narcisse bared his teeth, yelling in pain, but did not allow it to distract him from what was important. *Bluebell — got to save Bluebell.* Rolling on the ground with the beast, he was able to maneuver the knife enough to strike. Tilting it upwards, he slammed it into the side of the wolf's jaw and out through the top of its head. Its small yelp was cut short.

Before he could brace himself for the next attack, the two remaining wolves pounced. With one on his back and the other held back in his outstretched arms, he fought for his life. The one in front of him went down easily; with a quick twist of its head, it fell to the ground in a heap. But the other refused to yield.

Narcisse spun this way and that, trying to gain ground enough to dislodge the frenzied beast. He could feel his skin tearing under sharp claws and teeth, but he had no time to register the pain. He had no choice but to keep fighting, lest he was to succumb to the wolf and in turn leave his wife and father-in-law to its mercy.

In a final push, he threw himself to the ground hard enough to rattle his teeth, taking the wolf by surprise and sending it hurtling over the frozen ground. The beast whined on impact, but leaped back to its feet in an instant, facing off Narcisse once more. Its head was lowered to the ground, its maw dripping with saliva, as if the taste of Narcisse's blood had sent it into a frenzy.

"Come on, then," Narcisse snarled, pushing up into a crouch.

The wolf lowered its head, spittle dripping from its maw. It sprang, hitting Narcisse square in the chest with such force that it pushed him back to the ground. Bluebell's horrified screams seemed to reach him as if she were miles away. Everything ached, and he was sure he was to die. His final memories would be the sounds of his wife's cries. But his chest continued to ache, tightening as he sucked cold air into his lungs, past the heavy form that lay on top of him, unmoving.

"Narcisse!" Bluebell dropped to her knees before him, caring little of the damp ground, nor the blood, as she pushed the dead weight from him.

He squinted past her, where the body of the wolf had landed. He had killed it, and yet had no recollection of how he had done it.

The blood that seeped through his clothing — blood or the wolf's blood, he wasn't quite sure — coated the soft skin of her hands. Her beautiful, pale skin, marred by that horrid color. . . He hated the sight, and yet he couldn't help relaxing into her touch as she splayed her sticky, slick hands over his cheeks, leaning forward until her loose hair blanketed him from the world.

"You're alive," she breathed, a slight hitch catching in her throat.

Narcisse smirked softly, ignoring the slight tug of pain the small movement caused. "Of course I'm alive, a pack of wolves isn't going to stop me."

She shook her head, exasperation clearly written on her face. "You're a mad-man."

"I need to be if I plan on keeping you alive," Narcisse's small laugh turned into a cough, and he doubled over as pain wracked his body.

"Shhh." Bluebell rubbed at the sweat beading his forehead. "Don't move, you're hurt."

"I'm fine," he lied.

"You're covered in blood, you're far from fine."

A smile tugged at Narcisse's lips as he stared up at his wife. "Bluebell. My Bluebell." He blinked up at her, his vision becoming a blur of shadows.

"Bell," she wiped at her eyes.

"Hmmm?"

"Call me Bell." Her amber-colored eyes were the last thing he saw as the shadows swallowed him whole.

Chapter Six

NARCISSE FELL IN AND out of consciousness, the steady pace of Ophie lolling him back into oblivion each time he opened his eyes.

"He's falling." Narcisse's eyes opened long enough to see Jacques steady him. The worried expression Bluebell wore burned into the back of his eyelids.

Time blurred. The world moved around him. One moment he was on the ground, the next he was in his bed. Everything ached. There was a strange pull, tugging at him each time he moved, each time he breathed. He wished for sleep to last forever, only so he could escape the pain that built the closer he got to consciousness.

I cannot stand this pain, please let me sleep until it is gone. . .But Bluebell.

"*Bell.*" His cry came out as an agonized whimper. Narcisse groaned against the explosion of pain as he became aware of the world around him. He awoke to the blinding light of mid-morning. *Bluebell. Where is Bell?*

Narcisse sat up groggily, slumping uselessly against the headboard, the agony growing unbearable. He needed to get up and ensure his wife was alive and well. The last time he had seen her he tried to save her from the clutches of crazed wolves. . .but had he succeeded? Narcisse's mind was foggy, and the ache that filled his body and soul did not help.

Narcisse squinted against the sunshine that filtered in through thick curtains that had been left wide open; curtains he knew all too well. He was home, in his bed, and much like the times he had overindulged himself at the tavern, he had no recollection of how he had gotten there.

"Narcisse." He cracked an eye. His father-in-law stood at the base of the bed, where he had hoped to find his wife, wringing his winter hat in his hands. "I owe you my life."

"You don't owe me anything." Narcisse waited for Bluebell to appear behind Jacques, but the doorway remained empty. "You have already given me enough."

"Bell is in the kitchen preparing your breakfast," Jacques reassured him, as if sensing his disappointment.

Narcisse's brows knitted together. "I don't need breakfast." He ignored the pain, ignored the niggling in the back of his head that told him he needed to rest. His motions were slow as he pushed the blankets back. He gritted his teeth, black stars sparking in his vision when he kicked his legs over the side of the bed. The room swayed as he stood. Narcisse held out an arm to steady himself, which only caused the pain to intensify.

"Nonsense." The old man reluctantly stood back. "You must be exhausted; you need to eat and regain your strength."

Jacques flinched when Narcisse clasped the old man on the shoulder, giving it a reassuring squeeze before he stepped around him to open the bedroom door. "You should sit!" Jacques fretted, racing after him.

"I need to see my wife." Narcisse grunted, making his way toward the clanging that came from the kitchen.

Bluebell scurried from the table to the stove and back again, her face red from the heat of the kitchen.

"Bluebell," Narcisse rasped, taking a step toward her.

She paused long enough to cast Narcisse a condemning look. "You shouldn't be up yet. You need to rest."

He eyed the platters of food she began piling on the table and raised his brows in question.

"Don't look at me like that." She stopped what she was doing, her hands going to her hips. "I planned to come wake you when breakfast was ready."

"I'm okay, Bluebell. Truly"

She watched him suspiciously for some time. "Please call me Bell," she said, and then went back to buttering some crusty bread.

"Bell?" Narcisse tested it.

"Everyone I care for calls me Bell." She looked up at him from under her eyelashes.

All words eluded him. Narcisse stood before the table watching her, his brows furrowing once more. "You care for me?"

Bell ignored his question, wrapping the butter up in cloth and wiping her hands on her apron. She eyed his bandages, now soaked through with blood, before speaking. "Breakfast is ready."

Narcisse gritted his teeth against the pain, lowering himself into the seat before her. "You care for me?" he asked once more.

Bell stared down at her empty plate, unmoving. He was sure she would not answer at all. Clearing her throat, she said, "I didn't think I would. *Ever.* But you're different than what you let on. You're not like how you let the world see. I know our marriage is only young, and that many things may impact how I see you, but there's something there, inside, that has begun to shift." She paused. "It only increased when you saved my life. When you saved papa's life."

"Of course I saved you — saved you both." He glanced between them.

"You put your own life in danger to not only come after us, but to wrestle those wolves." Bell shook her head. "It was incredible."

You're incredible, he thought to himself, saying instead, "I would do it again in a heartbeat."

Bell simply nodded, silent as she dished eggs and sausages onto the plates before them.

"It was reckless for you to go after your father, but I understand why you did it. I would do the same for my parents if they were still alive." He bit into a piece of buttered bread he had layered with cheese. "Please don't do it again, though."

Bell looked up at him, her mouth open to retort.

"Come find me first, and I will help." When Bell said nothing, he added, "I know you like your independence and enjoy doing things for yourself, but there is a point where you have to draw a line. I'm your husband now, which means I'm here for you too. I can help with the hard stuff. I want to help." His eyes were clear, but there was a lump in his throat. "When I came home and found your note, when you didn't come back. . ." He ran his hand through his dark hair, his fingers coming away dirty from the oils he had used the day before. "I thought you had been taken or killed. With all these townspeople going missing, I really didn't know what to think." *If it weren't for that nosey neighbor, I wouldn't have known where to look.*

Jacques watched them eye each other off for some time before he spoke. "He's right, Bell. This was dangerous, and you could have been hurt, or worse. I don't want that happening to you. You are married now, which means you don't have to rely on yourself anymore. You must start relying on each other."

Bell bit at her lip, brows drawn in thought.

Narcisse picked at his plate while he watched her. He was glad Jacques agreed with him. Bell needed to start relying on him, rather than taking on the world alone. She wanted to do things herself, do things her own way, but it didn't mean she couldn't accept his help along the way.

Her shoulders slumped in submission. Narcisse's eyes widened at the gesture, but his heart calmed. "You must realize that I will do whatever it takes to make you happy here. I will take care of y—"

"I don't need to be taken care of," Bell interrupted him with a sigh.

He watched her for a moment, considering his words. "We will take care of each other. That's what a marriage means, is it not? To have someone beside you who will take on the world for you? Take on the world *with* you?"

"To most, no. Marriage means having someone who will take care of them in a different way to what you mean. A man marries so he will always be cooked for, cleaned after. They want a maid and someone to produce an heir, nothing more."

It was true enough. Marriages often began as an arrangement. There was no love, rarely friendship. But there were many an instance where what started as a marriage, grew into something much more. Love could take time to develop, but Narcisse had witnessed it enough to see it was possible. His chest tightened when he recalled his parents, and the love they shared for one another. The smiles exchanged, the laughter, the soft touches. He had longed for that.

But then alcohol took hold of his father, and his love was lost in a sea of whiskey. The smiles turned to growls, the laughter to shouts and cries. His father's anger had shaped him to become the man he was today, the man he so desperately wanted to avoid. Narcisse had longed for the love his parents once shared, but as he grew, he began to resent the world thanks to his father's short temper, and it was when he reached manhood that his thoughts on marriage changed completely. He wished for an accessory, for someone to clean after him and cook, pleasure him and nothing more. He did not believe in love.

And yet...

"For some, maybe," he said. "Not for me."

Bell's mouth twitched, "I'm sure."

"Believe what you will, but I want what my mother and father had," he closed his eyes, choosing not to mention the arguments.

Narcisse jumped at Bell's touch. She had leaned across the table, her hand resting softly atop his. "And what did they have?" she asked.

"Love." The warmth of Bell's hand urged him to continue. "Love. Trust. Security." *Hurt. Anger. But most of all,* love.

Bell nodded, looking at her father. "My parents had the same."

A sadness Narcisse had not seen before marred Jacques' features and it was a prolonged moment before he spoke. "My marriage started much like yours," he motioned between them. "She was intent that I married her only because of her social standing. Which was the case, for the most part. She was the doctor's daughter, and she was beautiful and talented, but she did not even know who I was. I was nothing but the widower's son who had to work in the fields to keep his mother alive." He paused, his eyes far away. "I visited the doctor more than I would like to admit. I wasn't good with machinery, and my body paid for it. That was the first time I saw her. Harriet." He smiled at her name. "She assisted in her father's surgery, and she was there as a wound I had received on my hand was stitched. I was only sixteen at the time, and I had never been sewn back together before. The pain was excruciating, and she was called in to help hold my arm down. She was beautiful, just like Bell." His eyes warmed as he looked at his daughter. "As soon as her hand touched mine, I knew I wanted her. But I didn't have money. Everything I earned in the field went to my mother so she could afford to feed us. I went home that night and that was when I made my first invention. I built a machine that made it easier to harvest, ensuring that the field workers weren't hurt anymore. It sold better than I was expecting, which gave me enough to buy a little house and approach Harriet's father."

Jacques stopped for a moment, taking a tentative sip from his tea only to cringe.

"Let me make you some more papa, you don't need to drink cold tea."

He nodded, waiting for her to replace his tea and fill a mug for Narcisse and herself before he continued.

"Her father had been approached by many who wanted Harriet for their wife, but he had turned them away. I was sure he would do the same for me. He agreed to it. Said that I was the hardest working man he had seen in a while, which meant I would work hard to ensure his daughter was happy and healthy."

"And you married her for her beauty?" Narcisse interrupted.

"Yes," he smiled. "I wanted her because she was beautiful. She knew that, and our marriage started off poorly because of it. But she grew to love me, just as I began to love her. It came to a point where we could not live without one another."

Bell's hands tightened around her mug. "When did you know?"

Jacques rubbed at the stubble coating his chin. "Well, if I recall correctly, it was I who fell for her first. I felt this strange spark every time I was near her. But I wanted her to feel the same." His eyes crinkled as he recalled his past. "Each morning I would go down to the fields and pick her favorite flower, bringing her a fresh posy every day. I did that until she loved me, and every day after that, until the day she died."

"Bluebells," Bell whispered, wiping at the dampness on her cheeks.

Narcisse balked. *She was named after her mother's favorite flower, and yet I had inwardly teased her about her name?* He suddenly felt bad for a whole other reason.

"How long did it take?" Narcisse's voice was low, his brows knitted in thought.

"We realized after Bell was born that we didn't hate one another nearly as much as we initially thought," he chuckled.

"That long?" Bell's eyes dropped down to her hand where it rested once more on Narcisse arm.

"It was worth the wait." Jacques' eyes clouded, and he shook his head.

Narcisse looked at her hand too, his eyes softening as he thought of the possibility that their love could become as strong as Jacques and Harriet's. Or his parents.

When he lifted his eyes to Bell, she was watching him too, her face softening when their eyes met. She squeezed his arm slightly, a reassuring gesture, as if she could see where his thoughts had wandered. But she dropped it all too soon, leaving his skin cold where hers had once rested.

"You are both lucky." Jacques took a sip from his own tea. "I can see the wall between the two of you dropping, brick by brick. You will have what we had in no time."

Jacques and Bell had finished eating long before Narcisse had, but they remained at the table with him while he regained some of the energy he had lost the night before. They talked happily between themselves, the continuous chatter surprisingly comforting while he ate.

Narcisse finished his plate, plus the leftovers that sat in the middle of the table, before he was satisfied enough to sit back, wiping his mouth on the back of his sleeve.

"I couldn't find napkins," Bell frowned, disapproval clear in her voice.

Narcisse dropped his hand. "I don't have any."

"I guessed as much."

Narcisse ignored the accusation, pushing his chair back, and making to stand. And then the injury, the pain, came flooding back. It hit him all at once, like a tidal wave tearing through his body. He doubled over, his arm held across his middle, and grabbed a hold of the table to keep himself from falling to the floor.

"Narcisse!" Bell's chair scraped over the stone. She rushed to Narcisse's side, throwing a supportive arm around him. "You need to be careful."

Narcisse's pleas for them to leave him be came out as startled growls when Jacques and Bell draped his arms over their shoulders and practically dragged him to the couch.

"Let me see." The demand in Bell's voice left him with little room to argue, but his pride pushed him to do so.

He glowered at her. "What, you didn't look while I was unconscious?"

Even the pain and dizziness he felt didn't stop him from noticing the embarrassment that Bell felt at his words, or the blush that crept up her slender neck and over her cheeks.

"I thought it was inappropriate to take off your clothes while you slept," she recoiled.

Narcisse smirked at the look on her face, despite his nausea. "You don't want to see your husband naked?"

Bell's cheeks only heated more when Narcisse waggled his brows at her. He was eager for his wife to demand he take his shirt off, and so he sat there, waiting impatiently for her to begin the assessment of his wounds.

"You need to take your shirt off." Jacques' gruff voice was not what he had in mind.

He frowned inwardly but did not argue. With his teeth gnawing at his lower lip, he reached for the hem of his shirt. Utter agony tore through his body; more pain than he had ever felt, causing black explosions to obscure his vision. He doubled over, his arms going around his waist, as if he could hold himself together, as stars danced behind his closed eyelids.

"Here, let me," Bell leant over him and pulled at his hem. She deftly removed it, pulling his red shirt over his head and tossing it to the floor by his feet.

Her eyes rounded as she stared at his muscular chest. He beamed internally when she looked away, pink creeping up her neck.

Bell examined him as if she had done it before, her fingers deft yet soft as she run them over his skin. "It's not as bad as I thought," she said, her shoulders relaxing slightly. "It's not good, but it's better than it could be."

"Sit forward if you can," Jacques said.

Narcisse gritted his teeth but leaned forward enough for them to inspect his back. He watched Jacques from the corner of his eye.

"There are some puncture wounds from the teeth, and some deep scratches. If we get some water boiled and clean them, they should heal fine."

"You're not a doctor," Narcisse growled. "How do you know?"

Jacques watched him for a moment before he spoke. "I helped at Harriet's family's surgery for many years. I picked up on a few things. It might have been a long time ago, but I remember a great deal."

Bell glared at him, no doubt for speaking to her father like so, but he ignored it and asked, "What about my chest?"

"Your chest hurts more than your back?" Jacques asked.

Narcisse nodded, leaning back into the soft embrace of the couch.

Jacques nodded slowly, bending over and inspecting his chest. "Hmmm," he looked up at him. "The puncture wounds are similar to your back and will heal.

It seems that the pain is coming from the bruising. If I'm not wrong, I would say you have a cracked rib or two."

Great. Narcisse had experienced a broken rib before, and he knew just how long it could take to heal.

"Should we bind them?" Bell asked.

"No, binding them won't do much. All that can be done is to let them heal on their own."

"And what of the pain?" They talked to one another as if he was not there at all.

"There isn't much that can be done about that either." He looked at Narcisse. "Unless. . ."

Bell looked at her father impatiently. "Unless what?"

"There is a salve that can be used for deep pain that your grandfather used to make. He had jars of it at the surgery, but I don't know if Doctor Salvatore continued making it when he took over the practice." Jacques stood, adding. "I'll go to the surgery now to inquire about it."

Neither of them spoke as he rushed from the house. Instead, Bell leaned over Narcisse, her hand over her mouth as she watched him struggle to breathe past the cracked rib.

"Are you okay?" he asked her.

"Me?" Bell frowned at him. "You're the one in immense pain and you are asking if *I'm* okay?"

Narcisse shrugged, the slight movement sending sparks of pain up his body, and then sat forward. He pushed his hands onto his thighs, needing the strength to stand. The pain was just as horrific, but he managed to stand without falling back onto the couch.

"What are you doing?" Bell moved to push him back to the chair but backed up once more as he stood.

"Whiskey," he grunted, holding his middle, and reaching for the whiskey decanter that sat on top of the fireplace mantel.

Bell eyed him as he removed the stopper, placed it to his lips and tipped his head back. The brown liquid burned on its way down, but the warmth that followed was a welcomed feeling. He sat on the arm of the chair and drank half of the bottle before Bell stopped him.

"Don't you think you've had enough?" She snagged the much lighter bottle and replaced it on the mantle.

He bit down on a retort to demand she leave him be. The whiskey had done its job. He was still in immense pain, but as the liquid hit his stomach, the pain went from an insistent throbbing to a dull ache. He swayed on his feet but was thankful for the distraction.

He floated toward Bell, and she made to move out of the way, but he grabbed her hand, stopping her from going any further.

"Bell," he said.

She watched him for a moment before she spoke. "Yes?"

"Oh, nothing. I just wanted to say your name." Red spread across her cheeks and down her neck as he looked at her and repeated her name over and over. "I like the way it sounds."

Jacques returned an hour later, his face flushed from the cold air. "Sorry," he huffed as he shouldered the front door open. "It took some convincing before Doctor Salvatore would allow me to take any of the salve. It seemed the salve my father-in-law used to make is old news. This is apparently a new formula that works even better than its predecessor!"

Only silence greeted Jacques, and he paused halfway through taking his coat off when he saw Bell asleep on a chair by the fire, Narcisse watching her, her chest slowly lifting with each breath.

"She got tired of watching me," Narcisse smiled softly.

"How long has she been asleep?" Jacques hung his coat and moved to warm his hands in front of the fire.

"It didn't take long once I lit the fire."

Jacques' brows lifted. "You lit the fire? What of the pain?"

"The whiskey helped."

Jacques eyed the almost empty decanter. "You will have to wait until tomorrow to use the salve," he said.

Narcisse didn't seem fazed, but he asked "why?"

"Doctor Salvatore said it should not be used in conjunction with alcohol or any other health remedies."

Strange, as it is just a salve. Narcisse gave a slight nod. "That is justified coming from a doctor."

"Rightly so," Jacques nodded. "I must be going," he reached for the coat he had only just hung up.

"So soon?" Bell walked toward the door with her father.

"I have some invention that aren't going to finished themselves."

His father-in-law didn't waste another minute. He faced his sleeping daughter, such love radiating in the soft way he watched her sleep. Then with a swift kiss to her cheek and a nod of his head, he was gone once more.

The bottle of slave had been placed on the fireplace mantle beside the whiskey and he stared at it in curiosity. What was in it that meant he couldn't use it once he had consumed alcohol?

Bell's soft groans drew his attention. He watched her as she awoke, her body straining against her clothing while she stretched.

Her cheeks seemed to color when she noticed his eyes on her. "Hi," she whispered, rubbing at her eyes.

"Hello, beautiful."

She held her bottom lip betwixt her teeth, unable to hide her pleasure at his words. His head swam at the way she looked at him from under her lashes, her stare so innocent it took his breath away. Keeping his hands off of her as he healed was going to be harder than he thought.

Chapter Seven

ACH MORNING AND RIGHT before bed Bell rubbed the salve into Narcisse's ribs. A slight tingle warmed his skin after each use, until the salve wore off at the end of the day, although the pain was improving immensely. But the more he used it, the stranger he felt. Some nights it felt as though he was going to sleep drunk. When he laid in bed his head swam as though he was floating through the sky.

More often than not, it was enough distraction to forget about the beautiful woman who slept beside him. They were yet to consummate their marriage, but each time his head hit his pillow, the hope diminished, and he would tumble away into a dreamless sleep.

"How are you feeling?" Bell was stretched out on the lounge, a book resting on her knees.

"Fantastic." He rotated his shoulders, feeling for the pull, for the jolt of pain that had him holding his breath, but it never came. "I feel nothing."

Bell watched him skeptically before she stood. She approached him and lifted his shirt. "Strange." Her cold hands trailed up his back. "The teeth marks are completely healed."

Narcisse watched her fuss over him, a smirk building as she kneaded his ribs like she would bread dough.

"Are you sure?"

"The bruising has gone, and the puncture wounds are nothing but scars."

He groaned inwardly when she dropped her hands, his skin now cold and bare.

"Impossible."

"Apparently not."

Narcisse reached for the jar of salve that sat on the coffee table, Bell having the same idea. Their hands met mid-air, her soft skin skimming over his callouses. Narcisse dropped his hand first, thrusting it into his pocket, and watched Bell bring the jar to her nose. She gave a tentative sniff, her brows knitting together.

"What is it?" Narcisse leaned over Bell's hand to sniff its contents.

She looked up at him. "Nothing."

"What do you mean?"

"It smells like any normal salve, but your injuries shouldn't have healed that fast."

"Isn't it a good thing?"

She scooped out a small amount of the salve, rubbing it between her thumb and forefinger. "I suppose."

Her words hung in the air between them. Narcisse shrugged; he had no reason to complain about his miraculous healing. "I may as well start working."

"Already?" Bell clutched the jar to her chest, worry creasing her forehead.

"I have some work I need to get done."

In fact, he had a hell of a lot of work to catch up on. Jacques and Bell had taken care of the farm animals, but he couldn't rely on them to complete his woodwork.

Sweat coated Narcisse from head to toe. He rubbed the back of his hand across his brow. He was exhausted. The sun had slowly begun to make its way toward the treetops when he stopped long enough to admire his work. It was turning out better than he hoped, and he couldn't wait to show his wife. He had said he was coming out here to work, and he was, but not for something anyone had commissioned. He was making something for Bell. A surprise he was sure would make her feel more at home. *Anything to make her feel like she belonged here, with me.*

He had spent most of the day carving and polishing pieces that he was yet to assemble. One by one he carried the large slabs of wood inside, calling out to Bell as he got to the door. She held the door wide for him, watching him curiously.

"What are you doing?" Bell asked.

"Building."

She glared at him. "I can see that. *What* are you building?"

"It's a surprise. Can you hold this up?"

Bell hesitated, reaching out for the wood that Narcisse had held against the wall in the parlor. Her delicate hands ensured it stayed in place while he hammered in the nails. He had her help for both sides, before asking her to prepare dinner while he finished up.

Dragging the coffee table across the floor, he stood atop it, hammering the remaining pieces of mahogany in place. With his hands on his hips, he stood back to admire his handiwork.

"Bell," he called.

"Yes?" She stayed in the kitchen, humming to the sounds of clanging pots.

"Would you come here, please?"

Narcisse could hear her muttering under her breath the closer she got to the living room. "If you want dinner done any time soon maybe you could stop working for a while and come he—" Her words trailed off when she rounded the corner. "What is that?" she whispered.

"A wedding gift." Narcisse stood to the side, giving her a better view.

"A gift? For me?"

"Yes, I thought it would make you feel more at home. That it would make you feel like you belonged here with me, if you had something here that was just yours. Somewhere where you could put your books."

Narcisse had built her a bookcase. Built right into the side wall of the parlor, from floor to ceiling. Bell's gulp was audible. "But you don't like women reading?"

Narcisse shrugged. "I like what makes my wife happy."

"I don't have enough books to fill it."

"I still need to make a step ladder so you can reach the upper shelves. Until I get that done you can use the lower shelves." He watched her move closer to the bookcase with slow and deliberate steps, inspecting each shelf. "I intend to make you a reading chair to sit here," he pointed at the blank wall by the shelf. "Then you'll have your own reading corner."

Bell turned to him. Narcisse hesitated, his words failing him. Tears trailed down her cheeks and fell onto the neck of her dress. "Thank you," she whispered. Narcisse could not have prepared himself as she threw herself into his arms. "Thank you so much."

"You're welco—" her lips mashed into his, swallowing his words.

With a hand fisted in his hair she kissed him deeply. Holding Bell against his body, he relaxed into the kiss. When she pulled away her cheeks were flushed. Bell made to step back, but Narcisse kept his hands firm on her hips, keeping her in arms reach.

There was a question in his eyes —one that he thought she would not answer. But she nodded at him, her mouth open as her breathing intensified. "After dinner," she said.

Narcisse didn't try to hide the strain in his trousers as she returned to the kitchen.

If I'd known that was the response I'd get, I would have made it sooner.

Dinner was nice. Bell had roasted a chicken and some potatoes and beans, and they ate in a weighted silence. Narcisse wondered if the pink that remained on Bell's cheeks and spread down her neck meant that she was as eager as he was. Only they knew they were yet to consummate the marriage, but they had been married for almost a month, and Narcisse had begun to lose hope. If others were to find out, would they be forced to separate?

Tonight was the night it would all change. He could feel his body responding to the thought of Bell's naked body under him and he coughed to try and hide his erratic breathing.

He stood and cleared the table, placing all the dirty dishes in the wash trough. When he turned back Bell was already at the bedroom door. She leaned on the doorframe, her hand reaching for the tie at the back of her dress.

Narcisse watched her from under his brow, his heart thumping as he prowled toward her in slow, deliberate steps. His chin lowered in feral delight at the way her breathing hitched.

Bell backed through the door, her eyes wide, innocent. She was afraid, but there was lust reflected in her eyes. Lust for him that caused his cock to harden instantly.

He slowed his steps when she sunk to the mattress. Her hands went to her thighs, her eyes dropping to the floor.

"Are you okay?"

Bell nodded, her eyes still not meeting his.

Narcisse could have kicked himself for his next words, but it felt the right thing to ask at the time. "Are you sure you want to do this?"

She nodded once more. "I do." She reached out for his arm, holding it in some sort of reassuring embrace. "I've never done this before." Her voice was barely a whisper.

Narcisse had guessed as much. Any respectable woman who expected to marry saved themselves for their husband. "I know," he gently pulled her hands from his arm as he stood to remove his shirt.

He could see the way her throat bobbed, her eyes cast down at her hands.

"I'll go slow," Narcisse said, "if you want to stop, we stop."

"You would do that?" Her eyes lifted to his.

"Of course. If you don't want to do something, I'm not going to force you. I want you to love me, not loath me."

Bell nodded slowly, as if thinking, then pushed back on the bed until she was lying with her head on the pillow.

"You want to stop?" he froze.

"What, no! We've just started."

He smirked at the way she lay on the bed, with her shoes and dress still on. She had undone the ties on the back, but they remained under her. His hands shook as he kicked off his boots and unbuttoned his breeches. Her eyes remained on his as his breeches pooled at his feet and he was left standing in his undergarments. Narcisse was sure he had never blushed before, but he felt his cheeks heat as her eyes scanned the length of his body. They paused on his undergarments as his hands worked on the drawstring and pushed them down.

Her eyes narrowed as she took him in. If it weren't for the fact that she had never seen a naked man before he would have felt embarrassed by the way she scrutinized him. With nothing but the dark scattering of body hair covering him, he walked around the room and blew out each candle until there was only one left. The single candle let out a soft glow that illuminated Bell's perfect, milky skin. She fidgeted, bringing her arms up to cover herself, although she was still fully dressed.

His mouth twitched up at one side, amused by the way she squirmed. With a glimmer of lust in his eyes, he stalked toward her.

Narcisse stood at the end of the bed, his hands on his hips. "I can't remove your clothing with your arms wrapped so tightly across your body," he murmured.

Bell's throat bobbed, but she lowered her arms and watched him from under her lashes.

He'd expected to find fear in her eyes as he lowered himself beside her and placed his hand on her thigh. Instead, her breathing seemed to speed up, her mouth opening in anticipation. His cock reacted to the way her nipples peaked against the soft fabric of her dress.

"Are you ready?" he asked, more so to himself than to Bell.

A slight nod from his wife was all he needed. Narcisse's heart beat loud in his ears as he gripped the sleeves of her dress and pulled. There was no resistance, the dress heaping by the bed. He was gentle, slow, deliberate, as he untied her shoes, the straps of her undergarments, and removed them, tossing them to the side with the others. He eyed his wife. *His* wife. She was utter perfection. Bell raised her arms to cover her nakedness, but Narcisse stopped her with a hand on her wrist.

"Don't cover yourself around me," he begged, voice cracking as his eyes trailed over her milky white skin. She hesitated, but dropped her arms to her sides. Narcisse's hands shook as he ran them over her thick thighs until they rested on her hips. The small indents at the top of her hips seemed the perfect fit for his hands, as if she had been made for him.

"Beautiful," he breathed.

Bell's blush spread down her neck, and Narcisse couldn't help the groan that escaped him as his cock twitched in excitement. Her stomach quivered slightly as he brushed his fingers across her sensitive skin, keeping one firmly on left her hip. He trailed them up her torso until his fingers rested beside her breast, his thumb flicking up to lay across her nipple. Bell's breathing sharpened at the touch, her back arching slightly.

"Better than I imagined."

"You've thought of me naked?" She bit her lip. *Oh, sweet, naïve Bell.*

"Often," he purred. It was no lie that he had lain in bed late at night, Bell's face in his mind as he pumped himself into his hand, pretending that it was hers instead of his.

Bell's eyes shouldered as she placed her hand over his and lifted it until it was fully encasing her breast. Narcisse moved forward, stretching his body over hers. He held himself above her on his elbow, every inch of his skin touching hers. The heat of Bell's body spread over his and he lowered himself enough to press his lips to hers. He started slowly; testing, tasting, teasing. Her lips felt like silk, and they parted on a soft moan as he ran his hand up the inside of her thigh, until his palm rested at the very apex.

Her breath washed over his face, his lips hovering above her as he watched her eyes glaze slightly. He was ready for her, yearned to feel her wrapped around him, but he urged himself to go slow. He wanted to explore her, discover what would pleasure her, what would make her scream his name into the darkness of the night.

His fingers ran over her delicate folds and his mouth opened as he watched her eyes go wide. He had heard stories at the tavern about how to make a woman feel the same pleasures a man felt during intercourse, but he had never put them to use. Narcisse definitely wasn't a virgin, especially when he had so many women throwing themselves at his feet. But he had never taken it upon himself to make sure they felt at ease or were pleasured just as they had pleasured him.

This was different. Bell was different. His cock strained against Bell's leg, and he ground his hips against hers as he slid his fingers along her dampness. She was ready for him, practically begging for him. His eyes bore into hers as he searched for that spot he had so eagerly listened about. He knew when he found it, as her hips jerked upward of their own accord, her breath hitching.

"What. . ." The way she looked at him then had him panting for air.

She hadn't explored her own body, as he had expected. He almost came simply at the knowledge that he was truly the first who would bring her this pleasure. The first and last.

"Shhh," he nuzzled his nose into her neck as he brushed his finger back and forth over that sweet spot.

Her hips bucked once more and he stretched his leg over hers to keep her in place, his cock pressed up against her thigh. Narcisse felt clumsy, but persisted as her hard breathing turned into moans. He could feel her muscles tense as he continued, his fingers moving faster, aided by the wetness that continued to build.

Bell's hand shot out and grabbed a hold of his arm, her fingers vices as she held him. Narcisse panted in her ear, his fingers slowing to a leisurely pace. She groaned in protest, her hips pumping in time with his movements.

"That's it," he breathed. "Let yourself go for me."

When her legs began to quiver, shaking uncontrollably, he quickened the pace once more. Her nails dug into his arm and her moan was surely loud enough to alert neighbors as her hips bucked and her eyes rolled into the back of her head.

Bell thrashed beneath him, and he held her down as he continued to work her. "Oh, God," she cried.

Her legs spasmed around his arms and he could feel her contract once, twice, thrice, and she moved away from his touch. He moved his fingers over her once more, eliciting one final moan, before he moved his hand to rest on her thigh.

"How are you feeling?" Narcisse placed a single kiss on her lower stomach.

"What — what was that?" Bell's chest rose and fell at a rapid pace.

"Unrestrained pleasure," he chuckled. "Did you like it?"

Bell watched him from under her lashes, but nodded softly, shyly. "It was intense."

"Indeed." He sat up enough to look down at Bell, reeling at her flushed skin. "Are you ready?"

Bell remained silent, watching him, her lips held between her teeth. She said nothing, nodding and motioning him to her. Narcisse hovered over her, looking down at the anticipation in her eyes. He could feel her stomach muscles tense, his cock poised at her entrance.

"Relax," he said, more so to himself.

"Will it hurt?" she whispered.

Narcisse paused, but nodded when he saw no fear in her eyes. "I believe it will. But I'll be gentle."

Narcisse thought that surely someone would have educated her in this, but then silently chastised himself when he remembered that her mother had died. He lowered himself slowly, moving his hips forward slightly so that he could glide through the dampness that waited for him. He hissed through his teeth as he pushed inside her opening. Her groan matched his, although hers was for an entirely different reason. Her slick warmth encased him inch by inch, and he kept pushing, slowly, steady, until he was sheathed to the hilt.

Bell shook beneath him, her eyes wide, filled with unshed tears. He paused, feeling her tense around him. "I can stop."

"Please don't," she rasped, holding his shoulders.

Narcisse sighed in relief, because he wasn't sure what would happen to his body if he had to stop. His pulse was a flutter under his skin, his breathing erratic. He held himself above Bell, still buried deep. He didn't move, waiting for her breathing to return to normal before he pulled himself out again. Narcisse slid out to the tip, and then eased himself back in. He continued like this until her muscles relaxed slightly and her eyes opened once more. They locked onto his, Bell's mouth open as he began to pump faster.

He could feel that addictive sensation building deep inside him, could feel his balls tightening, but he refused to cum so soon. What first impression would he give off if he lost control so soon? Bell slung her arms around his neck, pulling him closer, deeper. His breath was a rasp, washing over her skin as he leaned into her, pumping harder.

"Fuck," he groaned into her mouth as she pushed her tongue against his.

His groans of pleasure goaded Bell. She mashed her hips into his, moving along to his thrusts. She met his thrusts with her own, their hips slapping one another in a delicious sound. Their movements were frantic, erratic. Narcisse lost control.

He fisted his hand in her hair, groaning into her neck. She bucked up to meet him just as pure ecstasy exploded inside his core. He felt it building from the moment he started touching her, but this feeling of utter pleasure was so new to him that his eyes lost focus and he roared. So intense, so unbridled, that he felt it deep in his very bones, felt his cock twitch and pulsate inside her. Felt himself spurt against her walls. She milked him for all he had, leaving him a panting mess as he collapsed on top of her.

"Wow," he murmured more to himself.

Narcisse had lost himself in countless women over his short adult life, and yet there was something that felt different about fucking his wife, rather than some random woman. It may have been that it had been weeks since he found such pleasure, or was it that after longing for Bell for so long, he had finally been able to fuck her?

Narcisse leaned forward, planting a single, soft kiss to his wife's sweaty brow, rolling onto his back on the bed. It was a strange feeling —fucking someone, and not kicking them out the moment it was done, like he had done so many times before. He put his arm around her shoulders and pulled her against him.

She laid her head on his chest, brushing her fingers through his thick scattering of chest hair, the strands slick with sweat. "That was. . .different than I expected."

"Hmm?" It was different than he'd expected, too. Better. Narcisse hadn't actually expected anything, especially to marry Bell in the first place and then to lay with her. If anything, he'd expected her to refuse. To laugh in his face and marry someone more fitting instead.

"I don't know. . ." She sat up slightly, her eyes meeting his. "I guess I wasn't expecting to feel. . . *that*." Her cheeks colored.

He grinned at her. "I guess most women don't know what to expect," he confessed. "They don't know they can. It's pleasurable for men, everyone knows that, but for most women it's simply a way to conceive."

Bell nodded in agreement, laying her head back on his chest.

He shrugged nonchalantly, lifting her head slightly with the movement. "There are books about them, ones not found in the main chamber of the library." He stared up at the darkened ceiling. "I must admit I heard of it talked about by drunken men at the tavern more than once. But to be honest, I had no idea what I was doing."

Bell giggled softly, her warm breath parting his chest hairs. "You and me both."

Narcisse smiled down at her, her lips pulling up in return. "It'll be a learning curve for both of us. Something to experience together."

"Not straight away, I hope." There was a tinge of amusement in her voice. "I'm a bit sore," she grimaced.

"I can wait," he smirked, grabbing a strand of Bell's hair and wrapping it lazily around his finger.

He hummed to himself, content in his marriage. He had snagged the most beautiful girl in town, and he had finally fucked her. Soon he would mold her into the wife society would approve of. He smiled, truly content.

Bell's breathing evened out, her hand limp on his stomach and mouth parted on soft a snore. He watched her chest rise and fall, safe in his arms. Did she still feel just as content? She had been more reluctant than he was to marry, and yet she seemed more content with him as the weeks passed.

Nothing could keep them apart now.

Or so he thought.

Chapter Eight

NARCISSE'S MUSCLES ACHED AS he sat up in bed, his ribs straining underneath his skin once more. He checked in his mirror to ensure the damage the wolves had caused hadn't come back magically overnight. It hadn't. He groaned as he stepped into his breeches. He fastened his shirt and adorned his hunting coat, before turning toward the bed. Bell still slept peacefully, her hand resting on his now empty pillow. Her soft snores followed him out the door.

The morning sun beat down on him the moment he stepped outside. He squinted up at the sky, noticing the cloudless expanse. Today was going to be a hot day.

With his axe slung over his shoulder, he tramped through his lands until he was standing at the very edge of his property. The tree line melded with the woods that surrounded much of this part of town. The trees here were larger, older, and he almost felt bad for chopping them down, but he needed the wood for his work.

His ribs ached as he swung the axe, the impact reverberating up his arms. A few swings and he was already exhausted, but he persisted.

That was until he saw them.

At the edge of the woods, where the trees became thicker, denser, and wilder, he saw a group of people.

"Hey!" he called, waving at them with his free hand.

They ignored him, disappearing into the woods until they were nothing but a memory.

He should leave them, go back to his work, but he couldn't do that. There were so many people missing now, gone without a trace, that he could not bring himself to be the reason more people vanished in this town.

"Hey!" Narcisse called again as he swung his axe, leaving it stuck out the side of a tree, trudging into the trees after them.

It didn't take long for him to catch up with them, but no matter how fast he walked, or ran, he was never quite close enough. He could see their hair, the backs of their coats and cloaks, he could even hear their soft breathing. . .but he could not reach them.

"Where are you going?" Narcisse couldn't help imagining the next time he was in town; the cries of the parents, wives, husbands, children who had lost their family member and couldn't explain where they went. He didn't want to have to tell anyone that he had seen them, and that he could not stop them.

When he thought he was gaining on them, they moved faster, always keeping the same distance between them. Narcisse knew he was far away from his property line by now, knew he was going too deep into the woods. He had explored these woods many a time when he was a child, but he had never gone this far alone. He wasn't even sure he knew his way back. Had he been running in a straight line?

"Wait!"

Narcisse stumbled ever so slightly, barely able to catch his footing.

"Hello." A soft voice, one as smooth as butter, came from behind him.

Someone had managed to sneak up on him. Swallowing his panic, he turned slowly, purposefully, until he faced an unfamiliar woman.

She was a beautiful woman, so fair skinned and seemingly so bright in the shadowed woods. She wore a black velvet cloak, her inky hair flowing out from the hood covering her, as if it were part of the fabric. Despite casting her in darkness, it did not obscure her raw beauty.

"Hello," she said once more, a smile forming on her lips in the shadows of her hood. Narcisse could not see her eyes, but he could almost feel the burn on them on his face.

Narcisse's heart froze in his chest, his breathing caught as he watched her come closer. He felt some kind of déjà vu; that he had been here before, or seen this beauty, but he could not put his finger on it. When he felt that he was close to remembering, his mind became muddled, and he could think of nothing but the soft, red lips before him.

"It has been an age since I saw you, dear Narcisse." The woman's mouth moved as she spoke, but it was as if her words came to him from all directions. They echoed inside his head, calling him forward, comforting him. Seducing him.

He blinked at her words, his mind foggy. *What was I doing? Why am I in the woods?*

"Who are you?" Narcisse managed to speak, but his throat felt raw, his words gravelly and unsure.

"You will find out soon enough."

The fog that filled his head grew thicker and denser until he could see nothing, hear nothing, be nothing. Narcisse blinked furiously until the fog was gone from his head. But when he could see the world around him once more, the woman was gone. It was as if she had never been there in the first place. He looked around, frantic to find the people who he had been following, but they were long gone. He walked a few paces, but gave up before he could really start again.

It was no use. They were gone and he could no longer hear the rustling of the forest floor.

With one final look in the direction the people had gone, Narcisse walked back the way he came. It took little thought, as if he had mentally memorized the path, even though he had barely paid any attention to it at the time.

Before he had time to gather his thoughts, he was back at the tree line, staring at the axe that still hung from the tree trunk. He felt sluggish when he pulled the axe from the wood. Narcisse had every intention of staying there, cutting down the tree, and then leaving it under the thick canopy of trees to dry out. But the hair on the back of his neck still stood on end, and he was sure someone or something was watching him.

Narcisse felt ridiculous, but he couldn't stay put. Something told him, urged him, to return closer to home. And so he did.

He found a nice outcropping of trees just behind the cottage, where he set up shop for the day. The feeling of being watched had abated the closer he got to home, but it hadn't left completely.

He took one final look in the direction he came from, sure he would find that beautiful woman shaded under a tree, smiling coldly at him. But there was no one there.

He shook his head, dislodging the image and got to work chopping down trees.

"Here."

Narcisse jumped, almost dropping his axe onto his foot. He hadn't seen Bell come out.

"How did you know I was here?" he panted, wiping his brow once more. Thank God she hadn't come out looking for him earlier, because she wouldn't have been able to find him.

"I could hear you chopping wood from the house. I practically felt the tree hit the ground." She frowned at him as she added, "Why didn't you tell me you were leaving to work?"

"You were sleeping." He took the cheese sandwich she extended to him. "Thanks."

"I would've come and helped if you'd only asked."

He took a large bite, his cheeks puffed out as he chewed. He forgot how hungry chopping wood could make him. "Help?" he mumbled.

She cocked a brow ever so slightly, as if she thought him stupid for even asking. "I'm not afraid of hard work, Narcisse. In fact, I enjoy it."

Narcisse eyed her as he took another bite of his sandwich. He didn't like the idea of his delicate wife working out in the yard with him. It wasn't entirely the fact that he thought her of better use in the kitchen, but more that he was worried she'd end up injured in one way or another. But his mind wandered, and he imagined Bell carrying wood to the house, her skin glistening with sweat, and it caused his cock to twitch inside his tight trousers.

"You can help if you wish. But I would prefer you not hurt yourself." Her hands went to her hips.

Narcisse's lips twitched. "There is nothing to be done now until the wood has dried, but if you want you can help carry it to the back of the house when it does."

She watched him for a moment before nodding and walking back in the direction of the house.

Narcisse finished the rest of his sandwich in one bite then followed after her. His long strides meant that he reached the door just as she went to close it. She grinned at him, standing in his way. Him standing at the bottom of the step meant that they were at the same height. The way her eyes shone wickedly had him rushing at her, swinging her up in his arms and carrying her to the couch. She squealed in delight as he dropped her to the soft couch, leant across her and danced his fingers over her body without mercy. Her surprised laughter filled the home. Something he had never heard here before. Something he could get used to.

While Bell prepared dinner, Narcisse stood by the fireplace, a snifter of whisky in his hand. He tilted his head back, downing it all before putting the glass back like he hadn't touched it. The pain he had experienced throughout the day only got worse, the adrenaline from chopping down trees gone the moment he put down his axe. Once he stepped inside and felt the warmth seep back into his cold bones, the pain truly hit him.

He didn't want to show his pain. He had just gotten over the injuries, and he wished to not worry anyone again, particularly Bluebell. But it seemed that he had overexerted himself more so than he should have. The last couple of days had finally caught up to him, and the healing he had done on the outside did not match the pain that radiated from inside.

He could hear Bell in the kitchen, her soft humming filtering through the closed door. So he resorted to self-medicating. He pulled the cork from the bottle that sat on his mantle, tipped his head back and took a deep drink of liquor. It burned a trail of fire down his throat and pooled in his stomach. Warmth filled him, spreading out from his core, and easing the stiffness.

But it wasn't enough.

He gritted his teeth, groaning loudly when he took a seat before the fireplace, just as Bell walked in from the kitchen.

"What's wrong?" she cried.

He shook his head, wishing to ignore the pain, rather than tell his wife. But she would have no bar of it. She knelt beside him, her hand on his knee. "What is it?" There was a real concern in her words that he just couldn't ignore.

"I thought I was completely healed. Perhaps I am, but I pushed myself too hard today." Narcisse rubbed at the sweat that beaded his brow. "The pain has returned."

Bell's hand rested on his knee, but she frowned at the salve that sat on the parlor mantle. "You did heal incredibly fast."

Narcisse nodded, still marveled at the lack of cuts and bruises.

"Perhaps you are still healing. . .if the wounds closed up that fast, maybe you are still knitting yourself back together under your skin."

"You could be right," he sighed, adding, "it feels like I'm being torn apart from the inside out." Like he had sutures that were pulling with every movement.

Bell looked down at where the gouges had been, as if she could see inside his body and watch the fat and muscle sew itself back together. With a slight squeeze of his shoulder, in comfort or reassurance he wasn't sure, Bell strode to the mantle. Narcisse hoped she wouldn't see the tumbler he had used, still wet from his drink.

Bell held the salve in a white-knuckled grip but said nothing. She had not seen the empty tumbler after all. Narcisse remembered Jacques' words advising him not to use the salve if he drank, but it was only a small swig after all. Narcisse watched his wife approach him and said nothing. He didn't know what the consequences would be for disobeying a simple instruction like that.

Without a word, Bell lifted his shirt over his head, pushing him back down into his chair when he made to stand. Her hands were steady as she stroked a hand over the muscles in his chest, long before she removed the cap on the salve.

"Bell?" He smiled at her from under his lashes as a light blush crept over her cheeks.

With nimble fingers, she removed the lid, dropped it in his lap and massaged large blobs of salve into his skin. The moment it soaked in he sighed in utter relief. The pain was gone in seconds, and he was left grinning as he took a hold of Bell's hand.

"Thank you," he breathed.

She nodded again and made to pull her hand away. Narcisse flashed his teeth at her in a wicked grin. Taking the jar from her, he discarded the salve and lid on the coffee table, and then pulled her into his lap. She squealed in delight as his lips pressed against her neck. Narcisse could feel her pulse beating against his tongue as he tasted her.

"Narcisse," she sighed. "Dinner will get cold."

He said nothing, his hands roaming over her body as his tongue turned ravenous. With greedy fingers he slid under the velveteen fabric of her dress, splaying his palms so he could feel every inch of her. She wrapped her arms around his shoulders, resting her face in the crook of his neck. Bell sighed, her warm breath washing over him. At the way her body relaxed against him, the way she breathed him in just as he had her, his hands slowed. He didn't remove them from beneath her dress. Instead, he wrapped his arms around her body, his hands devouring the warmth of her skin.

He had every intention of kissing her when there was a hesitant knock at the door. He hmphed, but lowered Bell to the ground, stalking to the door.

"Narcisse!" Louis greeted, looking past him to Bell, who had quickly busied herself in the kitchen once more. "We haven't seen you down at the tavern for quite some time."

Narcisse shrugged, even though it was true. He had not been back since the night of his wedding. He missed the company of his drunkard friends. He used to go to drink away his loneliness in company. Narcisse had thought many times about shoving his feet into his boots and marching off to the tavern, but he had been quite distracted.

He stepped to the side. waving Louis in.

Louis didn't need his invitation, he usually just barged in and made himself at home, but Narcisse thought it best that he stopped feeling that comfortable now that he had a lady living with him.

Louis watched Bell move about the kitchen, then faced Narcisse, waggling his brows at him.

Huffing through his nose, he shut the door and glared at the back of his friend's head as he followed him into the kitchen.

"Hello, Bluebell!" His cheerfulness seemed to irk him more than usual.

Bell smiled sweetly at Louis, her eyes crinkling when she saw the way Narcisse watched him. "Hello. Are you joining us for dinner?"

"Yes," Louis said eagerly, just as Narcisse growled, "No."

Bell ignored the latter, grabbing out an extra place setting. "I hope you like game."

Of course he did. Narcisse hadn't ever seen him turn down any food. He'd eat anything, especially if he didn't have to make it himself. That was why he still lived with his parents. Narcisse smirked at his friend.

Louis noticed the amusement in Narcisse's face and tilted his head in question. Narcisse simply sat back in the chair he had occupied before his friend interrupted. Louis sat on the other side of the table, watching as Bell fussed with the food. His eyes remained on Bell as he spoke. "Where have you been?"

"Working." Narcisse shrugged, not seeing why he was being questioned in the first place.

Louis said nothing further about the matter when Bell placed a plate pilled with roasted venison and vegetables in front of him.

After placing one in front of Narcisse and filling some glasses with water, she joined them at the table, sitting beside him. They remained silent as they ate, Bell's eyes cast down at her plate clearly struggling to find something to talk about. Louis ate quite fast, shoveling the vegetables in without stopping for a single breath.

Narcisse bit into a baby carrot, glancing between his wife and his friend. He was about to do something about the silence when he paused, frowning down at the plate of food before him.

Bizarre. There was something off about what he ate, and he wondered if perhaps the food had gone sour before his wife had had a chance to cook it. Narcisse pushed the food around his plate, looking for any signs of rot or mold.

There was none. *Strange.*

Narcisse sat there silently for some time before Bell leaned toward him, looking down at the mess he had made of his dinner.

"Are you okay?" she asked, her soft voice causing him to jump.

"Fine," he gasped, lifting his water to his mouth. "Just fine, dear."

His fingers felt weak, as if they were too weak to hold onto the glass and it would slip from his grasp at any moment. His hand shook as he tightened his grip. But that wasn't weakness Narcisse felt. Something different coursed through his veins.

He cocked his head, watching his fingers tense around the glass. It shattered beneath his fingers, bursting out from his hand and showering down like a starburst. He felt nothing, could think of nothing, as he looked at his hand and the blood that seeped through his fingers.

Bell shrieked, Louis even yelled, jumping up from his seat. Narcisse looked down at the glass that now covered his dinner. *Pity.*

"You're bleeding!" Bell rushed to his side.

"I am?" He narrowed his eyes slightly as he stared at the blood that coated his hand.

She grabbed his hand in hers, not caring for the blood that coated her own skin. She turned it back and forth, frowning at what she saw.

"What is it?" Louis asked. "Is it bad?" Narcisse laughed slightly watching his closest friend, *only* friend, turn pale at the sight of blood.

"I—." Bell used her white apron to wipe at the blood. Narcisse flinched, expecting to feel glass grate into his skin. Instead, he felt nothing. "I can't believe it," she stared in disbelief. "There's nothing here. No cuts, not even a scratch."

"But there's so much blood." Louis came closer, leaning over Narcisse and inspecting it himself.

"I can't explain it." Bell was quiet as she wiped the remaining blood from his hand. She dropped the apron, but kept his hand in hers, eyes narrowing as she ran her fingers over his callused palms. "Does it hurt?"

It took a moment to realize she was talking to him. Narcisse flexed his hand, bringing it to his face. He felt nothing of the strength or whatever it was he had felt earlier, nor did he feel any kind of pain. Not even a tingle.

"Fine," he said. "I feel fine."

"But the blood," Louis squeaked.

"I'm going to call for the doctor," Bell rushed to the door.

"But I'm not hurt." Narcisse rose from his chair, intent on stopping her.

She said nothing. Wrapping a shawl around her shoulders, she walked out into the dark, cool night and shut the door.

"I don't need to see a doctor," he said to himself.

Louis frowned down at Narcisse's hand. Narcisse flexed it, sure his friend would try to grab it. Instead, he merely shook his head, rubbing the stubble that lined his jaw. "Getting a second opinion wouldn't hurt."

"I don't have a first opinion, why would I need a second?"

Louis shrugged, going back to the table to finish his dinner like nothing had happened. But nothing *had* happened, had it? He broke a glass; wouldn't any strong man like himself be able to break one without a thought? Narcisse lifted the glass Bell had set out for herself and tested the strength of the glass.

"Hmm," he mused. It was quite thick.

Narcisse leant against the kitchen counter, a thick piece of leftover meat held in his hand, the other stretched out on the counter behind him. Louis remained seated, every now and then looking up at Narcisse as if he would speak.

They waited.

Neither of them spoke as they anticipated Bell to return with the doctor. Barely twenty minutes had passed when she rushed through the front door, Doctor Salvatore in tow.

"Louis, Narcisse." The doctor removed his hat from his head, holding it to his chest as he nodded in greeting.

Narcisse dipped his head toward the medical bag the doctor carried. "I'm fine, Doctor, I don't need any medical attention."

Doctor Salvatore said nothing. He placed his bag on the table, pausing when he noticed the glass shards that still sprinkled the table and Narcisse's food. "Bell explained to me what occurred. I thought it best to take a look."

"Sit," Bell pulled out a chair, her tone leaving no room to argue.

Narcisse wiped the meat residue on his breeches and dropped down into the seat.

"Which hand?" The doctor took a pair of magnifying glasses out of his bag and set them over his eyes.

Narcisse said nothing, holding out his right hand.

Doctor Salvatore made humming noises and he looked at Narcisse's hand, moving it about as he did. "I can see small amounts of dried blood."

Bell removed her shawl and pointed to the blood-stained apron she still wore. "This is from his hand," she said. Doctor Salvatore pushed the glasses away from his eyes, his brow cocking as he took in just how much blood there was.

"Where are the wounds?"

"I told you, they just weren't there."

The doctor looked back down at his hand, confusion lacing his expression, before some sort of clarity seemed to click in his eyes. He stood, leaning over Narcisse and sniffing at his clothes.

"Hey!" Narcisse leaned away from him in protest.

"You used the salve today." Not a question.

"Yes, he was in a lot of pain," Bell answered for him.

"Did you consume any alcohol?"

No, stuck in Narcisse's throat. Instead, he looked away as he said, "Yes."

"Narcisse!" He refused to look at his wife, afraid he'd find disappointment there.

"That's the problem," the doctor tsked. "I warned you not to have alcohol while using the salve, because there can be severe consequences."

"What, exactly, are the consequences?" Bell rested her hand on Narcisse's shoulder, squeezing in reassurance, as if she understood that he had drank because of the pain.

"For me to explain that I will need to explain what is in it and why I have it." He looked toward the fireplace that lit the living room in soft shadows. "Shall we?" He waited for Bell to nod before walking into the room and sinking down into a leather chair. Narcisse looked from Bell to Louis, shrugged and then joined the doctor in the living room. He waved his hand out to Bell, motioning her to the last free chair. She smiled softly before sitting across from Salvatore.

"Where to begin. . ." Salvatore rubbed at the stubble that coated his jaw.

Louis was the last to enter the living room, his eyes narrowed as if he wasn't prepared to believe anything. He stood shoulder to shoulder with Narcisse, the latter moving slightly so he could feel the heat of the fire, rather than the heat of his friend's skin.

"As you know, I acquired the medical practice after Bluebell's mother passed." He tipped his head at Bell, a slight recognition. "And as you are aware, during my time as a practitioner, there have been many times that civil unrest has broken out in our small town. One of those times, not long after I set up shop, was the worst of all."

Narcisse knew which time he was speaking of before he even spoke. He was young, but if he had got his timelines right, it was not long after Bell's mother died. A time of turmoil, of fear and uncertainty. Fear for the future, for what was to come of their town when they had no leader.

"During that time there was more than words slung over drinks. Civil unrest turned into civil war. Brother fought against brother, son against father, neighbor against church. It was a terrible sight to see. But I saw a lot more. The injured began piling up in my practice, the floor transformed into makeshift gurneys. I managed to tend to some, but others. . ." He swallowed hard, looking away from them.

Narcisse could recall seeing all the blood. Could hear the wails of the injured in the back of his mind.

"There were some far too injured, far too gone, to save. The bullet wounds, the facial injuries. . .they were unrecognizable. My practice was slowly transforming from somewhere I could save lives, to a mass grave. At least five died in the first day. I couldn't stand it. The blood reeked of iron; the vomit was nothing but whiskey. I left that night, leaving the healing to an apprentice who had little idea what he was doing."

"You left them to die?" Bell's eyes were wide with disbelief.

"I had no choice," Doctor Salvatore smiled sadly at Bell. "I had to do something, and slowing the inevitable wasn't one of them." The doctor leveled a stare at each of them before he continued. "I went to the castle."

Bell's eyebrows lifted in disbelief. "The abandoned one? Hasn't that been fenced off for at least one hundred years?"

"It has been, yes. But that doesn't mean it is abandoned. There are many of us who know who really resides in that castle."

"Someone *lives* in there?" Narcisse couldn't fathom that. The castle itself was dark and derelict, too dangerous to attempt to break into.

"It's an enchantment."

"What is?"

"There is a powerful enchantment on the castle, making all who stumble across it see nothing but ruins." When Narcisse blinked at him, the doctor added, "An enchantress lives there. Has lived there for many, many years."

"Sorcery is nothing but childish fairy tales," Bell whispered.

Doctor Salvatore nodded. "I used to believe that too, until I lost all hope during the civil war and sort out to find the enchantress myself."

"You went to the castle?" Louis balked.

"I did more than that. I went inside, looked around, touched things I shouldn't have. . . I called out to her, and the enchantment around the castle fell. I was standing in a beautiful well-lit dining room, and seated at the head of the table was the sorceress. She invited me to dine with her. Insisted I should. I sat beside her, admiring the beautiful angles of her face, the way her eyes shone in the firelight. But I didn't dally, I said what I needed to say, asked what I needed to ask.

"I told her I needed help. She watched me with intelligence and cunning. She knew what I sought before I asked. When she spoke, her voice was like a siren's melodic timbre, echoing around the room. She said, "You seek help to heal the wounded, to heal those very near death." I don't know how she knew before I asked. I nodded, unable to speak, unable to move and she stood from her chair and walked across the room. She returned with a small, clear glass jar and sat it in front of me. She urged me to open it. And so I did.

"I twisted the lid, but when I looked inside it was empty. I looked up at her, but she nodded back to the jar, and as I watched, the jar filled before my very eyes. It started out as a clear jelly-like substance. When I asked exactly what it was, she informed me it was simply aloe vera from her gardens. But then with a wave of her hand and a flick of her wrists, the clear substance took on a purple hue, getting darker and darker the more she put inside it."

"What was it?" Narcisse realized he had unconsciously crept closer to the doctor, curiosity getting the better of him.

"It was magic. She had jarred her magic, mixing it with the gel to create a healing tonic that seeps into the skin and heals what cannot be healed. With a click of her fingers, she set multiple jars before me. As I left with the jars, she said she would come for the payment when the time suited her."

"What kind of payment?"

"There has been many," Doctor Salvatore looked ashamed. "I didn't know that asking for her help would be so troublesome, but I had to save the townsfolk."

"What kind of payment?" Narcisse repeated.

"At the moment, she asks for only monetary payments. She keeps the jars stocked, and I pay her fifty percent of my yearly earnings."

"Fifty percent!" Louis exclaimed.

"She said she would come for the real payment soon."

Narcisse didn't want to ask again, but it seemed that the doctor was skating around the subject. "*What* payment?"

"A year from my life for every jar she has given me. Since the civil war I have obtained many jars. The magic works so well that not much is needed, but she continued to bring them."

Something hard, solid, formed in Narcisse's throat. He stared at the jar that sat on his mantle. . . the jar he had nearly used all of. The jar that held one year of Doctor Salvatore's life.

"The enchantress will take those years, or however many she deems fit, from my lifespan. She will come for me and take my life when she thinks I have lived enough."

"That's awful," Bell cried.

"Indeed," the doctor nodded. "But now to explain the alcohol. The alcohol seems to intensify the magic in the salve. I found out the hard way," he chuckled. "It messes with the immune system, making the recipient quite strong. Rumor has it, that the sorceress has guards watching the castle grounds who are supernaturally strong and fast, and if rumors are true, I'll bet she uses a magic with a similar technique on them."

"Jarred magic, superhuman strength, your life for the lives of others." Bell stared at the pile of books she had on the bookshelf, as if she couldn't quite fathom that this wasn't a story in one of them. It was too hard to believe.

And yet. . .the salve had healed his wounds too fast, beyond humanly possible. And the way he could smash that glass in the palm of his hand, as if he too had gained some sort of superhuman ability.

"Here." Narcisse disappeared into the dining room and returned with the salve. "Take this."

There wasn't much left, but he couldn't live with the idea of using it after what Salvatore had told him.

The doctor said nothing as he took the jar and placed it inside his medicine bag before standing.

"Does she still live there?" Bell stood to follow him to the front door.

"She does."

"What happens to those who venture there now?"

Doctor Salvatore paused, looking at Bell from under his brows. "I believe no one has been imprudent enough to do so since me."

Or so he thought.

Chapter Nine

"**Y**OU DID?" BELL'S BROWS crinkled. "But Doctor Salvatore said no one had gone there since him."

Narcisse's eyes flicked to Louis, almost completely involuntary. The small movement was enough to make Bell pause. Louis was smart enough to look away, as if he hadn't noticed at all. But Narcisse knew he had.

"*We* did," Narcisse said, dipping his head toward Louis.

Louis glared at Narcisse, but said nothing, refusing to admit to anything. Bell, on the other hand, folded her arms across her chest, looking between the two men from under her furrowed brow. There was utter outrage reflected in the tension in her body, the fear in her eyes. "What do you mean?" her voice quavered.

There was no point hiding something they'd done as children; it had no consequence on them now as adults. "We were fifteen when we went to the castle," he said. "We didn't go inside like Salvatore had, but we explored the lands surrounding it. We obviously had no idea who was living inside at the time."

"No, we did not," Louis barked, "but the intense fear makes more sense now."

Bell sat by the fire, the orange light casting her in shadows. "I feel for the doctor," she said, staring into the hearth. "He gave away any chance of a long life to save others."

"A very selfless thing to do," Louis whispered in agreement.

Narcisse joined Bell beside the fire, though his mind was elsewhere.

The three of them pushed through a thicket of brambles, the thorns sticking to their clothes, like tiny hands trying to stop them from going any further. One scratched at his cheek with a slight sting, but it was forgotten as they emerged onto the castle grounds. Louis turned to Narcisse; his white teeth flashed in a grin that was a stark contrast to the darkness surrounding them. But it was his other friend, Peter, who had Narcisse smug as they paused in the courtyard. He shook, although it was the middle of summer. His fear was almost palpable, like he expected a monster to jump out of the castle at any moment.

"Wow," Narcisse breathed as his eyes scanned the dark stone walls of the castle. It was huge. The walls towered over them, tall enough to peek over the top of the trees and just be visible to the village. It looked bigger in person. Intimidating. Narcisse didn't know what he'd expected to find when Louis approached him with the idea of exploring the derelict grounds. But whatever he'd expected, this was even better. There was a thick darkness that clung to the castle, spreading out and stretching toward them, as if the shadows were alive. The light from the moon above them barely lit the grounds, as if there was something preventing any light from touching it.

Narcisse's heart pounded loudly in his ears, getting louder the closer he got to the daunting stone walls.

"We've seen it, can we go now?" Peter hadn't moved from the spot he'd occupied when they stepped from the trees. Narcisse noticed the way he held his arms close to his body, the way his eyes refused to look up at the castle.

"Are you scared?" Louis didn't sound like he mocked his friend, only curious. It was as if he were too ashamed to admit that he was scared also.

Narcisse didn't blame them. The castle had been abandoned for such a long time, there could be anything hiding in the shadows. Did wolves roam the grounds, *waiting for children like themselves to stumble upon them? Could there be vagabonds or a gang of thieves living inside the castle?*

His gulp was audible as he turned back to face the castle, imagining large men with knives and blackened teeth coming out to take their coin purses.

"Yes, let's turn back," Louis squeaked. Was he imagining the same as Narcisse?

Narcisse nodded, not able to speak. He had gotten closer to the castle, and he was afraid his voice would travel inside the darkened fortress.

He forced his steps to remain slow and unhurried as he returned to his friends, although fear was eating him. Idiot, being afraid of an empty house. . .that's all it was after all. Louis and Peter barely waited for Narcisse to reach them before they disappeared back inside the woods. He had the urge to rush after them, but something had him pause at the tree line. Brows furrowed; he turned back toward the castle.

He refused to look at the door, picturing it swinging open as soon as his back was turned. But that wasn't what had made him pause. There were a lot of windows covering the expanse of the castle, each and every one so dark they looked like ink stains against the grey stone. All except one.

Light flickered from the window on the very top of the castle, as if there was a single candle lit in the room. The dim orange glow wasn't enough to cast any light outside of the castle, but just enough to see shadows dancing past the windows.

Narcisse's heart fell to his feet when one of the shadows seemed to solidify, moving differently, more fluidly, than the others. His legs were stiff, his hands shaking. He couldn't move, couldn't take his eyes from the flickering light as the shadow grew, slinking closer to the window. As he stared, something moved in front of the candlelight, blocking the orange glow from view. Someone, something, stood at the window, watching him as he stared back.

"Are you coming?" Peter called from the trees.

Narcisse jumped. He'd almost forgotten his friends had been waiting for him. "Sorry," he said too loud.

"Come on," Louis' face appeared between some oaks and grinned at Narcisse, as if he could see the fear in his eyes.

But the fear that filled him body and soul, was not caused by the sudden reappearance of his friends, but something much more disturbing.

For when he turned back to the castle, looking at the window one last time, it was utterly black. There was no candlelight, no obscure figure standing in the window frame. And as he stepped into the trees and tried not to run back to the village, he swore he could feel someone watching him.

"Narcisse?" Bell's hands were warm against his cheeks, her eyes searching his face.

"Hmm?"

He was thankful that she didn't remove her hands as she spoke. "Are you okay?"

It wasn't often Narcisse thought about that time in his life. In fact, he couldn't remember the last time he recalled the memories.

"Im fine," he blinked.

Had the shadow he'd seen in the window of the castle when he was fifteen been the enchantress? Had he known someone lived there all along? When Narcisse and his friends got back to the village he hadn't told anyone what he'd seen, not even Louis. He'd believed it was simply his mind playing tricks on him. As much as he liked to think himself a fearless man at fifteen, he had indeed been scared the moment they stepped into the courtyard that night. Fear had messed with his mind, his eyes. He had seen nothing but shadows.

"You don't seem fine," Louis murmured.

The tan that was a constant on Narcisse's skin, thanks to his work outdoors every day, was suddenly gone. He could almost feel the color drain from him as he stared in the direction of the castle, as if he could see all the way there, through walls and trees.

He had forgotten about it for all these years, but Salvatore's confession had awoken the fear all over again, and he could recall the exact way the candle flickered inside the room, the shadows dancing along the walls.

Narcisse could feel the eyes on him, could see the way they watched him, waiting for him to speak. But what was he meant to say?

"I should be going." Louis stood from his seat, stretching his short arms above his head. "It's getting late."

How late was it? The wood in the hearth was nothing but smoldering ashes. Narcisse shook his head to dislodge his sudden fear and stood, walking with Louis to the front door.

"Come to the tavern tomorrow night?" Louis asked from the porch.

Narcisse had every intention of saying no, but found himself saying "Yes, I will be there after dinner."

Louis strode off in the direction of his house. Narcisse found himself standing on his porch and couldn't help looking out over the trees in the distance, his eyes falling on the silhouette of the castle, barely visible in the dark.

"It's like it has eyes, watching the village." Bell was beside him, leaning against his side as she spoke. "I wish someone would tear it down."

The blankets tangled like vines around his legs, restricting him, holding him as he flailed about. Sweat coated him, making the sheets damp and sticky. Everything seemed to hold him, keeping him from waking. His breathing came in short, panicked bursts. It felt like a fist clenched around his heart, suffocating him as he tried so desperately to awaken. Narcisse yelped as he shot up in bed, his hand pressed hard against his chest, and tried to calm his breathing. He couldn't remember the last time he'd had a nightmare, and this one had felt so real it left him panting on his sweat-soaked bed like a dog.

He squinted in the darkness, sure he'd find Bell's eyes on him. Instead, he found her fast asleep, her arm thrown over her eyes.

His nightmare still clung to him as he stood on shaky legs. *Water.* He needed to wash away the stench of fear that hung in the air around him.

He walked through the dark house, dropping down into his favorite chair with a glass of water in hand. The fire was out, but some glowing embers still remained, lighting the living room in a soft orange glow. He placed a small log into the hearth, stoking the fire back to life as he swallowed the last of the water.

There was still a couple of hours left until sunrise, but the nightmare was still fresh in his mind, and there was no way he could go back to sleep with the risk of starting it all over again. He leaned back in his chair, staring into the dancing flames. *How had the doctor so willingly sold his life to help others?* Could Narcisse do the same if given the chance? *No way in hell.*

How old *was* Doctor Salvatore? He had given the enchantress a year of his life for every jar, but how many had he had? Was he fifty? Sixty? Narcisse had never been good at guessing someone's age, but if Salvatore were only to live to sixty like many here, could he die at any moment? How would it happen? Narcisse imagined Doctor Salvatore suddenly aging, withering on the spot and floating away like ash in the wind. Or perhaps the enchantress would come for him, dragging him away in the dead of the night? But would she take him back to the castle or dispose of him in some other sinister way?

His stomach lurched so suddenly he was sure he would vomit in his lap. He rushed for the front door, falling to his knees in the damp grass.

That could have been me. He wanted to scream. *She could have caught me and made me pay for trespassing.* He heaved violently but nothing came out. *That could have been Louis or Peter!* The ground swayed under his knees and acid singed his throat as he vomited. The sounds of his heaving filled the silent night air. Narcisse was no longer friends with Peter, after he moved abroad, but he couldn't help imagining the shy, fearful lad he had been so close to. *If he'd been caught there.*

If Louis. . . Vomit splashed from the grass and sprayed over his hands as he leaned over his knees.

Narcisse would have given his life to save his friends. Sure, he was a selfish man, who thought mainly of himself. But he was also a reckless teenager who wanted to be a man, and that meant facing off with some monster in the woods to show just how manly he was.

"I was hoping you'd be awake," a hushed voice called through the darkness.

Narcisse's heart skipped a beat as he imagined the sorceress stepping out from trees, like he and his friends had done so long ago. But it wasn't a woman's voice that sounded to the side of him.

"What are you doing here?" Narcisse stood, stepping away from the vomit at his feet. "It's late."

"Late, or early?" Jacques chuckled softly.

Narcisse said nothing as he looked at his father-in-law over from head to toe, checking for some sign of distress or reasoning as to why he would be here at this time. But Jacques was dressed, his hair and beard combed, as if it were a reasonable hour.

"I'm leaving," he said. "I have another fair to attend, but I wanted to speak to you first."

Narcisse looked out into the dark trees and the shadows that still clung to the morning. "Do you think it wise to travel alone this early in the morning when so many people have gone missing the last few weeks?"

"It's at least a three-hour ride, and I need time to set up. But don't worry; I don't need to take any of the paths in the woods to get there this time. You won't have to come riding after me." Amusement shone in his eyes.

"I'm glad to hear I won't need to fight wolves this time."

Jacques looked at the window to Narcisse's bedroom. "Is Bell awake?"

"No one sane is awake at this hour."

"You're clearly not sane then." Jacques chuckled again "I came to speak with you both, but as my daughter is sleeping, would you be so kind to pass on what I have to say?"

"I should be asleep now myself. What would you have done if you came to find I was?"

"I would have knocked and waited patiently." Jacques took a long, measured look at Narcisse. "I wanted to tell Bell that I was leaving for the fair, so that she didn't assume I was missing like all those other people. I didn't want her to worry." He frowned. "I hadn't planned on going to the fair at all. It was all very last minute, otherwise I would have come a lot sooner."

"You came out here at this time to tell us you are leaving? You couldn't have left a note instead?"

"I could have, but my leaving isn't what I wanted to talk to you about."

"What is it?" Narcisse's brows knitted at the way his father-in-law rubbed his hands together anxiously. "Out with it."

"I was in town yesterday and I ran into Doctor Salvatore." Jacques stepped out of the shadows; his hands held before him in surrender. "He told me what had happened with the salve. But, Narcisse, I swear I had nothing to do with it. I had no idea what was in the salve."

Narcisse watched warily with narrowed eyes, taking note of the way he moved with such purpose.

"The Doctor told me how he acquired it, about the witch and the magic. The salve I recommended, I had used it long before Harriet had passed. It wasn't spelled; it was just a simple salve, made with herbs."

"We know," Narcisse replied.

"I just don't want her name associated with anything of that nature."

"I can assure you, Jacques, that thought had never come to mind. Bell would never think her father that foolish, to mess around with magic." But there was something in the way Jacques sagged in relief, the tension never really leaving his face. There was something he wasn't saying, something he was hiding, and Narcisse couldn't help the wave of suspicion that rushed through him.

The old man was hiding something.

Jacques was quiet, his mouth pursed. "Do you really think it foolish, that he saved so many people?"

"In a sense it was heroic and brave, but it was foolish nonetheless."

"Even fools can do the right thing," Jacques mused, before adding, "I would have told you the salve was magic if I'd known."

"But you did warn me not to consume alcohol while using it?"

"I was simply relaying a message from the doctor."

"And you didn't think to question it?"

"You didn't think to question the accelerated healing?"

Narcisse couldn't help the smile that tugged at his lips. He had a point. Narcisse had questioned it, but once the wounds were gone, he was too distracted by being able to move without tearing them back open to care.

"I should be off now. I need to get back home and check I have everything packed before I leave. Please tell Bell where I have gone so that she doesn't come to visit and find me gone. And please tell her I didn't know about the salve."

"When should we expect you back?" Narcisse moved toward the door.

"The morning after next." Jacques vanished into the darkness, but his voice was clear as he added, "Why were you sick?"

"A nightmare," Narcisse shrugged. "Nothing serious."

"Adieu," Jacques called.

Narcisse waited by the front door, ensuring he was gone, before slinking back inside. The cool night air had cleared his head, chasing back the memories of the night he had ventured to the castle grounds. Of course he had seen nothing but shadows. There was nothing there then, and if he had witnessed the sorceress in her window, he would not be here now to tell the tale.

By the time Narcisse cleaned himself up, stoked the fire, and set water onto the stove, the sun had just begun to peak over the top of the trees and the sky was streaked with orange and purple.

The house was quiet, so quiet that he could just make out Bell's small, shallow snores from the other room. Narcisse smiled to himself. Her quiet snores brought him happiness in the strangest of ways.

Narcisse made quick work of his coffee and stepped back outside to greet the morning. He frowned down at the vomit patch to the side of the porch and hoped it would rain today to wash it away. The day had barely begun; the sky was a wispy blue while Narcisse fed the animals and went to check on the wood he had set to dry the day before.

The wood was drying well, but it would still be a long while before he could make anything, without the possibility of shrinkage. He checked the stockpile of smaller pieces, scratching the back of his neck as he scrutinized the small pile.

"I'll put some together today and sell them to people at the tavern tonight," he said to himself. *What better way to convince someone they need more furniture, what better way to make money?*

He remained around the side of the house, prepping the tools he would need.

His ears pricked up each time he heard noise, hoping that Bell would come outside and offer to help once more. Carpentry could be a lonely trade, and he imagined he would quite enjoy the company more often than not.

He couldn't help the way his heartbeat sped up when he heard the front door bang open and close.

"You're up earlier than usual," Bell yawned. She stood in a wrinkled dress, as if she'd just thrown it on to come outside, her hair pulled back from her face.

"I couldn't sleep." He scanned the pile of wood again, but his mind remained on Bell.

"How long have you been awake?"

"Long enough for your father to visit well before the sun was up." He wiped the back of his hand against his brow. "He wanted to inform us that he was leaving to attend a fair."

Bell's brow wrinkled ever so slightly. "I had heard about the fair, but I thought he would find it safer to stay home, what with all the disappearances and all." She stood silently, unblinking, unmoving.

"Bluebell?" Narcisse's voice sounded harsh in the silence. "Are you okay?"

"Oh, yes." She shook her head, pushing strands of sleep-messed hair. "What are you making?"

"I'm going to make some chopping boards and candle sconces to sell in town tonight."

"Tonight? I wasn't aware the markets were on."

"They're not. I'm meeting Louis at the tavern tonight, so I'll take a satchel of them down with me and try my luck there."

"Are we low on money?"

"Of course not!" Narcisse was appalled at the thought. "We have plenty of money. In fact, I have a lot of it. But I like to make money to live on week by week, so to not spend into our savings."

"And you mean to make some money from drunkards?"

Narcisse winked. "Easy pickings."

"How cruel of you." Bell made to look appalled, but it turned into a strangled laugh.

Narcisse found himself watching her in quiet admiration at how her eyes crinkled.

"I'm sorry." But she continued to chuckle between words. "I hope I haven't offended you."

"Quite the opposite, actually." Her easy teasing made his heart soar.

The sky was now wholly blue, the daylight lighting up the way Bell's cheeks heated as he watched her.

He scanned her face, the way her eyes filled with heat, the soft coloring to her round cheeks, until they settled on her lips. They opened slightly.

"Bell," he breathed as she bound toward him and threw herself into his arms.

He was so taken by surprise that he barely had time to catch her, his arms wrapping around her waist and lifted her. He carried her so that she was soon sitting on the table behind the house. Her knees parted, an invitation for him to settle there.

A soft moan washed over his lips as he pushed his mouth against hers. His right hand was flat against the base of her spine, while his other was fisted messily in her hair.

She pulled her mouth away from his long enough to pant, "The neighbors will see."

He flashed his teeth in a feral grin in response. His lips trailed over her jaw. He sprinkled her in soft, passionate kisses, scraping his teeth over the sensitive skin behind her ear. Bell arched her back, pressing herself against him.

His cock was hard in an instant, the fabric of his breeches straining him from unleashing his length. He pulled Bell closer until he was pressed against her warmth, and he could feel the answering dampness through her undergarments. She moaned inside his mouth at the contact, grinding herself into him. His cock twitched almost hard enough to break through the rough material of his breeches.

"Should we go inside?" she gasped, closing her eyes as he rubbed himself against her.

"Mmm." But Narcisse didn't take her back to the house. He picked her up, her legs wrapping around his waist, and walked her into the small feed shed that sat beside the house.

He used his foot to kick the door shut, the small windows only letting in the smallest amount of light. Bell said nothing when he lowered her to the ground, setting her on the loose hay he kept for the horses. She laid there, her eyes full of lust as he removed his hunting jacket, unbuttoned his shirt and stared down at her from under his lashes.

"I never thought this would be happening," he breathed. "I never could have imagined that I'd be here with you, let alone about to fuck you in the feed shed."

Bell's cheeks heated, her embarrassment mixing with the color of desire that already washed over her milky skin.

"Who said you're going to *fuck* me in the feed shed?"

Narcisse paused, watching Bell as she wriggled under his stare, sprawled in the straw. It was such a vulgar word coming from her hot little mouth. He growled in hunger.

Bell's hand flew to her mouth, as if she hadn't realized she'd said it aloud. Giving her no time to overthink it, he pounced, dropping to his knees by her feet. With an evil look, he slid his hands up her legs, feeling the soft fabric of her stockings catch on his calluses. In a swift motion he tore a hole in them, leaving her bare in the most important place.

The morning air was crisp, covering his exposed skin in goose bumps. His eyes bore into her as he unbuttoned his breeches. He pulled them down to his knees, unleashing the full length of him. His cock throbbed in his hand. Bell squirmed in the straw; her lip caught betwixt her teeth.

There was no slow, easing Bell into this time. He moved toward her, his finger brushing over her to make sure she was ready. In one swift motion he leaned over her and then thrust until he was buried to the hilt. Bell gasped beneath him; her breath pained. But she said nothing, only dug her nails into his back, and pulled him closer to her.

Narcisse wrapped his arm underneath her, his fingers splayed over her plump ass, pushing her against him, the cool morning forgotten. Their warm breaths mingled in the frigid air, his sweat slick skin slapping against hers.

He ground his hips into her, pushing deeper and deeper, her thighs growing wider and wider with each thrust. She welcomed him, took all of him, and begged him to go harder, deeper, harder, until she screamed. He didn't stop; couldn't stop the heat that built the harder he fucked her. Had he hurt her? *No.* There was nothing but raw, unadulterated pleasure in her eyes, the redness in her cheeks, the unrestrained moans that escaped her. He went wild. His thrusts were wild, animistic, pushing her into the straw.

Bell's cries of pleasure were his undoing. "Damn, Bell!" he groaned, feeling her tense around him.

Bell's head tipped back, her eyes rolling into the back of her head. Her moan caught in her throat, and she arched up toward him, her breasts pressed so hard against his chest he could feel her heart beating. Her moans exploded from her once more, and she dug her nails into his shoulder, pulling him closer still, and she pulsated around him, forcing his own undoing. The warmth that built deep inside him was enough to cause his moans to rival hers, and he lost all sense of himself. He pounded his hips into her, riding out his orgasm, pushing her legs even wider to welcome all of him.

Bell's mouth contorted in pain momentarily, as if she couldn't get her legs open more than she had, but it smoothed out into ecstasy as Narcisse's cock found the spot he had been looking for. His wife's moans became louder and less controlled as he pounded harder, faster, riding her through one release and straight into another.

He watched her face contort, her mouth open on a silent scream, felt her tighten around him. She arched against him even further, as if trying to get away from his cock and wanting to take more of him all at once. He opened the top of her dress and sucked a nipple into his mouth, biting slightly, nipping and sucking until he felt her tighten around him even further, almost holding him in place, and then spasmed uncontrollably, as if she had been electrocuted. He rode her through it, through his own re-release that continued to give, until he grunted through his teeth, slamming his palm into the hard ground to keep himself up as his legs shook.

Narcisse buried his face in her neck, biting softly as he collapsed on top of her. He could feel Bell's breasts rising and falling beneath his chest, could feel her hard nipples against his skin. A different kind of warmth filled his body when his wife nuzzled her cheek against him, closing her eyes.

She shifted underneath him, pulling her arm free to rest her hand on his cheek. "You should put your shirt and jacket back on before you catch a chill."

Narcisse nodded, pulling her up with him, shivering at the sudden loss of contact. He dressed fast, the rough fabric of his pants grating over his sensitive cock. He looked back up at Bell and couldn't help the laugh that shook his shoulders.

"What?" She crossed her arms.

"How are you so perfect?" he asked, picking straw from her hair.

She looked away bashfully.

"You should go get changed before you give someone a fright," he said, motioning to the ripped tights beneath her dress.

Bell seemed to suddenly remember her immodesty, and she made to cover herself up. "I'll leave you to your work," she squeaked.

Narcisse's eyes smoldered as he grinned up at her. She turned and disappeared out the shed, leaving Narcisse standing there, his cock aching once more.

"Wait!" he called after her.

She was almost at the front door when she stopped. "What is it?" she asked, worry in her tone.

"Care to join me at the tavern tonight? You could help me bamboozle drunkards out of their hard-earned coin."

"The tavern doesn't seem like a safe or respectable place for ladies to be seen."

"I would look after you while we were there, and no one would dare approach you with me by your side."

Bell watched him, speaking slowly with a smile. "And how will you take care of me and protect me from the drunks if you're going to be one of them?"

"Hey!" Narcisse retorted in mock outrage. "I'm not a drunk."

But Bell was already through the front door, her laughter trailing behind her.

Chapter Ten

NARCISSE HADN'T BEEN TO the tavern in some time, having decided instead to spend his time at home with his new wife, but it was exactly how he left it. There was noise to rival a circus, and it was filled to the brim with merry men and a handful of women. Most of the women were barmaids and those wishing to take money from the drunkards by exploiting their bodies.

"It's loud," Bell said, holding his arm tightly as he navigated through the crowd, finding his usual table at the back of the room.

Louis sat by himself, a beer already in his hand. As Narcisse approached, his friend's eyes flashed with surprise, then disappointment when he saw Bell with him.

"Louis," Narcisse said, clapping his friend on the shoulder.

"Hello," he said, tipping his head toward Bell questioningly.

Narcisse ignored his friend's implied question, motioning Bell to sit on the side closest to the wall so he could keep her from the view of any amorous man.

Bell wrung her hands before her, frowning ever so slightly, sinking down to the chair. "There's an awful lot of people here I've never seen before," she whispered. "Do they even live here?"

"Some are farmers. They come into town for the tavern," Louis answered.

Narcisse's hand rested on Bell's knee under the table, comforting her as he flagged down the barmaid.

The short, plump woman approached the table, the tavern lighting illuminating the sweat on her brow. "Narcisse, we haven't seen you here in some time," she said in way of greeting.

Narcisse smiled tightly, but it did not reach his eyes. Surely he hadn't spent *that* much time here that they noticed his absence.

"Marriage keeps him occupied!" Louis was the only one who laughed, beer foaming out of his nose.

The barmaid smiled softly at Bell, noticing her wide eyes and tight posture. "Three beers then?" she asked.

"Just the two." He could not imagine Bell guzzling down a beer with them nor the tinge of it on her breath.

But when the barmaid returned, she placed three beers on the table anyway, one directly in front of Bell. "It will calm your nerves," she assured his wife before disappearing back behind the bar.

Narcisse said nothing, grabbing his own tankard as he watched Bell. She brought the drink to her nose, sniffing ever so slightly. Her nose scrunched up in disgust. He expected her to place the tankard back on the table. But he paused, his drink frozen before him as she brought it to her lips. Her sip was small, tentative, but her whole face drained of color as she coughed on it.

"The taste isn't for everyone," he said, still watching her carefully as she recovered herself. Bell nodded, as if she intended to say that anyone who liked the taste was out of their minds.

"I like the taste though," he said, more to himself than anyone else.

Bell took another sip, the color returning to her cheeks as she drank more deeply this time. When she returned the tankard to the table, foam coated her lips and nose. Narcisse couldn't help but chuckle as he used the sleeve of his hunting jacket to wipe her face. He really couldn't believe he had brought her here with him. She seemed so out of place.

Bell glared at him from under her lashes, but there was amusement in her eyes as she swatted his hand away. She had relaxed slightly in this loud place, as if the small amount of beer she had consumed gave her the courage she needed.

"What brings you here?" Louis asked, not even attempting to hide the disappointment in his voice.

"Narcisse asked me to come," she shrugged.

"A tavern doesn't seem like the place for a lady," Louis muttered.

"Watch it," Narcisse warned.

"And you think it *is* the place for a gentleman? Or do you not consider yourself one?" Bell smirked around the tankard as she took another sip.

Louis's mouth open and closed, his retort lost on his tongue. He shook his head, clearly exasperated, and a hearty laugh burst from him. "I see that you can handle yourself."

She could, it seemed. Narcisse was impressed.

The barmaid returned moments later, placing platters of stew and bread in front of them. Narcisse hadn't even asked, but he was thankful. Dinner hadn't even crossed his mind.

"Marriage becomes you," the barmaid said as she left.

Narcisse stared after her, blinking.

"I'm not going to lie, it does," Louis said with a huff. "I wasn't sure, but seeing the two of you together — still alive, mind you — has changed my mind."

Heat crept over his skin as he noticed the men closest to them nodding in agreement. He hid his embarrassment by shoveling food into his mouth.

Bell pouted, looking from Louis to the retreating barmaid. "Thank you," she said, nodding at his friend. "I hadn't thought much of it, but you're right. I'm enjoying our marriage." The smile that graced her soft, plump lips was not one Narcisse had expected at all — it did not crinkle her eyes as he had seen every so often.

Louis waggled his eyebrows, clearly not noticing the tension in her smile. Bell looked away, a slight blush creeping up from the neckline of her dress. *Did she still have reservations?*

"Now," Bell mused, attempting to change the subject. "When would you like to start taking the drunkards' money?"

"Eat. We can do that before we leave."

"Why not start now?" Bell leaned over Narcisse, reaching down into the satchel he had placed at his feet. "Louis! How would you like to buy a new cutting board? It would be the perfect gift for your mother."

Louis gulped down his food, glaring at Narcisse for telling Bell he still lived with his parents. "Not today."

"Come on, I'll give you a friends discount," she urged.

"I don't give discounts, friend or other." Narcisse scoffed at the idea.

"*You* don't have to, but *I'm* offering my friend a discount on this beautifully made cutting board." She smiled sweeting at Louis, batting her lashes.

"Your friend?" Louis looked between Bell and Narcisse, his cheeks coloring.

"Of course. Now that Narcisse and I are married, we share everything. That means I got his friends in the marriage, and he gets my father."

"A wonderful trade," Narcisse quipped, not able to keep his grin at bay.

Bell glared at Narcisse before smiling sweetly at Louis. "Five silver coins, what do you say?"

Louis' sigh was audible over the din. "Fine." He pulled out his coin bag and placed five silver pieces on the table.

Narcisse sold his cutting boards for four silvers, but he said nothing, pocketing the coins. "Enjoy," Bell beamed. She swept from her seat, grabbing the satchel, and wandering into the crowd before he could stop her.

"It's a good thing she doesn't look like the prostitutes, otherwise she might get into trouble," Louis mused.

Indeed, she was dressed like a lady, and her stance said that any who messed with her would be dealt with accordingly. Meanwhile, the other women wore dresses that pushed up their breasts, as well as dark rouge and kohl around their eyes.

Narcisse stood, towering above the masses to keep an eye on his wife. It appeared the beer had given her liquid courage.

"A light drunk," Louis mused.

Narcisse chuckled, watching as Bell sauntered from table to table, advertising Narcisse's cutting boards and wall fittings.

Only a few refused. Others took some persuading, but soon Bell returned to the table with an empty satchel and a pocket full of coins.

"A great success, I see." Narcisse sat back in his chair, pulling Bell into the seat beside him.

"I sold every single piece," she said, but her tone was off.

"Huh." Narcisse watched her warily, noticing the way her shoulders slumped, the sparkle missing from her eyes.

"How much did you make?" Curiosity laced Louis' voice.

"I sold the cutting boards for eight silver pieces and the walling fittings for five."

Narcisse stared at her. "How on earth did you manage to sell them for double?"

"Threats, mostly," she said, her voice becoming hollower the more she spoke.

Louis thumped a fist on the table as he laughed, causing the table to shake. But Bell did not share in the amusement. In fact, she looked back at the tavern goers, scanning the crowd for God only knew what.

"What is it?" Narcisse's voice was soft. He pulled his chair closer to hers, gripping her chin with his calloused fingers.

She looked up at him from under her lashes; an entirely different implication than the other times she had done so.

"I overheard some gossip while I was working the crowd."

Louis was oddly silent, the amused laughter dying on his lips as he waited for her to speak. Bell wriggled in her seat, moving forward slightly to ensure no one outside their table would hear what she had to say.

Narcisse placed a gentle hand on her thigh, nodding to urge her on.

She gulped multiple times before she was able to speak clearly. "There have been more disappearances."

"More?" Louis scooted closer in his own chair, his elbows resting on the table.

Bell nodded slowly, her eyes flicking to his. "Many more." She chewed her lip. "Maybe they were enticed by the enchantress? No one seems to know it's her. Young woman, men, even children, missing." Bell rubbed at her eyes. "Some of the drunkards here are parents, husbands, all drinking away their sorrows. Some think they ran away, and some think they were abducted."

"No one has caught wind of the witch, then?" Narcisse glanced about, noticing the red-rimmed eyes and the worry that plagued so many.

"No one," Bell echoed. "This is a disaster, and no one has suspected anything."

Louis stood abruptly, nodded toward the door. "I'm going to check on my mother."

No one stopped him, but Narcisse wondered how his friend would break the news to his parents without spreading mass hysteria over the whole town.

It was a long night, and an even longer walk back home, with Bell at his side. After Louis left, Bell ordered beer after beer, drowning out the gossip of the missing townsfolk that circulated through the bar.

Narcisse had drunk just as much, wanting to blind himself to the tears and tales he heard for the remainder of his time at the tavern.

It was when the barmaid came to clear their empty tankards, and Bell had ordered more, that he decided enough was enough— both the drinking and the disappearances. He had to do something about it. So he drank water and watched his wife become merrier by the minute, until he was brave enough to drag her home.

She didn't resist.

They walked under the moonlight in silence, Bell swaying at his side.

"Bell," Narcisse warned, right before she slipped on the damp ground. Her feet went out from under her, falling on her rear with a splat.

She sat in the mud, her arms crossed. She glared at the ground and then at Narcisse, as if unable to decide whose fault it was that her dress was now wet through.

"Beer does not become you." Narcisse tried but failed to hold in his amusement as he helped Bell to her feet.

"I didn't drink that much," she pouted, accepting Narcisse's arm.

He didn't disagree. She had only had two tankards in total, and by the end of the first one she began speaking louder and laughing at everything Louis had said, hanging on his every word. *He's not* that *funny.*

Even with Narcisse's arm linked in hers Bell was sliding and stumbling. He smirked, a smug sense of satisfaction overwhelming him as she squeezed his muscles to stay on her feet. If it weren't for his masculine build he was sure he would have ended up on the ground with her.

"Can I tell you a secret?" she rasped.

"You can tell me anything," he replied, although he paused to look around them and ensure they were alone. God only knows what she would say in this condition.

Bell opened her mouth and a hiccup wracked her body. She paused before him, grabbing a hold of his upper arms and squeezing in appreciation. He said nothing, waiting for her to speak. After one last squeeze, she leaned in, her beer-laced breath washing over his face.

"I think I lo-o-ve you," she slurred, licking at her lips. "There, I said it!" Bell proceeded to place her hands on her hips, looking around the trees that surrounded them, instantly distracted.

He was utterly speechless. He shook his head, trying to clear his brain enough to trudge after Bell who had begun wandering toward their cottage.

She *loved* him?

Do I love her? Narcisse knew his heart had expanded, making room for her very soon after they married, but he wasn't entirely certain he loved her. Not yet anyway. Narcisse didn't love anyone, save for his parents. And they were dead.

"Thank you?" he called after her, running to catch up.

Bell stopped so suddenly that Narcisse had to grab onto her shoulders to keep himself from tackling her to the ground. She faced him once more, crossing her arms over her chest, accentuating her generous breasts.

Bell poked his chest, her finger pressing in as she leant forward slightly. "Thank you, for what?" she rasped.

Narcisse wanted to deny it. He wanted to laugh it off and pretend like she hadn't said anything at all. But going by her glassy, vacant eyes, her cheeks colored from the beer, he didn't have to say anything. She watched him, flashing her teeth in a grin he hadn't seen from her.

His brows cocked as he looked down at his beautiful wife and the mischief that shone in her eyes. The alcohol had fueled her courage in more ways than one tonight.

"I like you." Her grin grew. "You're f-funny."

With little warning, Narcisse swung Bell up in his arms, one around her back and the other hooked under her legs. She squealed in delight, grabbing his shirt. He cradled her like she was wounded and began walking toward home once more.

He nuzzled his face in her hair, his eyes closed in contentment as he took in his wife's floral scent, marred by beer. The path remained solid under his feet despite his distraction.

"I like you, too," he whispered into the crook of her neck.

"Of course you do," she giggled, her tongue lashing out to lick against the side of his face. She leaned her head against his chest, her eyes closed, but her teeth shone in the moonlight as she grinned. He had never seen her smile so widely, so openly. "I know," she breathed.

"How touching."

Narcisse's steps fumbled and he almost dropped Bell as the distorted voice wrapped around them. It was as if the voice came on a wind, from somewhere far away. It was both old and young, close and not close.

Narcisse blinked into the darkness, but could see nothing, no one.

"And here I thought you only liked yourself." The voice wrapped around him, as if it could strangle him.

He lowered Bell to the ground. She clung to him, desperately, her nails digging into his arms. She was afraid, and so was he. He pulled Bell behind him and drew out the hunting knife he kept strapped to his belt. He held it before him, in a loose grip, assessing the situation.

A figure materialized from the darkness, stopping in front of them. A woman Narcisse had never seen before. Shadows clung to her, moving around her as if alive.

"Who are you?" Bell whispered, popping her head around Narcisse's arm.

"I think you know who I am." But from the way Bell stared. He knew she had no idea.

She was beautiful and dark. Despite Narcisse knowing who this woman was, he hissed, "She asked you a question." His hand tightened around the handle of his hunting knife.

"Surely you recognize me," she smirked. "It hasn't been that long since I caught you trespassing in my yard, has it?"

Narcisse blinked at the woman. He knew who she was, and yet. . .

The single candle that lit up the window was barely enough to see, especially from where Narcisse stood at the base of the castle. But he could see the flame dance from the breeze, and the way the shadows flickered around it. As if from a nightmare, those dancing shadows solidified, until the candlelight was almost completely blocked from view. It moved toward the window, as if brought there by the breeze that had caused the light to flicker. He backed away on instinct, as the shadows continued to become darker, denser, until he was staring at a woman. A beautiful woman with hair the color of ink and bronze skin. Her teeth shone in the moonlight and Narcisse turned tail and ran after his friends, disappearing back into the woods.

"I saw you in the window." Narcisse breathed.

Bell glanced between them, as if she could piece it together without his input but failed. "Who is she?" she whispered.

"The witch." Narcisse answered and Bell gasped, moving further behind him. "The witch who has been tricking people, stealing them, taking them for herself."

"I prefer enchantress or sorceress," the woman shrugged, "but the notion is the same."

Narcisse had expected her to laugh at the accusation, not confirm it. "What do you want?"

"Don't look so afraid," she smiled. "I have forgiven you for your indiscretion. Just don't do it again. Next time I catch you, or your kin, on my land, I will not hold back."

"Why did you?" It was Bell who spoke for him, as if they shared the same mind.

"He didn't come looking for me, like so many others have. He and his friends were merely exploring, which is not what I can say about the other selfish souls." When neither of them spoke, she added, "Oh, don't look so shocked! I'm not the bad person that everyone sees me as. I don't need to be feared. Respected, yes, but not feared."

"But what of the doctor?" Bell asked, "And what of all the others you have taken?"

"It is the price for magic. Magic isn't free, something must be given. When I use it, I give a piece of myself every time. When others come for my help, they must give something of their self in return."

"That is why I have come." She stepped further from the trees, the shadows following her like the way fog clung to the lake during winter.

"To take something from *us*? We had no idea the salve had magic in it!" Narcisse grabbed Bell's arm in warning. She shook against his back, her breathing loudly in his ear.

"I have come for Doctor Salvatore. His time has come to make payment for what he has taken from me."

"He's not here," Narcisse said.

"I can see that. I was told he was with you a few days ago. No one has seen him since. It seems he has run, feeling his time would soon come."

"We haven't seen him in days," Narcisse glowered. "If we see him, we'll be sure to send him your way."

The sorceress watched them, her mouth cocking up the more she stared. "Be sure that you do." Her eyes went to Narcisse's chest, staring through him to his cowering wife behind him. "What a beauty you have become. And here we thought you wouldn't make it." She chuckled. "A pleasure to see you alive and well after all these years. If I find that you have helped him in any way, then I will indeed come for you both, bargain or not."

"What do you mean?" Bell gulped, but the sorceress was gone, swallowed by her shadows.

Life returned to the woods the instant she was gone. The shadows disappeared with her, and they were left staring into an empty space.

"That was frightening," Bell breathed, fear sobering her some. "What on earth could she have meant by that?"

Narcisse said nothing. He turned to face Bell, his heart breaking as he saw the tears that ran down her cheeks. With a gentleness he didn't know he possessed he rested his hands on the sides of her face and used his thumbs to wipe away the tears that fell.

"Shhh," he soothed. Swinging his wife up in his arms once more, he walked toward their home.

"I can walk," she whispered, as if she was too afraid to speak in case it brought the sorceress to them again.

"I know." He didn't want to let her go though. He used her warmth, her presence, to ground himself and to clear his mind of the shadows that remained.

He walked the rest of the way home with Bell in his arms, her head against his shoulder. Narcisse said nothing further until he walked through the front door and fell to the couch with her still in his arms. He held her against his chest, his face buried in her neck.

Sweat coated his hands, his back, his brow. His heart still beat sporadically in his chest. Narcisse had never felt such fear before, and it wasn't for himself. It was for Bell.

Marrying had become both a blessing and a curse.

"You won't really tell her if you find Doctor Salvatore, *right*?" Bell mumbled against his chest.

"No," he reassured her, but it was no soothing thought. If the sorceress wanted him, she could find Salvatore herself.

Chapter Eleven

THE WOOD NARCISSE HAD chopped and covered was yet to dry out completely. The cold, frigid air covered his land in dew each morning, seeming to find its way into the covered wood, and extending the drying time even further. Sure, it had dried slightly since he'd cut the tree down, but if he were to wait for it to dry out completely, like he would have preferred, then he would be waiting another six months.

"It'll do," he said to Bell as she helped him carry some of the larger pieces to his woodworking station at the back of the house. "The moisture isn't ideal, but there isn't much we can do about it."

"Why does the wood have to dry, anyway?" Bell grunted behind him.

Narcisse turned to answer his wife, but paused, his lips curled into a smile as she struggled to carry a smaller stump. "The furniture will shrink as the moisture leaves the wood."

"What will you do?"

"I'll have to ensure the fixings are extra tight and secure so that as it shrinks the pieces move together, rather than leaving large gaps, and potentially breaking apart entirely."

Bell wiped her brow. "Do you know how to do that?"

Narcisse frowned in mock offense. "I've been making furniture for years, dear."

She nodded, turning on her heel to fetch more wood. When she returned, her arms loaded, she asked, "Where did you learn to make furniture?"

Narcisse was struck dumb, if only momentarily. No one had ever bothered to ask him. "My father. He created things for people all over town, and he taught me. When he died, I took over his regular clientele, as well as getting some of my own."

Bell wiped her hands together and then placed them on her hips. "Is that enough wood?" she panted.

"Plenty." He had carried over what he needed, the smaller pieces adding to his large mound on the table. "Thank you for your help."

She seemed satisfied with his praise as she turned and left with a soft smile on her face. Narcisse heard the front door shut before he began sizing up the pieces and sanding them. He had only just begun assembling the base when he heard voices in the distance; they grew louder the longer he worked.

He stopped his work, folding his arms across his burly chest. The voices only grew as he waited, until there was a knock on the front door. Narcisse groaned but wiped his hands and forehead on a cloth before stepping out from behind the back of the house.

Three men in large, hooded coats stood before an opened door. He watched as Bell welcomed them into their home. He dropped the cloth to the ground, racing to the front door before Bell closed it.

He sighed inwardly at whom he found. Jacques and Louis stood in his kitchen, the former removing his coat. But it was the village mayor — *self-appointed* — that had him pausing.

The three men turned to face Narcisse, Louis smiling apologetically. "How can I help you?" Narcisse asked, removing his work apron and hanging it by the door.

Louis followed suit, taking a seat at the kitchen table. "The mayor was on his way here. When I heard why I decided to tag along."

"As did I." Jacques sat beside Louis.

"Yes, when I told them why I sought you out, they insisted on coming."

Narcisse smirked at his friend and father-in-law and the annoyance the mayor wasn't trying to hide. He motioned the mayor to take a seat, while Bell busied herself in the kitchen, preparing tea.

"Why *are* you here?" Narcisse sat at the head of the table, his hands steepled in front of him.

"Wait for the tea, it's almost ready," Bell mused.

"I don't think this is a topic for ladies," the mayor said, though his eyes scanned Bell appreciatively. Narcisse tensed, glowering at the mayor's unsavory glances.

"You will come to realize that anything said to me will be discussed with my wife once you leave." Narcisse grimaced. "We will wait for Bell to finish the tea; it will save me repeating it again."

The mayor frowned in disapproval but shrugged. "Very well."

Bell sat a steaming teapot on the table, along with a stack of teacups. When she was seated to the side of Narcisse, she began pouring tea and sliding the teacups across the table. Both Louis and her father thanked her, but the mayor ignored her kind gesture and leaned back in the chair. He eyed Narcisse, as if evaluating him.

"It isn't often that I visit villagers' homes," he said. Narcisse almost growled. They knew all too well that the self-appointed mayor felt too important to visit any of them. Something must have been quite awry for him to be here now. He sat in his large home on the top of the hill overlooking the apple orchard and ignored the village until he had no choice but to intervene. "Something has been brought to my attention."

"What is it?" Bell looked to her father, waiting for him to chime in. He remained quiet, his eyes on the mayor as he spoke.

"As you are aware, many of the villagers have gone missing over the last few months." The mayor eyed them, as if they had something to do with it. "More and more people, young and old, going missing without any indication as to what has happened to them."

Narcisse knew all too well, thanks to the enchantress and her recent visit. He furrowed his brows, watching the mayor.

"Now Doctor Salvatore has gone missing."

Narcisse was quiet, waiting for the accusation.

"When the first people started to disappear, I could have believed that they ran off together, but not the doctor. He wouldn't have up and left the town without a physician." He eyed Narcisse suspiciously. "I have investigated it, and it has been made apparent that he was last seen here. Can you tell me why he was here?"

"Surely you're not saying we had something to do with his disappearance?" Bell squeaked.

"I'm simply piecing together a picture of his last hours so that we may find out what happened to him."

"Bullshit," Narcisse spat. "You're accusing us."

"I'm not accusing you of anything. Just tell me why he was here."

"You've never cared about any of us before, why start now?"

The mayor looked as though he would deny it, but instead he shrugged. Even he knew he cared only for himself. "He is our only physician. We need him."

Narcisse wasn't sure where he was — he had no idea if the enchantress was telling the truth that he had gotten away. "He was here to inform us of a mistake he made, and to assist after if affected me." Narcisse was careful to be vague, unwilling to tell him anything further if he didn't have to. "He left after that, and I haven't seen him since."

The mayor narrowed his eyes, scanning Narcisse. "And what mistake, pray tell, is that?"

Narcisse couldn't tell him. If the mayor didn't know what the doctor had done, what he had sacrificed for the town, then that was not his story to tell. He was grateful when Jacques spoke, drawing the mayor's attention away from him.

"I saw him in town the next day," Jacques chimed in, shrinking into his own self when the mayor faced him. "He seemed panicked. He was in a rush to get home."

"Are you—"

"You know who lives in that castle," Narcisse interrupted.

The mayor balked, fear flashing in his eyes before leveling out to indifference. "It's an abandoned castle, nothing more."

"We all know that's not true." When everyone else remained quiet Narcisse admitted, "She came to us a few nights ago."

"She *what*?" Jacques was on his feet in an instant, rushing to Bell's side. There was true fear in his eyes then, and he examined his daughter as if checking to make sure she had not been harmed. But there was something more to that fear—something that the older man was hiding. Something Narcisse would pry from him as soon as the mayor left.

Narcisse blinked, looking away from Jacques and leveling a stare at the mayor. "We were walking home late one night, and she just materialized from the shadows." He shook his head, clearing the shadows that built around him as he spoke. "She also wanted to know where the doctor was."

"And why did she approach *you* to find him?"

"The same reason you have. Apparently, no one knows where he is, and we were one of the last people to see him."

The mayor watched Narcisse suspiciously, as if deciding whether Narcisse was at fault here.

"This gets out to no one," the mayor said, standing abruptly and making for the front door. "We don't need the town finding out who lives there."

In the quiet that accompanied the absence of the mayor, Narcisse remembered the stories told to him as a child to scare him away from going to the castle. That had just enticed him and his friends, and he'd made the mistake of trespassing.

"Maybe the town needs to know." Bell stood, emptying the teapot into the sink.

"It's not wise," her father said.

"Perhaps if more people knew about the castle, they wouldn't make the same mistake so many others had made. They wouldn't sell their lives to the enchantress for a small taste of her magic."

Narcisse had to admit, she did have a point. But he knew what people were like. It might just entice them to seek her out.

"Leave it for now," he said, rising from his own chair. "I believe it's best to keep them in the dark for now, otherwise they will only approach her for themselves. We'll just go about things like normal." He shrugged. "Then if things escalate, we'll tell them exactly who they're messing with."

"And you truly don't know where Doctor Salvatore is?" Jacques asked.

Narcisse glowered at him, causing the older man to squirm under his stare. "What is it you think I have done to the doctor?"

"Nothing," Jacques held his hands before him. "I just mean perhaps you know he is hiding. Perhaps *you* are hiding him?"

"Why would I put my wife at risk? I don't want my wife anywhere near that hag, and hiding Salvatore would only bring her back here."

Jacques nodded, his shoulders sagging in relief. "Good, keep it that way."

Louis looked between them. "If I were him, I would have fled and never looked back."

His words echoed through Narcisse's head. *Louis isn't the only one who would run if their life was at stake. I would leave. I would take Bell, maybe even Louis and Jacques, and I'd run as far as I could, until I was sure she'd never find me.* It seemed like the only rational thing to do, unless Doctor Salvatore thought taking his own life would save him from whatever she had planned for him.

"You're probably right," Narcisse nodded. "He had a feeling his time was coming soon, and he knew that the best thing to do was to run. He's probably somewhere far away right now, safe from the sorceress' reach."

Bell huffed in frustration. "How do you know she doesn't have him locked up right as we speak?"

"Because if he's smart, he'll be in hiding. Somewhere where the witch wouldn't think to look."

Jacques was standing by the front door now, and Louis went to join him. They eyed each other, as if coming to terms with what may have just happened to Doctor Salvatore. She didn't seem the type to brag if she had captured him, so would they ever truly know what happened to him? He could be rotting away in her dungeons at this very moment.

"I guess now that the mayor's gone, I won't need this." Louis produced a stick from his pocket, dropping it onto the table.

"Why on earth were you carrying a stick?"

"If he was going to accuse you of having anything to do with Doctor Salvatore's disappearance, I planned to bonk him over the head with it."

Narcisse could see Bell cover her mouth behind Louis, her eyes crinkling at the corners.

"Let me get this straight," Narcisse grinned. "You were going to attack the mayor with a stick? Then what? Were you planning on killing him or just knocking him unconscious?"

"It depends how hard I hit him in the heat of the moment, I guess."

Narcisse could feel his skin prickling as he held in his laughter. "And what did you plan on doing with his body if you had killed him? Bury it in my garden?"

Louis shrugged, but Narcisse could see he hadn't planned anything at all, besides looking out for his friend. Narcisse grabbed Louis by the elbow and tugged him into his arms.

"You're a good friend," he said, using his knuckles to mess his hair.

"Wait," Bell giggled, holding up her hands. "What would you have done if you'd managed to knock him unconscious? Drag him outside and hope he didn't remember you hit him over the head with a stick?"

Louis shrugged again, his face heating.

"Imagine if you hit him with it and he didn't get knocked out. What if he just stood there, glaring at you for hitting him with a stick?"

Laughter rumbled from Narcisse's chest, his shoulders shaking.

Louis's face grew redder, but soon he was laughing with them. "I guess I didn't think that far. All I know is that if he was going to blame you for this, he was going to go missing, like the doctor."

Narcisse looked at his friend in horror, but then Louis laughed again, winking as Narcisse shook his head. He wasn't entirely sure he was joking.

No one had seen or heard from Doctor Salvatore. Although there were now many villagers missing with no word from any of them, people had started to spread rumors about his disappearance. Narcisse knew they were simply doing it to pass time, and to reassure themselves that he would return, but the rumors were starting to get rather ridiculous. One in particular had Narcisse frowning. Many were saying that he had run away with one of his nurses, although the only two nurses he had in his employ were still there.

"Maybe someone should look for him,' Bell said one morning, on their way into town. "Make sure he's safe."

"It's too risky. If she hasn't already found him, she will be led straight to him."

Bell and Narcisse walked arm in arm through the bustling town center. They could hear the hushed whispers that spread around town, and Narcisse was content to ignore them, until he noticed the many eyes turned toward them.

"Do you think they know we were the last to see him?" Narcisse whispered, his eyes on his wife.

"Looks like it."

But they were far from right.

The eyes had not been on them at all, but rather the old cottage that stood behind them.

Doctor Salvatore's house was one of the oldest in this town; the beautiful stone and wood building reflecting the town's past. The doctor had inherited the home from his family, and he had always been one to look after the old cottage, ensuring it would last another hundred years.

Narcisse turned to the house, sighing at how the beautiful home now stood cold and empty. The door was wide open and seemed to creak and rock in the wind, an eerie site to behold.

"What happened?" Narcisse asked a man who passed by.

The man shrugged, taking a step away from Narcisse to look back at the doctor's cottage. "The strangest thing," he said, rubbing the back of his neck. "I didn't see it myself, but my neighbor said he saw a beautiful woman cloaked in shadow kick down the door as if it were nothing." He looked behind him, as if he expected to find her standing there, ready to kick him down. "She raided his home and was there for quite some time but left without a single thing."

"No one tried to stop her?" Bell whispered.

"Not with the way she barged in there." The man shook his head. He turned to leave, but Narcisse stopped him again with a hand on his arm.

"What did she look like?"

"Rumor has it that her hair was dark as tar, her glowing skin the color of coffee." The man leaned in, as if afraid to say anything else above a whisper. "She was the most beautiful woman ever seen, but there was a rage in her that twisted her face. People were afraid of her. She burst from the house, screaming in what can only be assumed as anger, elbowed past people, pushing some to the ground as she retreated. No one stopped her. Then she disappeared like so." The man clicked his fingers. "Poof, and she was gone."

"The mayor is in there now, looking to see if she may have taken something, but her hands were empty when she passed us," a woman chimed in.

Narcisse nodded his thanks, walking toward the hanging door. "If she came here and raided the place, it must mean she hasn't found him yet."

Bell nodded, stopping at the bottom of the stairs. "I'm not going in there," she said, scowling at the rubble that covered the floor.

"Of course. How rude of me to try and drag my wife into a crime scene." He was a moment away from unhooking his arm from hers so he could go inside alone when the mayor stepped outside.

"Narcisse," he said, his face a mask. The mayor looked disheveled, his hair out of place and his cheeks red. "I didn't expect to see you here." He nodded toward Bell, "Madam."

Bell smiled, despite her obvious unease, although it did not meet her eyes. "What happened?" she asked.

The mayor looked out at the townspeople who had gathered around the house. "Nothing to be troubled about, just a love affair gone wrong!" he called out, before placing a shaking hand on Narcisse's elbow and leading him to the side of the house.

"Was it her?" Bell hissed, following close behind them. "Was it the witch?"

"Shhh" The mayor held up his hands, silencing them. He looked behind them, scanning the empty alley before he spoke.

"It seems that way, yes."

"Are you sure?" Narcisse asked.

"We've gathered information from all those who witnessed the break-in and all the descriptions are the same. Plus, we found this."

Narcisse squinted at the small hessian bag he held in front of their faces. "What is it?"

"We're not certain, but it seems to be buzzing with magic. She is the only person we know who holds magic in our town. It must be her."

Bell took a step back. "Should you be touching it then?"

"Put it back," Narcisse said at the same time. He ignored the mayor's glower, adding, "Maybe it's best to leave it where she put it, so that she doesn't know others are aware of what she is."

The mayor was quiet as he mulled it over. "Perhaps you're right. It will give us the upper hand." He said nothing further before turning on his heels and disappearing back inside Doctor Salvatore's home and medical practice.

"Do you think they know who or what she is?" Bell whispered, looking out at the villagers who still milled around the house.

"There are many who don't, but some of the older generation seem to know. I recall my grandparents telling me stories about the monster who lived in the castle. I thought they were old wife's tales to keep us in line and out of the woods, but they must have been referring to her."

"What do you think she'll do to the doctor when she finds him?"

Narcisse linked his arm with his wife once more and began a casual stroll toward the market. "You think she'll find him?"

Bell kept her voice low as she said, "I do. It's not a matter of if; it's a matter of *when* she finds him. She has magic, and he has nothing."

"Let's hope she doesn't find him until he's an old man and his life is truly ready to end." But somehow Narcisse knew it wouldn't be the case.

"But what do you think she'll do to him?" Bell asked again.

"I can't imagine her being merciful. Maybe she will keep him as her slave until he dies. Maybe she will torture him, or maybe she will absorb his life force, his soul, to regain the magic he borrowed. Who knows? If it's inevitable, let's hope for a quick and painless ending for Doctor Salvatore."

The market was buzzing as usual, but the gossip had turned to what had come of Doctor Salvatore and who the woman was. Narcisse noticed a group of older villagers, the age his grandparents would have been if they were still alive, standing together, away from the noise. Their eyes scanned the younger crowd with fear in the eyes. They knew who she was, they had to. Narcisse couldn't help recalling the fanciful tales his grandmother had told him in front of the fireplace before bed. Her eyes had shone not only from the flames, but perhaps from wonder as she spoke of magic.

"Once upon a time, in this time and the time before, there lived a beautiful woman. She resided in a large white castle, covered in smoke and shadows, guarded by gargoyles. She watched the world outside through their eyes, you see.

"You said this story was going to be about monsters, not princesses." Narcisse crossed his arms, ever a defiant five-year-old.

"But it is. You see, the beautiful woman wasn't a princess at all. She was only disguised as a beautiful woman, when really, she was a terrifying monster who held the power to destroy us all. Inside those walls she kept innocent people who she had tricked with her beauty. They stayed in her dungeon, wasting away until they were nothing but an empty shell. Then she ate the husks, feeding her beauty with what was left of them. Others, the beautiful young ones, she devoured the moment she called on them, never allowing their beauty to go to waste. For you see, she used their life, their beauty, their youth, to stay young and beautiful forever."

Narcisse had grinned like the little terror he was when his grandmother told him of the wicked monster who lived from the lives of others, but his stomach churned now as he recalled what she had said. His grandmother's face dissolved before his eyes, and he was staring at the group of older people. Narcisse jumped slightly when he realized he now stood in front of them.

"Forgive me," he said. "I was distracted."

Why was it that older eyes always seemed wiser than most? They watched him as he backed away, as if they had witnessed his memories and discerned that he knew of the witch just as they did.

"We should get home."

"We just got here," Bell frowned.

"I know. But I don't want us to be here if she decides to come back."

Bell watched Narcisse, her eyes searching his.

Narcisse remained silent, lost in his past, for most of the walk back. He couldn't shake the knowing stares of the older gentleman who watched him retreat with his wife. They had reminded him of his grandmother's.

Was it true what his grandmother had said in the stories she told him at such a young age? The sorceress was older than anyone in this town, and she was able to stay so youthful by taking the lives of others. How many people did she have held captive in her castle, and how many had she killed?

Narcisse couldn't stop the raw fear that twisted his stomach. He worried for the doctor, and what the enchantress would do once she got her hands on him.

Chapter Twelve

T HE MATTRESS OPENED UP, melding around him to swallow his large form, encasing his arms and legs. He was trapped.

Narcisse tried to move, but couldn't. He couldn't shut his eyes, couldn't scream. All he could do was stare as the enchantress appeared from the shadows. A smirk stretched across her face as she stood over him. His mouth hung open, and he tried so desperately to call out to his wife, but Bell slept soundly beside him, unaware of his distress.

Narcisse's chest ached from the force it took to suck down a breath as the mattress continued to constrict him. It was alive – a tar-like substance, oozing and pulsating against him, stretched over his muscled body until he was nothing but a face. The enchantress moved toward him like liquid through the night, shadows lifting from her skin like steam over boiling water.

"I knew from the moment I saw you, gawking up at me from my gardens, that you would be trouble," she said.

What do you want? His words echoed inside his head, but he could not speak them aloud. The sorceress grinned menacingly down at him, her eyes full of delight as she watched the mattress inch over his face.

Pain laced through his body, but he was able to fist his hands at his side. He tried in vain to pull from the trap, but it was no use. *It was no use.* The mattress moved over his face like ocean water over a rock. His breath continued to come out in panicked bursts, until the mattress completely covered his nose and mouth.

The last thing he saw as the darkness spread over his eyes was the enchantress hovering above Bell, a hand poised above his wife's heart, as if she would tear it right from her chest. Then the world was nothing but darkness and shadows. Narcisse felt the darkness fill him, body and soul, like hot coals simmering within him - a dark so black it was oblivion.

He was nothing.

A jolt of pain shot through Narcisse as though he'd plunged into ice water, and he sat up so fast he tumbled to the floor, hitting the cold ground so hard it reverberated through his teeth. He lay on the floor, his chest heaving.

It was a dream, he told himself.

But he wasn't so sure. He scanned the room, focusing on the shadows that gathered in the corners. Nothing; they were alone. There was no enchantress there, but he felt wrong-- as though he could feel her on him, feel her in the air around them.

"Narcisse?" Bell groaned, sitting up in bed. Her eyes narrowed in confusion when she found him on the floor.

"I'm fine." He stood on shaky legs, wiping his sweat-soaked palms on his bare legs. "Just a bad dream, go back to sleep."

"Another one?" Bell asked softly, much like she would to a child.

"Don't pity me," he growled.

Her concern transformed into annoyance. "It's not pity, Narcisse. It's *worry* for my husband. Is it Doctor Salvatore going missing that's gotten to you?"

"No. It hasn't gotten to me." But it had. Whenever Narcisse was left alone to his own thoughts, he was suffocated with "what-ifs". What if the sorceress hadn't let him leave the castle as a child? What if he and his friends had tried to enter the castle itself? What if he had been dealt the same fate as Doctor Salvatore?

What if I had been kept there and never given the chance to meet Bell?

"If you say so." Bell sighed, a strangled noise of frustration, pulling the blankets up to her chin. "I'm going back to sleep."

Narcisse swallowed to a retort. She had every right to be upset at how he had spoken to her. But he wasn't annoyed at Bell for pitying him; he was annoyed at himself for allowing this to get to him. Men shouldn't feel so vulnerable, so *weak*.

There was nothing he could do about it. Doctor Salvatore was a fool for offering his life for the use of her magic, after all. Yet, what he had done was selfless and had saved so many other lives.

Was one life worth the lives of twenty?

"What is wrong with me?" he whispered into the silence.

"You're a stubborn man," Bell answered him.

Narcisse shook his head, suppressing his grin. "Is that not why you love me?"

"I don't love you," she scoffed.

"Come on now, love, even you know that's a lie."

Bell's soft laughter washed over Narcisse like warm honey, taking away some of the fear that still clung to him. "Come back to bed or stop talking so I can sleep."

He had every intention of going back to bed, but the darkness that encased the room held tightly to his nightmare. Bell said nothing as he lit a candle that sat on the table beside his bed. A single candle, the warm orange glow enough to rid the shadows of the power they currently held over him.

As tired as Narcisse was, he couldn't help but watch the doorway that led to the living room, half expecting the sorceress to materialize from the shadows like she had done so before. He had left the door open when they'd come to bed, and now it seemed to mock him, the darkness beyond watching him back.

A loud, unrelenting racket tore Narcisse from a fitful sleep, the world crashing back around him at the crude banging.

"Someone's at the door," Bell whispered beside him.

Narcisse swore under his breath. The sound was indeed rude, hurried knocking. He groaned, rubbing his sore, aching eyes. The knocking continued until

Narcisse pulled on a pair of trousers, stomped into the living room and yanked open the front door.

"What is it?" he snapped.

Louis stood before him, his fist raised, ready to knock again. Louis' cheeks were red, his chest heaving, as if he had run all the way there.

Narcisse stepped aside and motioned Louis inside as he asked, "What happened?"

"Y-you are not going to be-lieve what is happening in town right now!" Louis held his hand to his chest. He threw the same hand in the air as he added, "The witch came back to town!"

Narcisse's chest tightened as the nightmare replayed alongside his friend's words. "When?"

"She's been there for about half an hour now. She's refusing to leave until Salvatore comes out of hiding or until someone takes her to him."

"Who is it?" Bell called from the bedroom.

"You should probably get dressed and join us in the living room," Narcisse yelled back.

Bell came out of the bedroom, the sounds of fabric brushing against her as she wrapped herself up in Narcisse's robe.

"Louis," she said warily in greeting. "What is it?"

Narcisse stepped toward her. He needed her beside him as he spoke. "The sorceress is in town, and she won't leave until she has the doctor,"

"What of the townspeople?" Bell wrung her hands by the unlit fireplace, as if she needed the idea of warmth to get through this conversation.

Louis paced before them. "Everyone has been called out into the town square. She's refusing to let anyone leave. I managed to sneak away while the mayor was distracting her."

"Father," Bell cried out, a hand flying to her mouth. "We have to go make sure he's safe."

"It's not a good idea, Bell," Louis frowned, pausing in front of her. "She's announced that if no one comes forward with Doctor Salvatore's location or any relevant information in the next hour, she will start prying it out of people by force."

"But she'll hurt the doctor!" Bell whispered, as if she were afraid to speak it allowed. "And what of the town if they refuse to talk?"

"The worst thing about it is that no one actually knows where he is. And they don't even know who *she* is."

"Surely they know now?" Narcisse could not imagine anyone questioning the sorceress if she stood in the middle of the town square with her shadows dancing around her.

"Oh, they do. I saw it firsthand." Louis shook his head as if he still couldn't believe it himself. "She came from nowhere, and when people tried to leave, she used her magic to keep them in place."

"Keep them in place?" *How on earth could she manage that?*

"It was like they were stuck in tar; they couldn't lift their feet from the ground."

Narcisse's dream came to mind once more, like a prediction of what was to come today.

"How does she plan to pry the information? By force?" Bell chewed her lip, likely thinking of her father.

"She didn't say, but whatever she does, I don't want to be on the receiving end."

What could she have planned? It would be impossible to torture information from people when they had none.

"Perhaps there is someone who knows where he is," Louis said, as if answering Narcisse's thoughts. "Someone might have seen him leave, or maybe he told one of his nurses where he was going. They might come forward before she hurts anyone."

"We should be there," Bell said, pacing behind Narcisse, who refused to let her close to the door.

Narcisse rested a hand on Bell's shoulder to stop her pacing. "There's nothing we can do. Being there is only going to make matters worse."

"How is us being there to help going to make anything worse? And Father, I need to make sure he's okay."

"I didn't see him in the town square," Louis chimed in. "Perhaps he is still at home."

"I don't want to take that chance. What if someone tells the witch that he spoke to Doctor Salvatore before he left? She could think he knows something the others don't. She'd try to force it out of him."

Narcisse moved his hand to his wife's cheek. She trembled beneath his touch, as if she struggled to keep still. There was no use trying to calm her, as her fear was what controlled her. To Narcisse's surprise, it was Louis who seemed to know what to do and what to say.

"I'm going back. I need to make sure my parents are okay, I'll look out for your father too," Louis said, moving toward the door.

Narcisse hesitated but moved to join him. "I'm coming with you."

"No!" Bell tugged at the sleeve of his hunting jacket as he swung it on. "Please don't go."

"You would risk yourself for your father, but worry for me?"

The look of distress in Bell's eyes made him pause. "I can't bear to have you both out there. She'll see you; she'll recognize you and hurt you. I just know it."

"Dear, don't underestimate me. I don't plan on being seen. I'll survey from the back, away from the view of the hag, and if I don't see your father I'll come back."

"I want to come with you," she pouted.

"No chance. I'm your husband and I protect you, taking you there will put you in harm's way, which is against everything I stand for."

Bell's hands went to her hips. "Being my husband doesn't mean you have to protect me."

"I'm not arguing this again. Just stay here and be safe." Narcisse gave her no room to argue as he backed out of the house and pulled the door shut on her glare.

"That was awkward," Louis muttered, scratching his scalp as they made their way into town on foot.

"If you say so."

Narcisse hoped this wouldn't cause any friction between Bell and himself. But more than that, he hoped she would actually listen to him and stay home.

"Do you think anyone knows more about Doctor Salvatore than they're letting on?" Louis asked.

"I think we need to remain quiet, who knows if she has ears or eyes in these woods."

Louis nodded, looking ahead. After a few minutes of silence he blurted, "Don't you think we should come up with a plan of action before we get there?"

"My plan is to get into town without being noticed, find Jacques and ensure he's safe, then get out of there."

Louis stopped, gazing sideways at Narcisse. "Where do I fit in with that plan?"

"You *don't*. You go find your parents and make sure they're okay. Then, stay hidden until the hag leaves."

His friend looked as though he would protest and insist they stay together. Instead, he snorted, "*Hag*. A title not befitting someone so beautiful, don't you think?"

"A title befitting a terrible person," Narcisse replied with a grimace.

Louis shook his head, exasperated. He began walking again before he spoke. "I hope someone comes forward."

"You hope someone turns in the doctor so the sorceress can take him and do whatever it is she has planned with him?"

"It's better than the alternative," Louis shrugged.

Narcisse supposed he was right. He tried to keep reminding himself that one life taken was better than the whole town being punished. After all, Doctor

Salvatore had apparently thought the same thing when he made the bargain. Now it seemed that he would rather live. Perhaps he thought he could find a way out of it. Had he known that the sorceress would come looking for him and put the whole town in danger?

Their footfalls were whispers, somehow growing quieter as they approached town. Narcisse tried to tread carefully, fearful that any noise would draw unwanted attention.

Louis was silent beside him; the only sound he made his own rushed footfalls. Narcisse eyed Louis sideways, noticing the sweat on his brow that matched his own, the breeze washing over his damp skin cooling his nerves.

Things had gone very wrong the last few weeks, and he was about to throw himself into the fold to rescue his father-in-law. But there was something inside of him, something niggling deep within, besides the need to rescue the Bell's father, that had him scared for what was to become of his small town if the enchantress wasn't stopped.

He feared for Jacques and Louis, he feared deeply for his wife, but more importantly—he feared for all the lives that would be taken if someone didn't step in.

What was I thinking?

Narcisse nodded once, reassuring himself. He was there to get Jacques and that was it, not rescue the whole town. He could do this.

Did abandoning the town make Narcisse a bad person? Maybe, but there were battles Narcisse knew he wouldn't win. He needed to choose them wisely, even if that meant ignoring the sorceress at this time.

The air grew thicker the closer to town they got. The cool morning breeze whipped at his sleep-mussed hair as he walked through the fog that clung to the ground. The moment Narcisse and Louis stepped from the trees and felt the town cobble stones beneath their feet, all sound disappeared – no birds or crickets, no chattering. Utter silence, as if the town were encased in a giant bubble, swallowing everything within.

"It's so quiet," Louis whispered as they stopped behind a stone building.

They were only a street away from the town square, and yet there was barely a whisper. Had the sorceress left after all?

"What's happening?" a voice whispered from behind them.

Narcisse span on his heels, his hand reaching for his hunting blade that was strapped to his belt. "For goodness sakes, Bell! I told you to stay home."

"I took it as a suggestion rather than a demand." She threw him a wane smile, but he could see her shake beneath her cloak.

"This is serious, Bell. It's not a game of husband-knows-best, this is your life."

"I know. I thought about what you said, and I decided that your life is worth just as much as mine. I want to protect you just as much as you want to protect me."

"Shh." Louis held his hand up, pointing in the direction of the town square.

Narcisse's eyes narrowed. In the past, Narcisse would have dragged Bell back to their cottage and locked her inside. But as he looked at his brave little wife, chin up, his heart swelled. He adored her courage, even if it terrified him. If she got hurt, he could never forgive himself, but he could not deny her being by his side. His shoulder's slumped in defeat.

Bell smirked, realizing she had won.

He moved forward until he was pressed up against the back of the grocers, then peeked around the corner. His heart fell to his feet.

Sure enough, the enchantress stood outside the town hall, her powerful presence towering over all who gathered there. Narcisse shivered as her voice washed over his skin.

A voice that had previously sounded like honey to him now left a bitter aftertaste and carried out further than humanly possible.

There was a condescending sweetness to her tone as she addressed those gathered. "I am giving you until sundown! If your peasant doctor isn't handed over, I will take a dozen people in his stead."

Narcisse looked to his wife and friend. Bell's hand had flown to her mouth.

"She can't," she rasped, her eyes wide.

"It seems she can," he whispered.

He crept forward, toward the buildings that surrounded the square and peered between them.

He could just make out those gathered there, some standing, some kneeling. He scanned the crowd for Jacques, but he was nowhere to be seen.

None of the villagers spoke. No one seemed willing to speak up; after a moment, twelve people shuffled forward. Narcisse's skin buzzed as he watched the witch drift between the townsfolk, staring each and every one of them down.

"So no one truly knows where he's gone to, then," Louis whispered beside him.

Narcisse wasn't so sure. Maybe no one did know, but he knew that if Louis had run he wouldn't have given his location away either. Perhaps one of the doctor's close friends or family members knew where he had gone and were hiding it a little too well?

Narcisse opened his mouth to whisper back to Louis but then a small figure stepped forward and his response died on his lips.

A tiny woman, barely five feet, waddled forward, the crowd parting around her. She threw her head back, staring the enchantress down, but her voice shook as she spoke. "I know where he is," she squeaked.

"No!" another voice called at the same time. "Please don't."

Narcisse could hear the enchantress hiss, sneering as she took a step toward the small woman.

The woman was not deterred. "Innocent people will *die* if we don't tell her. There are children here! I will not stand back while that coward hides, leaving us to take the brunt of his punishment for using the devil's magic."

The following silence thick as mud, and Narcisse had to stifle a cough as it choked him. The tension that followed was alive, a kind of electricity that grew as Narcisse snuck closer to the town square. He slipped between buildings, his heavy boots falling silently on the grass and gravel that lined his path. Bell and Louis followed close behind.

"She's got a point," Louis whispered, popping up beside Narcisse once more. "He took advantage of something that shouldn't be used by anyone, then tried to run from the consequences, leaving everyone else to deal with the witch's wrath."

The old woman cowered before the enchantress, her hands held protectively before her face. No one moved and no one protested, leaving the woman to deal with the ire that was directed at her.

Narcisse was close enough now that he could make out the shine of the enchantress' eyes. She stared the woman down, a smirk appearing as the older woman squirmed.

"Out with it!" the sorceress hissed, her hand lashing out to grab a hold of the women's wrist.

"You w-on't hurt anyone here if I tell you?" the old woman begged in a whispery gasp. "Promise you won't h-arm them and I'll tell you."

Brave, but stupid of her to make such demands, Narcisse winced.

The sorceress' unamused snicker reached Narcisse, setting his skin crawling.

"You're brave," the sorceress mused, echoing Narcisse's thoughts. "Perhaps stupid, but brave. I will not harm anyone here if you give me useful information. If what you tell me is a lie, or I find it less than useful, then I will kill everyone here and bathe in their blood."

A collective gasp filled the town square, and the crowd rippled as everyone moved to back away. If it weren't for the sorceress' growl of warning and the flash of magic in her palm, Narcisse was sure that they all would have fled. His stomach clenched as he watched the exchange from the shadows.

"I know where he is," the woman cried.

"And who are *you* to the doctor?" The sorceress sneered down at the old woman, as if assessing her worth.

"I'm a nurse at his medical practice. I have been helping him for fifteen years now, assisting with surgeries and procedures."

The sorceress held her hand before her, shadow dancing menacingly in her fingers as she waited silently for the woman to speak.

"I was at the practice the day he left." The nurse wrung her hands. "He ran inside like a madman, his eyes wild and his hair unkempt. He rushed around grabbing things and shoving them into a satchel before he noticed me there." She paused, remembering. "He was in a panic when he asked me what I was doing there on my day off. I was preparing the practice for the surgery that was scheduled for the next day, you see."

"Spare me the details," The enchantress closed her fingers into a fist, the shadows spreading out around her, winding around the woman.

The nurse recoiled as if she'd been struck, then nodded. "I asked him why he was in such a rush and where he could be off to. It took him some time to collect himself enough to speak. When he did, he was rambling, and I couldn't understand him. I had to shake him before he'd stop for one moment and tell me what was wrong."

The sorceress narrowed her eyes at the rambling woman but waited, her face awash with impatience. Narcisse also wished to shake the old woman; to demand she get on with it.

"He told me about the castle then. About the war. He said that during the civil unrest many people died. His use of medicine and knowledge of the anatomy wasn't enough to stop the badly injured from passing." She hesitated, gulping. "He didn't even have the means at the time to ease the pain of those passing. Family fought family, and fathers lost children, sons lost their fathers. There was nothing he could do to stop the fighting, there was nothing he could do to stop the death, to help the injured.

"He heard rumors of y-ou," the woman paused, taking in the look of impatience the sorceress wore. Said he begged for your help. You offered him a way to help, but in return you wanted his life."

"You think I don't know any of this?" the sorceress spat. "If you don't tell me where he is now, I will *end* you!" Narcisse took an involuntary step back, as if the sorceress had been speaking to him. He couldn't understand why someone as powerful as her would get so worked up over one life.

The woman backed away in fear, but the sorceress still held her wrist, stopping her from retreating any further. "He said as he got older he could feel his time was coming, the time that you would come for him. He was scared, anyone who saw him in the final week could see that in his eyes and the way his voice shook. He ran."

"Of course he did," the enchantress said, clearly having expected no different from him.

"He left. He thought he could get away with it. He packed up what he could, then took a mare from the community stables."

The sorceress' eyes shone with rage as her hand tightened around the woman's arm. "But where did he *go*, you stupid woman!"

"He has family the next town over," she screamed, from pain or fear, Narcisse couldn't tell. "He's staying with them!"

The witch dropped her arm, stepping back slightly. Cruel fury radiated from her, her shadows writhing as if they were alive. "That fool!" she spat. "Humans are selfish in nature, but to go back on a bargain is unfathomable."

"P-please don't hurt him," the woman sniffled.

"Oh, I plan on doing much more than hurt him. He will suffer for trying to take magic from me without paying his due."

"This is bad." Bell stepped closer to Narcisse, her rasp causing him to jump. He swore silently. "I can't believe she gave away his location."

"What did you expect her to do?" Louis' brows furrowed. "She threatened so many lives if he wasn't handed over."

"But she said he is staying with his family. What if she goes there and hurts or kills them for helping him?" Bell shot her husband a panicked glance. He reached out silently, taking her hand into hers and squeezing it reassuringly. At least, he hoped it was.

"The woman had her swear she wouldn't hurt the townspeople if she told her," Louis said.

Narcisse shook his head. "She only said she wouldn't hurt the people here, not in the next town."

The three of them were silent as they watched the sorceress retreat. A smug grin transformed her face as she stared out at the people still gathered. "You are all free to go. But if you are lying to me," she pointed to the woman, "I will come back here and kill you all, no exceptions."

The older woman approached the sorceress again, her eyes downcast. "What will you do to him?"

The sorceress glared at the woman. Her mouth puckered as she no doubt thought about what to do with her for being so insolent. "You're treading in dangerous waters, woman," the sorceress said. "Your prying and blatant disrespect is stupid, even for your lot."

"I'm sorry," the woman said, backing away and standing with who Narcisse could only guess were her family.

The sorceress glared after her, but answered, "I decided long ago what was to come of Doctor Salvatore. I said I would take fifteen years of his life but I didn't say in what way I would take it. The way he had acted this last week has made me less inclined to mercy. If he can make up for the insult he has caused by fleeing, then I will allow him to live for now. If not, then his death will be as painful as the trouble he caused me."

In a flash of lightning, the sorceress was enveloped by black shadows, the tendrils lifting from her skin and surrounding her in a darkness so deep they could no longer see her. The townsfolk cried in fear as the shadows lifted, pluming around them and sinking into the ground. Where the sorceress had once stood was empty and nothing but a small wisp of smoke remained.

Chapter Thirteen

THE MOOD WAS SOMBER as Narcisse, Louis and Bell walked toward her father's home, the wind relentlessly picking at their hair and clothing adding to the atmosphere. He could feel Bell's relief when they found that Jacques had not been in the town square during the visit from the enchantress. In fact, no one had seen him.

Townsfolk rushed around them, disappearing into the safety of their homes, their obvious fear leaving a strange taste in Narcisse's mouth.

Why was getting her hands on Doctor Salvatore so important? Was the life of one man worth all this trouble? Was she that evil?

Clearly, he snorted.

But was she really in the wrong if the doctor had run out on their bargain? She had been made to be a fool. He pondered it, picking it apart in his mind.

Selling her magic to unsuspecting people was unfathomable, but the doctor had done a stupid thing by taking from her and trying to run from his payment.

Narcisse shook his head, the hair that hung loose around his face kissing his eyelids. *What Salvatore had done was stupid, but he did not deserve to be hunted down like a wild animal.* One of the women had said it was devil's magic, but he had used it to save so many people. If he hadn't, there was a chance that many of them wouldn't have been alive today to turn him in.

"Do you think his family will fight for him, or do you think they will turn him over the moment they see her?" Louis mused aloud. The shorter man's mouth was pulled at the corner, as if he worried the inside of his cheek.

"I wonder if he even told them why he's staying there in the first place." Bell's shoulders slumped as she rubbed her hands together against the cold. Less contemplative than Louis appeared, Narcisse's wife did not have her usual fiery spark. There was a hollowness to her words, to her voice.

"Perhaps he's not even there," Narcisse suggested. He forced a swagger to his step, a false bravado for the other two. "Maybe he thought better of it and went somewhere the witch wouldn't be able to hurt others."

Bell lifted her head, a glint of hope in her eyes. "Where would he go? He doesn't come across as the kind of man to live in the wild and survive on berries." She peered up at Narcisse as they pushed through the gate to her old home. "Once, Papa said the doctor cried as a boy when he had to have no milk with his tea."

"Whether the witch finds him or not, whatever she plans to do with him, is not our concern." Narcisse stomped up the muddied path to Jacques' front door. He kicked his boots against the step, using the cover of shaking the mud free to hide the shaky breath he exhaled.

"Do you expect us to just go back home and pretend like she hasn't gone to take an innocent man's life and do with it whatever she pleases?"

"Not entirely innocent," Louis murmured, taking it upon himself to knock on the front door.

Narcisse could see the fire reignite in his wife as she spoke. Bell, who knew full well how it felt to have this town not care about her wellbeing. Bell, who he could see would fight tooth and nail for anyone that was treated as unjustly. He welled with pride as his wife stared down Louis, who seemed eager to avoid her gaze. However, Bell said nothing further as the front door swung open, revealing a disheveled Jacques.

Bell immediately rushed forward, grasping her father's forearms, searching over him frantically. "Father! Are you alright, are you hurt?" There were scrapes and bruises along his arms. Narcisse thought they seemed minor enough, watching as his wife turned Jacques' arms this way and that with a gentleness that tightened his chest.

"What? Of course not. I've been downstairs working on another invention for the fair next week." Jacques was wide-eyed as he took in the trio, as if he had just noticed they were on his stoop.

"You've been here this whole time?" Bell demanded, shifting closer to the light spilling from the open doorway.

"Yes, why?" Jacques gently pried his daughter's hands off so he could wipe his hands on his stained apron. "Has something happened?"

Narcisse's mouth lifted in a crooked smirk as he was flooded with relief. "You're a mystery, old man!" he said, clapping his father-in-law on the shoulder. "The sorceress has been in the town square for the last hour threatening everyone with death if Doctor Salvatore wasn't handed over, and you had no clue she was there!"

Jacques blinked up at Narcisse, unbridled fear flashing in his eyes "Was?"

"Indeed, she was! His nurse turned him in."

"Huh." Jacques looked over Narcisse's shoulder, as if he could see all the way to the town square.

"I was so frightened," Bell whispered, scanning her father from head to toe. "I thought you were there. I thought, maybe you'd do something stupid to draw her attention, to help."

"I'm not quite that daft, dear. I know when it is the right time to stand back and observe, rather than interfere."

Narcisse smirked at the dark oil spots that covered most of his father-in-law's face, and the magnifying glasses that were pushed back over his hair. "You were saying you're off to the fair next week? That's so soon."

"You're quite right, boy, but I need to make a living one way or another. No one will buy my inventions if I sit home with them all day."

"Has anyone ever bought your inventions?" Louis blurted, peering at the older man from over Bell's shoulder.

Jacques startled, his eyes narrowing slightly. But he said ignored the jab at his profession as he returned his attention to his daughter, comforting her with soothing placations the way only a parent could.

Narcisse had yet to see any of the contraptions his father-in-law tinkered with, but he couldn't help wondering the same thing. *Did anyone see the need to buy such outlandish things?* He scoffed silently. *He has no need to sell anything now that I pay for him to live.*

"Is she gone?" Jacques asked.

"Yes. She left the moment she learned Doctor Salvatore's location."

"Poor doctor," he shook his head, the magnifying glasses coming dangerously close to falling. "What is she to do with him when she finds him? Perhaps she will show some mercy."

"From what I witnessed, Papa, I don't think she will." Bell grimaced. "She threatened to kill a dozen people if he wasn't handed over, so I don't think there is any mercy in her."

Jacques' eyes narrowed, his fist clenching at his side. Narcisse noted the change in his stance, and wondered if perhaps there was something he wasn't telling them. Jacques didn't look as clumsy and fearful as he had at other times. Narcisse wasn't entirely sure, but he wondered if perhaps this wasn't the look of a man who was worried for the town doctor, but of something else entirely. He eyed his father-in-law suspiciously. The older man caught his stare. Jacques' expression smoothed, like a blank page.

"I need a drink," Narcisse sighed, rubbing at his face. It had been a long evening, suffice to say.

"What?" Bell frowned. "It's barely morning." She eyed the dark skies overhead. "The sun is barely up."

"It may only be early morning, but it's been one hell of a day."

Louis pivoted and stomped back down the path. He called over his shoulder, "I'm going to check on my parents now that we know Bell's father is safe." He lifted a single hand in farewell. "I'll meet you at the tavern."

Bell hesitated, watching their friend disappear around a bend in the path. She opened her mouth as if to protest, but Narcisse cut her off before she had the chance.

"Come on, old man. You look like you could do with a stiff drink, too." He clapped Jacques on the shoulder and threw a nod over his shoulder at his wife in beckoning. Jacques' eyes lit up, if only for a moment, as he rushed after Narcisse. Bell remained on her father's porch, her arms crossed as she stared after them.

Narcisse heard her groan of frustration as she slammed the cottage door shut and scampered after them. She intertwined her arm with his, motioning for him to lean down as they followed the dips of the valley to town. He obliged as Jacques bounced along on his other side. "You're a bad influence on my father," she whispered to Narcisse.

Narcisse's teeth flashed in the in the predawn light as he grinned wickedly.

The tavern was a lot less crowded than Narcisse had experienced before, but given the circumstances he wasn't surprised. He held the door open for his wife and friends, ducking in after them. There were a few regulars dispersed around different tables, but it seemed that everyone else had locked themselves safely in their homes, fearful of the witch's return.

From the frown on Bell's face, it seemed that she agreed with them, wanting to be home safe. Narcisse knew it wasn't a good idea to be here after what they'd just witnessed, but he really needed a stiff drink. Or three. Maybe seven, he thought wryly as he glanced about.

The barmaid was wiping down tables, trying to keep busy. She looked up when they took their usual table, smiling in relief, clearly grateful for the increase in numbers. Jacques beelined for the barmaid, scooching into one of the seats at the table she cleaned. She shot the older man a smile.

"Four brandies, if you please," Louis said, appearing behind them from nowhere, and dropping down beside Jacques.

When Narcisse wanted a stiff drink he gravitated toward gin, but he, didn't complain when a snifter of brandy was placed before him. The taste was intoxicating; the soft, sweet fruits and spices washed down his throat and almost pushed out the worry that was overwhelming him. *Almost. . .* Until he saw the way Jacques watched his daughter, the crease in Louis forehead, the tightness in Bell's shoulders, the uncomfortable silence that surrounded them.

"What is it?" Bell asked, her hand reaching for Jacques' fidgeting hands. Narcisse raised a brow, silently echoing her question. Jacques glanced around uncomfortably, lowering his voice as he spoke.

"There is something I must tell you. Something that may change the way you think of me."

Bell rested a hand on her father's arm. "Nothing you say could ever change the way I think of you, Papa."

Narcisse straightened up. He had become quite fond of this weird little inventor. If Bell had faith in him then he would too. But what he said next, none of them could've prepared for.

"I knew about the witch. Before Salvatore and all of this." He waved his hand before him for emphasis.

Narcisse sat back in shock as Bell asked, "What on earth do you mean?"

Jacques sat there frozen, as if he couldn't answer her. Eventually he sighed, a loud rush of air coming from somewhere deep inside him. Narcisse wondered at the sound, at the part of Jacques that was buried deep enough for that sound to come from. The part of him that hid what he knew about the witch before now.

"I have seen her before, on two occasions." Jacques paused again, staring off into space. Narcisse wanted to throttle the old man for his hesitation, and for keeping this from them. The old man was clearly struggling, however.

Bell removed her hand from her father's arm to rest it on Narcisse's; as if she needed his presence to steady her, to prepare her for whatever it was her father would say.

"It was twenty-two years ago the first time I saw her." His eyes were glassy; he was lost in the past, seeing something that Narcisse could not. "Not even a month after you were born, you were sick. So small, so ill, my dear little Bluebell."

Bell stilled, eyes wide at her father's words. Her breath hitched in her chest, a small gasp. Narcisse gently clasped his free hand over the one on his arm. She hadn't known.

"Scarlet fever." Jacques gulped audibly, his throat bobbing behind his collar. "It came out of nowhere. One day you were our healthy, babbling babe, and the next you were so deathly ill, we knew that we would lose you any day."

"I-I don't remember," Bell whispered. "You never told me."

Jacques looked away, shame coloring his cheeks. "I didn't want you to know—"

"Why?" Bell's voice rose slightly, an edge to it that Narcisse had never heard. "Why wouldn't you tell me? If you say I almost died, don't you think that is something I deserve to know?"

"Let me finish." Jacques looked away from the hurt reflected in his daughter's eyes. "Your mother and I tried to prepare for the worst. Your grandfather warned us, consoled us, because there was nothing we could do." Jacques' voice cracked but he continued, whispering slightly. Narcisse leaned in, better to hear him speak.

"I spent every moment I could with you in my arms. I held my breath constantly, waiting for you to take your last. But I was exhausted, emotionally and physically, and I passed out. I was sleeping beside your crib, until your cries startled me awake."

"She would have died that night?" Louis looked to Bell, and then back to Jacques, as if he expected to see her drop dead that very moment. *Perhaps he thought her a wraith.* At any other time, Narcisse might have guffawed at his own joke. He bit his tongue, squeezing his wife's hand.

"I thought that cry was to be her last." Jacques shook his head as he pressed on. "But when I leaned over her crib, the cry grew louder, stronger. The paleness of creeping death abated, and pink spread from her cheeks until she was the healthy wee babe I had seen my wife welcome into the world."

Bell sniffled beside him, but Narcisse couldn't take his eyes from his father-in-law, mesmerized.

"It was a miracle. At least I thought it was. Giselle came up behind me, a blanket wrapped around her shoulders and snow in her hair. I hadn't even known she'd left the cottage. I didn't even care, we just held each other and cried. God had finally answered our prayers and saved our only daughter. But I was wrong, so very wrong."

Jacques was quiet for some time, and Narcisse tensed, ready to order another round of drinks to wash down the depressing tale, but the old man hadn't finished.

"We had a whole week of bliss before I realized what the miracle had been." Jacques took a deep drink from his glass. "I woke up one morning to find your mother gone and a scribbled note tacked to the back of the front door. Your mother, my beautiful wife, had sold her soul to that *witch* to save yours."

"She didn't," Bell rasped, her voice hoarse with disbelief. "She couldn't have."

Jacques nodded slowly, as though he didn't quite believe it either. "On the night you almost died, she went to that cursed castle to beg for your life as I slept. The witch was kind enough," he spat, "to give your mother a week with her babe, a week with me. And then the witch came for her payment." Jacques' voice caught in his throat, the tell-tale sob of a man who had lost so much. Narcisse squeezed Bell's hand, fearful that this new information would tear her apart.

"I left you with your grandfather. Then I jumped on my horse and raced to the castle. I had to get to her, save her from what the enchantress had planned for her. When I got there, the door was open and the castle was empty, so I followed a path of light, and there I found Giselle, locked up in the tower. She was alive. I couldn't find a way to free her, and she was adamant that I didn't try, so that the witch didn't go back on her word and take your life." His words were thick with sorrow as he continued. "The enchantress found us, forced me out with her magic and the threat to take back her 'gift' to us."

"You left her for dead?" Bell cried out.

"No, of course not! I went back that night with a group of men I had convinced to help me. But when we got there, it. . .it was too late. I found your mother in the tower once more, but what I found there, what I saw, I will never forget."

"What was it? What did you see?" It was Louis who asked. He was leaning toward Jacques, hanging on to his every word.

"Giselle, my sweet, perfect Giselle." A single tear fell from his eye. "She laid on a bed, but she had aged tremendously. She was nothing but a withered old lady. The witch came up beside me laughing, and I could see your mother's beauty reflected within her eyes. The witch had sucked out her life, fed on her beauty, and had killed her. All that was left was her body. She was gone." Jacques closed his eyes, as if trying to squeeze the memories away. "I turned on the witch, ready to give my life to avenge my wife, but she too was gone. I never saw her again after that."

Neither of them spoke, Narcisse almost couldn't breathe. Jacques had known about the witch this whole time, had been scarred by her, and had not shared it with them.

Ashamed, Jacques bowed his head, refusing to meet any of their eyes. "I am truly sorry I didn't tell you," he whispered, reaching for his drink, staring into space once more.

Glancing at Narcisse, Bell removed her hand from his arm to place it on her father's once more. She rested it hesitantly on his, stopping him from lifting his glass. "I forgive you, Papa," she said, her soft voice loud in the quiet of the tavern. "I would have done the same."

Narcisse glowered at Jacques, unsure whether he would have forgiven him so easily. But then again, the sin was not against him.

As if sensing the tension, the barmaid reappeared at their table, dispersing large tankards of beer. She nodded to Narcisse, though her eyes moved around the tavern, taking in the somber mood. "These are strange times," she noted, before disappearing back into the crowd.

"Strange times, indeed."

Louis eyed Jacques, questioning why no one was pounding the older man harder for what he had withheld. At least, that's how Narcisse chose to interpret the small man's stare. After a pointed look from Narcisse, he shrugged, nursing his beer. "Do you think she's found the doctor already?" Louis questioned, changing the subject.

Narcisse answered with his own shrug. "Who can say? She's able to appear and disappear into her shadows as if walking through a door, so she doesn't need to account for travel."

"Perhaps it's all smoke and mirrors, and she can't actually do that?" Bell guessed, staring down into her tankard.

"I don't think she is the type to fool us all with cheap tricks. I say what would take others a day to arrive in the next town, would take her mere seconds."

"Perhaps she will give him the day and find him tomorrow?" Louis suggested.

Narcisse drank deeply from his own tankard, wiping his mouth with the back of his hand. "The sorceress would be stupid to leave it that long before going after him. That gives someone enough time to travel there and warn him. He'd be gone once more before she had the chance to get her hands on him."

"Enough talk of Doctor Salvatore!" Bell groaned. "I thought you dragged us here to forget about what just occurred. We can't do that if you bring him up with every breath you take."

Narcisse's eyes darkened with heat at the demand in Bell's voice and the challenge in her stare, but he couldn't help worrying for her even as she aroused him. Did she want to drink away this mess with the doctor, or the emotions that were no doubt warring inside her? "My wife is right. Let us forget about the hag by washing down the memory with liquor!"

"Perhaps this isn't a good idea." Jacques frowned.

"The witch isn't going to just pop up in the middle of our drinking, old man," Narcisse noted.

"Stop calling my father old man!"

"I-I don't mind it, Bell dear."

Narcisse waggled his eyebrows at his wife, *daring* her to correct him again. The challenge that met him once more had his cock hardening in his trousers. He squirmed in his chair against the uncomfortable friction.

"What's the matter?" she purred, noting the way he squirmed.

The stare he leveled back at her was pure animalistic, and a promise. *I'll deal with you later.*

Narcisse hadn't noticed the silence that filled the already quiet tavern, until the sickening scent of aftershave hit him, almost curling his nose hairs. He wasn't surprised to see the mayor walk through the door – though he was taken aback to see his purist wife at his side.

"What is he doing here?" Louis whispered.

Narcisse shook his head. They had no doubt been safe in their large hilltop manor when the enchantress appeared.

"I have been informed of the frightening events that unfolded today," the mayor announced, his loud timber echoing in the empty tavern. "I have no words for how sorry I am that I was not here to stop it."

"He's not sorry at all," Narcisse hissed. "He would have received word long before now."

"I bet the coward was too scared to come down and face her like the others were forced to do," Bell whispered.

"We rushed here as soon as I heard. This is unacceptable, and I will do everything in my power to prevent it from happening again."

"How?" Narcisse yelled, shoving his chair back. It toppled to the ground with a resounding thud. The muscles in Narcisse's biceps tightened as he hammered his fists on the table. "How do you plan to go against a witch when you were too coward to meet her as we all did?"

The mayor blinked. Clearly he had not expected to be questioned. His eyes fell on Narcisse, and he spoke, as if addressing only him. "I will go to the castle and speak with the witch."

Someone else spoke up before Narcisse could reply. "Do you plan on bargaining away part of your life just as the doctor had? We'd be in the very same mess as we are now!" Raucous agreement filled the room at his words.

The mayor opened and closed his mouth, fumbling for words. He looked around the room, eying each and every person who was there. "I must admit, I don't know what to do. I will think of something, though, because I do not want to see anyone else hurt." He held his hands before him. "I want this temptation gone. I don't want to see anyone else bargain with her." A harsh expression etched itself across his face as he glanced back up. "Until I figure out what to do, no one can seek her out. This will be on the town's shoulders too; you must all swear to leave her to me. Just pretend she doesn't exist, so that I can eliminate the threat."

No one spoke. The mayor stood, waiting for all to agree, but it was no use. Narcisse almost felt bad for the man.

"Until then, the next three rounds are on me!" the mayor called, dropping a sack of coins onto the bar before turning tail, scurrying away with his wife in tow.

"He sure knows how to win over the town," Louis smirked as the tavern cheered. "Too bad most of the town are home."

Narcisse watched as the barmaid took the coin bag and began filling tankards and jugs to distribute around the tavern.

"What do you think the sorceress will do when the mayor turns up on her doorstep demanding she stay out of the town?" Louis asked.

"Whatever she does, I daresay won't be pretty," Bell said, worrying creasing her eyes.

They were at the tavern drowning their fear and self-medicating for hours. The longer they stayed, the more people filed in, and soon the tavern was almost at its usual capacity. Narcisse watched as his wife swayed in her seat, intoxicated.

"We should go, I think you've had enough," Narcisse mused, reaching for the half-empty tankard Bell cradled in her hands. She glowered at him, holding her tankard out of reach. Bell's protests were interrupted as the door was thrown open hard enough to bounce from the side wall.

A disheveled man raced in, his eyes wild as he yelled, "She's found him!" The silence was deafening. All eyes focused on the man, who panted in exertion, unwilling to move as they waited.

"The sorceress has found Doctor Salvatore!"

Chapter Fourteen

THE AIR IN THE tavern was thick enough to choke. Narcisse found himself rubbing his throat, as if he could feel or taste the heaviness of the stranger's words.

"The sorceress has found Doctor Salvatore," the man repeated, his words coming out rushed and panicked. No one spoke; no one dared move.

"How do you know she has him?" someone finally asked.

"I saw her!" The man looked as though he would vomit at any moment, his hands shaking as he lifted them to his face. "I was out in the woods cutting down trees to prepare for the winter. I saw her. I saw the sorceress dragging Doctor Salvatore through the woods."

"Where did she take him?" Jacques asked.

"To her castle, I am sure. I followed them part of the way. She dragged him like he weighed nothing, as if he was merely a sack of potatoes. He was kicking and screaming the whole way. I heard his screams long after I lost sight of them."

"But he was alive when you saw him last?" Narcisse approached the man, noting the mayor had skulked back in after the panicked man. "Salvatore was alive?"

The man leant against one of the tables by the door, his eyes rounded in fear. "Yes." The man swallowed hard, the word difficult to speak.

"We must do something." Narcisse jumped when he realized *he* was the one who had spoken. "We must go after him." He blanched; he had spoken without thinking, moving as though he no longer had control of himself.

"Narcisse is right. We must go after the doctor," the mayor agreed, chiming in now that he thought it safe. *Coward.*

A woman called out from beside the bar, "But he brought this upon himself, did he not?"

"Shut it, woman," another man growled.

"Whether he brought this on himself or not, he doesn't deserve it." Narcisse stood up, walking to the middle of the room. Every step was light, as if he was floating. *How peculiar.* "I won't let anything come to Doctor Salvatore, whether anyone else agrees or not." *Why was he volunteering himself like this?*

Narcisse felt a small presence sidle up beside him and he grimaced down at his wife. Bell wore an air of confidence, though he could see the underlying fear in her stance. "Are you crazy?" she whispered, ensuring no one else could hear. "You could be killed if you run after the witch, all guns blazing."

"And how else do you expect us to get him out?"

"Distraction," Bell mouthed. She then stood back, raising her voice for all to hear. "Someone distracts her while another goes in unnoticed and gets him out. She will have no idea he's gone until he's fled once more." She sounded more confident than she looked, her porcelain skin wane, as though the idea made her ill.

"What of the others?" the mayor asked. Like a mouse, he had slipped through the room quietly, weaseling his way beside Bell unnoticed. "All of those who have gone missing. . . she could have them locked away."

The tavern grew louder until each and every person present was arguing on top of one another.

"If we distract her long enough, we could save them all."

Louis spoke for the first time, but there was a pitch to his voice that had Narcisse do a double take. "If we take the doctor out from under her nose, she will do more than threaten everyone. She will torture us all. She will kill innocent people until he is found again."

"And what do you suggest we do instead?" Bell crossed her arms, ever the defiant woman.

The mayor cleared his throat to interrupt. "I suggest we form a mob. We charge her castle, using brute force. We will overwhelm her, capture her ourselves and then get Salvatore out of there."

Bell cocked a brow, looking from the mayor to Narcisse, like she couldn't tell who was crazier. "What of the witch after we capture her?"

The mayor's eyes were hard, and Narcisse could see there would be no persuading him otherwise as he said, "We kill her."

"How could it be that simple?" Bell shook her head. "She has magic, we have nothing."

"We have manpower and weapons; we can stop her before she has the chance to do anything." The mayor spoke with bravado now; he had bought his own promise.

"So, what? We run in with pitchforks and torches raised and expect her to succumb? She will throw everything she has at us, just as we would her."

Suddenly the mayor and Bell were talking over the top of one another, neither of them willing to see what the other had to say.

"It's barbaric!"

"It's all we hav—"

"Enough!" Narcisse roared, loud enough that the whole of the tavern grew quiet once more, all heads swiveling his way. "Fighting will only make the situation worse. We need to stand together if we wish to do anything about the doctor, about any others she may have trapped in her castle."

"You're right," the mayor frowned. "I apologize."

A wave of courage and determination washed over Narcisse. He swept his arm out, pushing tankards to the ground as he leapt up onto a table. The tavern seemed to grow even quieter as all eyes turned to Narcisse. People buzzed with anticipation as they waited to see what he had to say.

"My friends!" he called out. "We must make a decision, and we need all of you to help. This is the worst news, hearing that Doctor Salvatore has been taken from the witch. We knew it was to happen, but it doesn't mean we have to sit back and accept whatever she has planned for him." Narcisse paused, looking at the frightened faces staring back at him. "Not only is Doctor Salvatore our only physician, but he is also a good man. What he did all those years ago was a foolish act, but he did it to save countless lives, disregarding his own!"

Narcisse waited atop the table. The crushing weight of silence that followed ignited a kernel of doubt in him, a hungry, mocking whisper. But then the tavern erupted into cheers. It seemed that they all felt the same way. Someone had to go after Salvatore—someone had to save him, and something had to be done about the witch before the same thing happened again.

He stared out over the crowd, grinning triumphantly as man after man stepped forward to volunteer to go to the castle with Narcisse. However, it was his wife who caught his eye. She stood beside the table, where he had left her. Her arms were crossed tightly across her chest, but it seemed more a self-soothing gesture than a defiant one. Bell's lips were a narrow line, her head down as she stared at the floor. That little kernel in his chest twitched again, the seed of doubt growing. Had Narcisse made a mistake in pushing for this? Perhaps he had put a new strain on his marriage. She cared for him, and he had put himself in the line of danger. As if she could hear his thoughts, Bell looked up, her eyes finding his. She smiled sadly, a slight nod of the head indicating that she agreed it was the right thing.

"For those who hesitate, I urge you to stay home, where it is safe," Narcisse called out. "And for those who wish to help, meet at the entrance to the woods at six o'clock in the evening. We wait for no one. Until then, go arm yourselves!"

Narcisse sprung down from the table, straight into his wife's arms. She almost barreled him over, but he caught her and pulled her against him tightly.

"You're a good man," she said. "But it doesn't mean I like what you're doing."

"I don't like it either."

"Then why are you willing to put yourself in danger to do it?" Her lips were turned down into an irresistible pout.

Narcisse took half a step back, tipping Bell's chin upward with a gentle touch. "Because everyone deserves a chance to be saved." *Just as you saved me.* Their eyes locked, and they spoke without words, searching one another.

"What will you do until we meet?" Louis interrupted as he appeared beside them.

Narcisse answered him without breaking his gaze away from Bell, "I'm going home to spend some time with my wife."

Louis harrumphed and muttered something as Bell smiled softly at Narcisse, a coy edge to it. His heart thudded against his chest, loud and wildly. It was she who broke their silent connection to nod goodbye to Louis. Narcisse tore his gaze away in time to see Louis wave and run from the tavern. He had not said whether he would come fight, but in that moment, he wished his oldest friend would not meet them at the woods and would instead stay locked away where it was safest.

"Come," Narcisse said, grabbing hold of Bell's hand.

Jacques caught up with them at the door. "I'll see you there, then?" he said.

Narcisse paused, taking in his father-in-law's determined stance. "No, you won't."

"Excuse me?" Jacques hesitated, clearly taken aback but the demand in Narcisse's voice.

"I want you to stay with Bell. Keep her safe, make sure she doesn't do anything stupid."

"I'm coming with you," Bell protested as Jacques said, "Very well." Narcisse stared down at his wife.

"You most certainly are not coming. I will be happier knowing you're safe at home. Having you there will only distract me."

"Fine." Bell's eyes narrowed into slits. She pulled her hand from Narcisse's, crossing her arms once more. Narcisse sighed inwardly.

"Shall I follow you back now?" Jacques asked.

"No, come just before six. I want some alone time with my wife before I leave."

The walk back to their home was a tense one, neither of them willing to speak. He could tell by her hurried steps, her slumped shudders, her hollow eyes, that Bell was hurting. He didn't overly understand either of their feelings, his own melancholy mood rivaling hers. It wasn't that he was afraid; he was far from that. He was sad for his wife, for the fear she seemed to be feeling on his behalf. Bell remained silent as Narcisse held the front door open for her. She pushed past him, disappearing into the bedroom with a quiet click of the door.

He waited a moment before taking a deep breath and following after her. He pushed on the door gently, peering around it into the darkened bedroom. She had shut the drapes, plunging the room into darkness and shadows. "Bell?"

He was about to call out once more when there was a strike of a match and a small candle lit up the room in a soft, warm glow.

His wife's face was haloed in the golden light, her dark hair blending into the shadows. She smiled sadly at Narcisse, glancing up at him through her eyelashes. Narcisse gulped, the sound loud in his ears. She looked beautiful, angelic, in the glow of the candlelight. He inched forward, lifting a trembling hand to rest his palm against her flushed face, and stroked his thumb over her temple.

"Bell?" Narcisse breathed, "Are you okay?"

She shook her head. "I will be." A small sob slipped from her lips.

Narcisse dropped his hand only to gather Bell up in his arms. He held her to his chest, his hand running through Bell's hair in short, comforting strokes.

Bell's strained, "I love you," vibrated against his chest.

His heart caught in his throat. "And I you." He nuzzled his chin into her hair, taking in the soft, floral scents he had come to recognize as his wife.

"This is strange," she mused through soft hiccups. "I never imagined I'd be in love, let alone with *Narcisse*. Now that I've come to terms with that, I must watch you go off and fight some crazy woman with lightning fingers."

Narcisse's whole body shook as he chuckled. "Lightning fingers!"

His wife waved her fingers in front of his face, making a "woooooo" sound as she wiggled them.

"I've never felt so alive since marrying you," he wheezed.

"You're welcome." Bell winked at Narcisse, her tears forgotten, before using all her force to push him back against the bed.

Narcisse fell gracelessly, despite his strength. He struggled with the coverings, trying to get back to his elbows as Bell climbed on top of him. His breath caught in his throat, his mouth opening of its own accord as she leaned forward and pushed her lips against his. He welcomed her, using his tongue to coax hers into his mouth. The weight of Bell on top of him and the sweet silkiness of their tongues sliding over one another was enough to make him instantly hard. He lifted his hips, rubbing his rough trousers against her, showing her exactly what she did to him.

Her fingers dug into the muscles of his biceps as he continued to grind his hips against her. Their clothes were a barrier between them, and Narcisse growled as he swung Bell from him just long enough to tear his trousers down. He kicked them to the floor, then in one swift motion Bell's dress was over her head and her underclothes piled with his.

Bell squeaked as Narcisse swung her by the hips and had her straddling his waist once more. Her eyes were wide, her mouth open. Narcisse held her above him, inches from making contact, and looked up at her from hooded eyes.

"I need to hear you say it," he said, his hands sweating as he held her.

"Yes," she nodded, her hair falling around her face like the drapes that covered the curtains.

It was all Narcisse needed. He lowered her down onto his waiting cock, slowly, savoring every inch. No doubt she had expected Narcisse to take her as he always did, but the way she had momentarily taken control caused his insides to tighten at the thought.

Narcisse could feel the way she tightened around him as she found the right position. Bell's hands were splayed over his chest to steady herself, her thighs spread wide around him.

"Like this," Narcisse groaned. He grabbed a hold of her hips, moving her back and forward, showing her exactly how to fuck him.

Bell moaned, her nipples peaking as he continued to slowly, deliberately slide her up and down. His grunts turned wild when she pushed his hands away and began fucking him at her own pace.

Her thighs shook, her hands digging into his chest as she thrust against him harder and faster. Narcisse couldn't take his eyes off of her, his cock twitching at the way her face held nothing but pleasure. Her eyes were closed, her mouth open on silent moans. Bell's cheeks were red, and her sweat coated skin glistened in the candlelight.

"Fuck, Bell!" Narcisse groaned, her insides tightening around him.

His moans seemed to coax her, because one moment her movements had some symmetry of control, the next they were almost clumsy.

Narcisse placed his hands on her hips again, splaying them enough so his thumb could just reach the apex of her thighs. He sat his thumb over her most sensitive area, the dampness helping her glide over his calluses with each thrust of her hips.

"Oh, god," she cried.

Narcisse could feel the way her thighs trembled against him, could see the way her arms shook from the effort it took to hold herself up. She was on the brink of losing control. He pressed his thumb down harder, moving it with Bell's hurried movements.

She threw her head back, her breasts covering in goosebumps, her nipples pebbled. "Narcisse!" she cried, just as he felt her contract around him.

In an instant Narcisse had Bell on her back. He rode her through her release, denying himself his own just yet. He continued to pound into her, the bed banging into the wall of the cabin from the force. He repositioned his hips, going even deeper, harder, until his wife trembled beneath him.

"I c-can't," she groaned, but her hips continued to meet his involuntarily.

Narcisse bit down on his lip, trying to hold in his release for just a moment longer. He needed to watch Bell, needed to see her lose control over and over. It would be an image he would take with him to the fight he was soon to have. *It seems I will fight with a hard cock!*

Bell's thighs shook out of her control, as she fought against her screams of pleasure. Her legs were opened as wide as they would go, his cock reaching someplace so deep he felt he would lose himself inside her at any moment.

"I d-d-on't know if I can," she stuttered, but her hips continued to tilt toward him.

Her eyes rolled into the back of her head as she arched from the bed, her breasts pressing against his chest. The bed coverings were fisted in her hands as her cries of pleasure turned into screams. Her insides quivered around Narcisse once more, tearing an orgasm from him so powerful it felt as though he would black out.

"Fuck, Bell!" Narcisse roared as Bell continued to milk him until there was nothing left. "Fuck!"

He fell on top of his wife, his cock still throbbing inside her. Bell's warm, quick breaths washed over his chest. With his face buried in her hair, he inhaled her scent, trying to slow his breathing.

"Wow," Bell whispered.

"Wow, indeed."

Narcisse was slick with sweat, his skin sticking to Bell's. She laughed softly as he pulled himself from her. He sat at the end of the bed, looking down at his naked wife. Her skin was red from exertion, her eyes bright. He felt strange having to leave her there to dress himself and prepare to leave.

"Are you bathing before you go?" she asked, stretching over the mattress.

"I don't think I have time." Narcisse opened the window coverings and saw that it was almost sunset. "I will need to leave very soon if I plan to meet them on time."

"Oh."

"It appears we lost track of time." Narcisse couldn't help but chuckle though. *What better way to spend my time?* "This way I can go to battle smelling of you."

Bell screwed her nose up at his statement, but said, "You don't think this will be a battle, do you? Surely she will give up when she sees how many of you have come for the doctor?"

Narcisse shrugged, looking back over at her as she sat up and swung her legs over the side of the bed. "Who can say? Hopefully that is the case, but we should prepare for the worst."

"If only someone here had magic to rival hers." Bell slipped from the bed and traipsed toward him, her feet sliding along the hardwood floors.

Narcisse opened his arms, and Bell ran into them. "That would be helpful, but who is to say they wouldn't use their magic against us?"

"I suppose you're right. Magic doesn't seem like something we can trust."

Narcisse held Bell at arm's length, taking in her worried expression and the sadness that shone deep in her eyes. "I must get ready."

"Do you have to?" she sniffled.

"Yes. If I don't show up, I have a feeling no one will go after Doctor Salvatore."

Bell stood in the corner of the room, her arms folded before her, as Narcisse dressed. Her eyes remained on him the whole time. It was when he shucked on his hunting jacket and strapped his rifle across his back that she ran into his arms once more.

"Please don't go!" He could hear the sorrow in her voice, but it was the tears that ran down her cheeks that caused him to hesitate, to second guess his plans. He paused long enough to run his thumb over her cheeks, wiping away her tears.

"Don't cry for me. I will be back."

"You don't know that."

"Such little faith you have for your husband," he tsked. "Your father will help distract you, and before you know it, I'll be back."

As if Narcisse's words were magic, there was a knock at the door. Bell's fingers were wrapped tightly around his hunting jacket, so all he could do was drape his robe around Bell and walk to the front door with her at his side.

"Bonjour," Jacques said as Narcisse threw the door open.

Narcisse nodded. "Jacques."

His father-in-law's eyes flicked to his daughters, no doubt taking in the tears that still ran down her face.

"I must go," Narcisse said. "Please make sure Bell doesn't come after me."

"Of course."

"Please don't go!" Bell cried once more.

Narcisse faced her, pressing his forehead to hers. "I will be back soon, my love."

"Please!" Her cries broke his heart in two as he pried her fingers from his jacket. "No!"

"Shhh." Narcisse rested his hands against her face, rubbing her tears away with his thumbs. "I will be back."

"I love you," Bell hiccuped.

Narcisse walked outside, pausing at the bottom of the steps as he said, "I love you more than you'll ever know."

Chapter Fifteen

"**I** WAS WONDERING IF you were going to show up," the mayor said in way of greeting.

"It was *my* idea."

Narcisse trudged up to the mouth of the woods to join the small group of men. As well as the mayor there were some other men that Narcisse knew well, having drunk with them on many occasions. He nodded to them and waited by the entrance for Louis and any other stragglers, the weight of his hunting dagger against his thigh a steady comfort.

The mayor drew his gold pocket watch from his breast pocket, frowning at it then up at the darkening sky. "Ten minutes until we march. I do hope more join us before then. . ." His words trailed off, tinged with fear and hesitation.

Me too, Narcisse agreed silently. There were only eight of them so far; far from enough to tackle an *enchantress*.

"Maybe we should wait until half past?" the mayor urged.

"No." Narcisse grimaced. If they wanted to be here they would have been. "We said six."

From where Narcisse stood, he could see the minute hand of the mayor's watch tick agonizingly towards the hour. His heart sank the longer they waited, hopes dashing with each *tick, tick* of the watch.

"Alright," Narcisse hissed through gritted teeth, taking a hesitant step toward the trees. The crunch of leaves under his boot was muffled by a familiar holler.

"Wait!" It was Louis. Narcisse closed his eyes, thankful for the short delay. Thankful that he wouldn't be marching towards idiocy for one more moment, however brief.

"Sorry!" Louis panted, skidding to a stop beside him. "I was gathering more men, but it took longer than I had hoped."

Hurried movement caught Narcisse's eye. Six men trailed after Louis, their pitchforks, guns and torches held before them. The darkened entrance of the woods lit up as they approached.

"No need to apologize," Narcisse grinned, slapping his friend on the shoulder in a warm greeting, although he was terrified. His heart roared in his chest, thudding against his ribs with such force he was sure the others could hear it. "Thank you all for joining us. I know this is dangerous, but the sorceress needs to be dealt with before others decide to seek her out just as the doctor had done."

The group grunted their agreements, lifting their weapons in the air.

"Let's go!" the mayor roared, confident now as the men whooped.

The entrance to the woods seemed darker than usual as they marched through; the light from the torches they carried only lighting a few feet in front of them before falling into dark shadows. The group of men was surprisingly quiet as they trudged through the woods, the enormity of the task ahead subduing them.

The path they treaded was familiar to Narcisse, vivid memories of his youthful mistakes haunting him. Thankfully though, strength in numbers meant they would likely be more than able to stave off any unexpected wolf attack.

"Do you think she knows we are coming?" Louis whispered at Narcisse's side.

The mayor had chosen to take the lead, marching at the head of the group. Narcisse and Louis hung by the back, keeping a look out for anyone who may sneak up on their rear.

"I hope not. The element of surprise would be in our favor." Narcisse gripped his gun that little bit tighter as he spoke.

It took less time than Narcisse remembered for the woods to open up to reveal the looming towers of the castle and its grounds. *Had her magic kept her hidden from everyone besides those desperate enough to need her?* By the mayor's watch, it took them twenty minutes to reach the outskirts of her lands, which was not nearly enough time to calm his thundering heart. Had he just misremembered his boyish misadventures? By the look on Louis' face as his friend glanced at the foreboding castle and at the woods behind them, he had not.

Louis gulped audibly. "Does this all seem eerily familiar to you?"

Narcisse chose not to reply, instead taking the opportunity to wind his way through the group until he stood beside the mayor. "I think it best if we sneak in, rather than running in, weapons out."

The mayor was silent for a time, staring out from the trees to the castle grounds. Uncertainty laced his words as he asked, "What would you suggest we do?"

"Let me go first." The words left his mouth before he had thought them through.

"What?" both the mayor and Louis shouted, although Louis' was more of a squeak than a demand. Narcisse hadn't realized his friend had come up from the rear with him.

"Let me go in and speak to her, keep her distracted while the rest of you sneak in. When I'm inside, two of you go look for Doctor Salvatore, the others, position yourselves and prepare for the worst. While her back is turned, you pounce. Restrain her and then tie her up." Bell's plan made the most sense, after all.

The mayor scratched at the stubble that lined his chin, the sound deafening in the muffled quiet. "It's not the worst idea. We've never faced someone who wields magic, so we will gag her and bind her hands, so that she has no way to use her magic if given the chance."

Narcisse grunted in agreement, before checking his rifle was loaded and ensuring he had his knife strapped to his belt. "I'll go now. Wait ten minutes, then sneak in."

"You don't have to do this alone," Louis whispered, grabbing a hold of Narcisse's hand as if he could stop him. Narcisse smiled sadly at his friend, squeezing his hand. It was softer than his, his work in the kitchen with his mother rather than outside leaving them less calloused.

"I know I don't. But I need you to help capture her once I have her distracted." Narcisse wanted — no, needed — to do it alone. There was a niggling feeling at the back of his mind demanding to know why the witch had allowed him and his friends to leave. So many others had trespassed, had paid the price, and yet, she had let them walk away. He needed to confront her. Why had she not taken something from him, like she had done with the doctor? He had guessed it was because he hadn't asked for her magic, but nothing he had since learned about her indicated that she was one to show mercy for trespassing. Seeing her in the window all those years ago had scared him senseless, but he squared his shoulders and swallowed that fear.

"Okay," he said, mentally preparing himself for the task ahead. "I'm going in."

"Good luck," Louis said, only now releasing his hand.

Narcisse nodded at the mayor, then to the men gathered behind him. "No less than ten minutes," he reminded them. He held the strap of his rifle close, pushing through bushes and low hanging branches as he felt his way forward in the darkness. Much like it had when he was younger, it felt as if small, clawed hands were grabbing at his hair and clothes.

With a grunt, Narcisse stepped from the woodland through a hole in a stone fence and emerged in the courtyard of the castle. He stood in the middle of a garden that had clearly not been maintained for some time. There were overgrown hedges scattered about and weeds covering much of the ground, coming up from cracks in the pavement. Long dead rose bushes filled much of the space, nothing but thorny brambles. It was the castle itself that had Narcisse pausing. The large, greying structure looked much the same as it had the first time he had seen it. But this time the shadows seemed to have grown in size, clinging to every inch of the castle, nearly obscuring it from sight.

Narcisse took a hesitant step toward the castle, stopping immediately as something caught his eye. The top right window, that had haunted his dreams for so long, was lit with soft orange candlelight. He squinted through the darkness, sure it was a residual memory.

But the soft glow remained.

As he stared at that one candle, the other windows began to light up, candle after candle lighting of their own accord. Did she know he was there? As he stared, the shadows that danced along the walls to the tune of the flickering flame seemed to solidify once more.

He wanted to look away, but it was as if his eyes were stuck on the shadows as they became one and moved to the window once more. One moment the solid darkness was nothing but shadows, and the next the sorceress stood in the window before him. A savage smirk grew over her face when her eyes met his.

"Narcisse," she said, her soft, velvet voice carried to him on an absent breeze.

It took all the strength he could muster to pry his eyes from the window. He forced his feet to move, one step at a time, until he was at the large dark wood door. The door was an intimidatingly two stories high, towering over him as he contemplated knocking.

The door opened before him as he reached out to grab the iron knocker. No one had opened it for him, the entryway empty. It was lit up with sconces, lining the foyer and the halls that led deeper into the castle. Giving himself no time to change his mind, Narcisse stepped inside. He jumped, cursing under his breath as the door slammed behind him.

"Narcisse." The sorceress appeared at the end of the hall, voice echoing in the large foyer, her teeth flashing as she grinned. "How kind of you to visit me. For what do I owe this pleasure?"

"Curiosity, mainly," he lied. "I wanted to speak about the night I visited, when I was a child." *Not a lie. I want to know.*

The sorceress' eyes narrowed slightly, assessing him to decide whether he was indeed telling the truth. "Come with me."

"Where?" But his feet were already moving, following the sorceress out of the foyer and down a dim hallway.

The witch walked slowly, her steps deliberate and unhurried. Narcisse was sure to keep a short distance between them. They entered inside a large dining hall, big enough to fit his whole cottage inside. There was a large spread of food on the long wooden table, and a half-eaten plate at the head of it. It seemed that Narcisse had interrupted her dinner.

"Take a seat," she said. "You will join me for dinner."

Not a question, but a demand. Narcisse nodded, taking up the seat on the other end of the table, rather than beside her. The sorceress chuckled softly at his decision, but said nothing as she swept to her seat.

She took a small bite of food before asking, "So, you wish to ask about why I didn't punish you or your cohort for trespassing?"

Narcisse nodded once more.

"I recall telling you and your pretty little wife that I am not as petty and cruel as everyone assumes, no?"

"That's right," Narcisse said. "But curiosity tends to get the better of me."

"Indeed." The sorceress took up a small crystal glass, swirling the contents and taking a sip before she spoke again. "Curiosity can get the better of most. But as I said, I am not cruel and unjust. I saw potential in you as a boy." She stared down into the dark red liquid that filled her glass. "It seems I was wrong."

Narcisse's breath caught in his throat. "I beg your pardon?"

The enchantress ignored him, changing topic as she examined her glass thoughtfully. "It's strange that you seek me out the very same day I bring the doctor to my castle, isn't it?"

Narcisse's gulp was loud in the strangled silence that followed her question.

Her eyes narrowed to mere slits, lip curling as she stared at him with indignation. "Are you not here to rescue the old fool?"

"No-I-no. . ." Narcisse fumbled for words but failed to find them.

"Hmmm." The sorceress slipped from her seat, slinking toward Narcisse like a beast sizing up its prey. "Are you here to rescue him?" she asked again.

Narcisse had to clear his throat multiple times before he could put a full sentence together. "Of course not. It is his own fault he is in this mess."

"Is that so?" She leaned over Narcisse, tilting her head, her eyes full of untamed hunger.

"Yes," he gulped. "He asked for something of you, agreed with the terms of payment you set out, but refused to pay when his time had come."

"You think my payments are fair."

"Oh, yes. More than fair. What the doctor asked of you seemed like it would take a lot to make. I think what you asked for in return was more than reasonable."

"Hmmm." The sorceress stood back, her hand on her hip as she examined Narcisse once more. Was his body language giving away his lies or fear?

"Do you want to know what I have done to the doctor?" she grinned.

No. "Yes."

"Do you think I am alone in this large castle, Narcisse?"

"I couldn't say." But he could hope.

"I am not. I have guards and servants like any worthy noble. Just as the nobles had before I took the castle from them."

Narcisse had heard stories about nobles ruling this land long before the castle was abandoned. He hadn't heard any version involving the sorceress *taking* it from them, or where they went when she did.

"What happened to the nobles?" He had to ask, curiosity getting the better of him. The enchantress chuckled, the light in her eyes dancing wickedly. The doors to the chamber burst open suddenly and men and women poured in, standing behind the sorceress, weapons in their hands. Narcisse had never seen them before. Their clothing was clean and well kept, their hair and skin shining in the candlelight. They said nothing. *Her guards*? They stared ahead, their eyes void of any emotion as they waited for her command. But she said nothing to them instead focusing back on Narcisse.

"It's a long story, Narcisse. Do you have time?" She tilted her head to the side, as if she could hear something in the distance that he could not. "I have been on my own since I was young, living off the land. One winter night, it became too cold to bear. I found this castle as I wandered around blindly. But when I asked for help, the young prince sneered at me and said he would not offer refuge to a *rat*. You see, he didn't know I held such magic. When he saw what I could do he begged for my mercy. I wouldn't allow him to have it."

"What did you do?"

"Nothing too dramatic," she smiled. "I turned him and his parents into doting servants."

The sorceress waved her hand at the three closest guards. Two men and a woman. Narcisse's stomach churned. Their eyes were fogged, much the same as the others standing behind the enchantress. But one detail only they seemed to have, as if the enchantress found them in need of a crueler punishment. Their mouths were sewn shut with thick brown yarn, the holes raw and weeping.

"But they haven't aged." The prince, he assumed, was young and handsome, his golden hair falling in waves to his shoulders, and his stormy ocean-colored eyes — as fogged and distant as they were — full of regret. He must have been only a year or two older than Narcisse.

"Yes, I have made it that way. They must serve me for all eternity."

"Have they not rebelled in all these years?" His voice was hoarse with terror as the words slipped from him.

"They may wish to, but it is impossible. They can think and feel like themselves, and may even wish for death, but their bodies will not do what their brains want them to do. They only do as I command, no matter what it is. They must bear witness to everything." She spoke nonchalantly, despite her horrifying words.

Narcisse could do nothing but stare at the poor souls who stood before him. They could understand what was happening but did nothing to stop it.

"You look pale, Narcisse. Is something the matter?" There was a wickedness that shone from the enchantress then, a glimpse of the terrible monster lurking beneath her pretty exterior. "There are others in the castle," she addressed a guard. "Unwelcome guests. See to it that they are brought to me."

Narcisse had no clue how she knew. His stomach twisted. Who had she detected? Narcisse thought better than to try and distract her, but maybe there was something else he could do to keep her preoccupied. He steeled himself, as he murmured, "You changed the subject."

The sorceress paused in her sneering. "Come again?"

"Just before, you changed the subject. You asked if I wanted to know what had come of the doctor, and I said yes. But you changed the subject, instead speaking of your servants."

A malicious grin spread over her face, and she leaned toward Narcisse once more. He refused to show any hint of fear, remaining in his seat at the table.

"I wasn't trying to change the subject; I have no reason not to tell you what I have done with Doctor Salvatore." She leant over him even further, until she was almost nose to nose with Narcisse. "I heard your little minions breaking in and I can hear them moving around like the disgusting vermin they are."

"My minions?" Narcisse shook his head. "I came alone."

"I can taste the lies seeping from your very pores," she spat.

Narcisse said nothing, staring up at the sorceress like he had far better things to do than argue with her.

She chuckled, licking at her lips. "Your bravery is quite charming."

"The doctor," Narcisse urged.

"Yes, of course. What have I done with your precious doctor," she tapped a finger on her chin. "You want to know if I killed him."

He did. He was waiting for her to tell him she had killed him the moment they entered the castle.

"I didn't kill him, Narcisse," she scoffed, "That would have been a waste of payment."

"Then where is he?" Narcisse looked behind the sorceress into the dark room beyond, as if he expected Doctor Salvatore to come walking out of the shadows.

"I see what you are trying to do here, Narcisse." A smile played at her lips. "You wish to distract me so I will forget about your friends breaking in."

Narcisse gulped but remained unmoved. Perhaps it was working, and she would stay with him until they got Salvatore out and then he could run.

"I will play along with your little game, as your impertinence amuses me." The enchantress straightened, but remained standing before Narcisse, blocking any chance of escape. "He is in the dungeons."

Narcisse paused. "And that is not a waste of payment?"

"He is there until I decide what I want to do with him. He will either be put into service with the others, as guard or servant. . . or he will be chained in the dungeons and tortured for fifteen years, until he is nothing but a shell — then I will consume his life force and fuel my youth. I haven't quite made up my mind yet."

His heart tightened in his chest at the thought of the old man being tortured with God knows what for the rest of his life, until she was ready to devour him. He wouldn't even be able die to escape the pain as the witch would keep him alive until she was ready for him to succumb.

Bile rose in his throat, burning his esophagus as he tried to force it back down. He would not show weakness in front of this sadistic wench. He wanted to ask if she had done the same to others before, but his throat contracted as he opened his mouth.

"Lost for words, I see," she chuckled.

There was a crash in the distance, followed by muffled cries. Narcisse kept his eyes on her, hoping his allies were dodging the guards who had run from the room. "Not lost for words, just appalled that someone so cruel could exist."

The sorceress was silent for a moment, her eyes distant as she too listened to the commotion occurring somewhere inside the castle. Her distant eyes soon filled with amusement. "Not cruel, *just*."

"Holding innocent people captive and forcing them into a lifetime of slavery and torture is just?"

"Innocent?" she spat, her piercing eyes suddenly full of rage. "They are not innocent! *I* am! I was minding my own business, simply living my life in this castle when they sought *me* out! They expected to use my magic without payment. If I gave away my power away without taking some of their life in return, I would be an old hag now."

Narcisse hesitated. "So, it is true. You suck the years from someone's life to stay young."

"Do you not think it cruel for all these people draining me of my own life force?"

Narcisse wanted to flee, to find his friends and get the hell out of here, but he needed to give them time to find the doctor without the hag's interruption. "What would happen if you didn't use your magic at all? Would you stay young without the need to take other's lives?"

She leveled a pointed glare at Narcisse as she said, "If I didn't use my magic I would live forever as a beautiful, youthful woman. I had no need to use my magic since I took this castle – until sniveling fools threw themselves at my feet and begged for my help."

Was she the victim after all? It seemed that for years she had been, but it had gotten out of control and now Narcisse could see that she was merely taking advantage of people who didn't really know the consequences. *She could refuse to help them, but instead she takes advantage of foolish villagers.*

"Will you let him go?" Narcisse demanded.

"Which one?" she smirked. "There are many men, women, and children locked in the dungeons. Which one do you wish for me to release?"

Children? Narcisse narrowed his eyes. "*All* of them."

The enchantress took a step back, her hand rising before her. Shadows rose from her skin, dancing around her fingers as she stared him down. Narcisse swallowed hard and pushed back slightly in his chair, the legs scraping on the marble floors.

She reached her hand out, shadows and all, and grabbed a hold on the chair, keeping Narcisse in place. He could feel the shadows weaving around him, their cold caresses.

"You're getting on my last nerve, Narcisse," the enchantress hissed, spittle hitting his heated skin. It burned where it touched, as if her saliva was acid.

Narcisse bared his teeth and kicked back the chair to stand up, ignoring the shadows that seemed to tighten around him. He refused to remain at a disadvantage sitting below her. He would face her standing, his weapons within reach. "And you think you aren't getting on mine? I came here to try and appeal to you, to discuss the doctor, but you've only proved yourself the cruel, crazy *hag* I knew you to be."

The enchantress' white teeth shone in the candlelight as she spat at Narcisse. Black hair lifted in an invisible wind, mixing with her shadows, and swaying around her face like live snakes.

"I warned you, rat. I gave you all many chances to leave me be." Her shadows continued to grow, until the room was thick with them. "I will kill you and all who you love, you impotent fool of a man."

Narcisse's clenched fists trembled at his sides, his scalp heating in anger. "You wouldn't dare," the sorceress screeched in anger, no longer the beautiful flower she had previously appeared to be. Her eyes began to glow red in the darkness, her hair snaking around her like lightning. "You dare challenge me?" Her voice echoed around the room, coming from all directions. "Not only did you come here and demand my prisoner be set free, but you also insulted me." The enchantress melded with her shadows, coming in and out of view. She stepped closer to Narcisse until he was forced back against the wall with nowhere to go. "Now you will pay! Guards, bring me the doctor!" Her demand was yelled beside him, splitting his eardrums, then it dropped to a seductive croon once more. "I will kill him slowly and painfully right before you, then I will kill you." Her voice wrapped around him and seeped within, soothing him, coaxing him to inaction. He couldn't move, couldn't think. But then she said something that Narcisse could not ignore. "I will drag your Bluebell here and suck every last drop of her beauty. Then she will join you in oblivion."

Narcisse roared; his lips pulled back in a terrifying mask of fury. He pushed away from the wall, taking her by surprise. She had expected him to succumb to death, to welcome it. But she had threatened his wife, his love, and she would pay. How dare her poisonous lips even utter Bell's name. He whipped his head forward, cracking his forehead into her nose. The satisfying crunch of bones mixed with her cry of shock and pain. It was enough of a distraction for Narcisse to push past her. He pulled open the main door to the dining room and found himself in a dark hallway. Without a second thought he tore off down the corridor, refusing to look behind him.

He could hear her cry of pain turn into a scream of rage, and he didn't have to look over his shoulder to know the enchantress was following after him. He expected her to appear before him, using her magic to jump through space. But he could feel her breathing down his neck, hear her manic laugh behind him, as if this game of cat and mouse amused her once more.

"Run, run, as fast as you can," she sang, her sudden child-like tone sucking any warmth from his body.

As he ran, he pulled the hunting rifle from his back, holding it to his chest. He sent up a silent prayer, throwing it into the ethos, as he dropped to a knee and spun around, levelling his gun in front of him. But when he turned, the hall behind him was empty. He cursed under his breath as the manic laughter washed around him once more.

Narcisse stood slowly, aiming the rifle as he spun, but the enchantress was not there. As he looked down the hall, sure she would suddenly appear before him, the candle sconces that lined the walls flickered. The shadows that danced in the narrow space watched him ominously, and he couldn't discern whether they were alive with her magic or simply stagnant shadows.

"Fear marinates one's essence," her voice called, as though she stood beside him, but the space remained empty. "And I have been looking forward to consuming your handsomeness for some time, you see."

Narcisse took an involuntary step back, his rifle shaking in his hands. "Then come face me, you coward," he called back, his voice trembling ever so slightly.

"When I am ready," she giggled.

He lowered his rifle, holding it to his side in one hand, and looked down both ends of the hall, not sure which way he had come from.

All sound seemed to dissipate, and Narcisse held his breath as the enchantress exploded from her shadows, materializing before him just as she tackled him to the ground. His head thwacked against the hard, cold floor, causing his vision to blur. He grunted in pain, blinking away the black splotches that floated around in his eyes. The enchantress rolled with Narcisse until she straddled him, holding him to the ground with unfathomable force. She splayed her fingers over her chest, her nails extending into jagged claws that pierced through his shirt. The sharp tips rested on his sweat soaked skin but did not go any deeper.

"Wish to know why I let you, trespassing brat, leave without punishment?" She leaned forwards, her icy breath sending goosebumps down his arms. "Because I knew you would grow into a strong, handsome man." She moved her hips slightly, leaning even closer until her lips were mere inches from Narcisse's. "And I was right." She brushed her mouth against Narcisse's very briefly, the contact burning him like a brand. "I will enjoy taking it from you."

"And I will enjoy taking yours from you," Narcisse rasped, as he pulled his small hunting dagger from his thigh and plunged it into the witch's back.

Her scream was ear splitting. She threw herself to the side, tearing the wound further as Narcisse kept a tight grip on the handle. She crawled to the side of the room, sprawling ungracefully into her awaiting shadows, and disappeared within.

Narcisse blinked away the pain in his head, fumbling with his knife as he got to his feet and staggered after her. But when he reached those shadows, deep in the corner, they were just that. . .shadows and nothing more. The enchantress had fled.

He searched around frantically on the verge of hysteria, when he heard foot-steps rushing up from behind him. Narcisse cocked his rifle, holding the butt of the gun against his shoulder.

"There you are!" Louis appeared from the shadows, his eyes on the rifle, a disgruntled mayor in toe. "We've been searching for you, but this place is like one big maze."

Narcisse huffed a sigh of relief, slinging the rifle across his back. "Took you long enough to find me," he groaned, his voice marred by pain. "Did you find him?"

"See for yourself." Louis nodded to the men who appeared behind him, assist-ing a limping doctor into the room.

Doctor Salvatore was covered head to toe in bruises and blood, his left eye swollen shut, but he was alive. Narcisse shoulders sagged in relief. They hadn't come here for nothing.

"We had to fight off some mute, vacant swine before I could get into the dungeon, but we got there in the end."

Narcisse noticed the blood that covered much of the men. "What of the others in the dungeon?"

Louis paused, shaking his head. "We'll come back for them."

"You couldn't free them?" Narcisse tried unsuccessfully to hide his outrage. No one deserved to remain in her dungeon.

"Salvatore's cell was open. I don't know why, so don't give me that look." Louis ran a hand through his hair. "It was as if she wanted us to get him out, just so she could lock him back up again. But the keys to the other cells are missing. I looked everywhere for them. . . but I think she has them."

Narcisse swore, tipping his head back to the sky, if only to say *why me?*

"Get the doctor out of here," Narcisse said, giving it no second thought. "I'll deal with the witch and release the prisoners."

"In that case, I'll deal with the guards," the mayor said, leaving Narcisse to face her alone once more.

"Don't hurt the guards," Narcisse demanded.

The mayor's brows knitted. "And why not? They attacked us and almost killed a few."

"They're not in their right minds; they're prisoners just the same and are being controlled by her magic."

The mayor looked as though he didn't believe him. He scoffed, "Who are they, then? They aren't the reported missing villagers, and I haven't seen any of them before." The mayor looked at the other men uneasily, as if looking for them to confirm as much.

"If she is telling the truth, then some are our previous rulers," Narcisse said. "The King, the Queen, and their son. Some it seems, are just poor souls who asked the sorceress for help."

"The King?" The mayor frowned, his eyes far away in thought. "I had heard of our royalty going missing, a very long time ago, but I thought it was just a story."

"They're trapped in her magic, forced to be her slaves while their brains are awake and aware of it all."

"How unfortunate." The mayor stared into the darkened halls. "But if that's proven to be true it means they are still the rightful rulers."

Was that underlining disappointment that he would no longer be mayor Narcisse could hear in his words. "How do we break the spell she has trapped them in?"

The mayor hesitated. "We kill her. If we kill her the magic will fall."

"How do you know it will work? What if we kill her and the prisoners are left trapped inside themselves?"

"It has to work." But he didn't seem so confident.

"But what if it doesn't? How do you know?"

"I don't. It is a hunch."

Narcisse swore, throwing his arms up. He turned away, closing his eyes to gather himself.

"We have the doctor, maybe we should just leave," Louis piped up.

"That is not wise the mayor growled. "We've taken Salvatore, angering her. She'll come after the whole town if we don't deal with her now."

Louis was jittery, his hands balled at his side. Narcisse knew he didn't want to run; his friend was just as afraid as everyone else. "Okay," he said, more to himself. "Okay."

"How many men do we have left?" Narcisse asked.

The mayor thrust a hand through his hair. "Three."

"Three! Where have they all gone?"

"I sent them to stand guard while we retrieved the doctor, to ensure the witch didn't escape."

"And what of us?" Narcisse frowned. "Do you not plan for us to get out of here alive?"

The mayor rubbed at the stubble lining his jaw, his fear and weariness weighing on him. "Surely five of us will be enough to overpower her?" But the mayor didn't seem so sure.

"Perhaps we haven't seen the extent of her magi—"

Loud, harrowing yells sounded from somewhere deep inside the castle. The clang of weapons followed, and Narcisse didn't let himself think before he ran toward it, Louis and the mayor following close behind He tracked the screams and grunts until he was in a large open room, darkened by the lack of candles. The remainder of their men, a whole three of them, stood in the foyer, their weapons raised before them. Their shoulders rose and fell in harsh breaths, blood covering their faces.

On the other side of the room stood a large group of men, clad in black leather and holding swords. Their eyes glowed eerily in the darkness. Narcisse's entrance distracted them only for a moment, before they raised their weapons again, ready to face the villagers.

"They're strong!" a burly villager yelled, his hands tightening on his pitchfork.

Narcisse's eyes narrowed as he looked back over the guards. Beneath the blood and sweat he could smell something strange, yet familiar. His nostrils flared as he tried to place the scent in his memories.

"The salve," the mayor gasped. "I would recognize the smell anywhere."

Narcisse raised his brows. Sure enough, he could smell the salve used to heal his wounds. "But why would they use it?"

"They haven't used it, but the magic flowing through them is one in the same. It makes them stronger." The sorceress appeared in a blackened doorway, only to grin and disappear once more. The door slammed closed behind her, the sound of a lock falling into place filling the quiet room.

"You take care of them!" Narcisse yelled. "I'll go after the witch."

The mayor simply nodded.

"Try not to kill them," Narcisse reiterated as the mayor lifted his gun once more.

The look of contempt the mayor shot Narcisse was pointed enough to kill. Narcisse didn't bother trying the handle, instead pulling his hunting dagger from its holster, and jamming it in the lock. The lock gave way with a soft click, the door swinging open before him.

Candles ignited as he stepped through, lighting the room up in a warm orange. He held his knife out in front of him as his eyes adjusted, expecting to find the enchantress. But she wasn't there. Narcisse found himself inside a utility room, filled with dried food and cleaning equipment.

Another door sat on the other side of the small room, hidden deep in shadow. As he stepped toward it, the door he had come through shut behind him with a loud bang. He swore under his breath, just as the door before him swung open.

Narcisse pulled his rifle from his back, again expecting someone to rush toward him as he entered the next room.

"I knew you'd come after me," the sorceress chuckled.

But there was no one in the room. He paused in the doorway, scanning the narrow hall for traps. The room was empty, save for a single narrow staircase that went to the level above. *A servant staircase.* Reason insisted he turn around, rather than rush through a darkened castle after a witch. But he swallowed his fear and glared at the end of the hall.

He thought of his wife and all he had to lose as he ran up the stairs, ignoring the fear in his head, crying for him to turn around and run the other way.

"It's strange, though," the sorceress continued to speak, her voice carried to Narcisse on an invisible wind. "Out of all the townsfolk, I hadn't expected you to care at all."

"Why wouldn't I care?" he said into the darkness.

"You are *Narcisse*. Your name is the talk of the town and has been for years. You are rude. . .narcissistic. A brute of a man who thinks of only yourself."

Narcisse's foot slipped on the stairs as her words struck true. He grabbed onto the handrail, the stairs swaying beneath him. *How could someone who hadn't even met me judge me so unfairly? It seems that everyone had misjudged me.?*

The sorceress' words continued to echo around him, but Narcisse was no longer listening. He stomped up the stairs at a run, almost falling to the floor as the stairs abruptly stopped and the ground evened out. He collected himself, then ran down another hall.

"What do you plan to do when you find me?" The enchantress' voice became soft, brushing against his skin.

Narcisse turned a sharp corner, finding himself in another narrow hallway. There was a small light down the end, haloing yet another set of stairs. As he walked toward it, the candles that hung along the walls ignited one at a time, lighting his way until he reached the bottom of the staircase.

All had gone silent. The enchantress' voice no longer called to him, and dread turned his blood to lead as he considered whatever that meant. *Am I going the wrong way?* The further he climbed, the harder his heart pounded in his ears.

A large wooden door framed in black iron waited at the top of the stairs. Narcisse paused before it, his hand outstretched. *This is a trap.* He knew it was a trap, could taste it, but he pushed the door open anyway.

As he stepped through the door, cold wind hit him square in the face like an anvil and he took an involuntary step back. Before him was the open night sky, the stars hidden by dark ominous clouds. He stood on the roof of the castle.

"There you are," The enchantress' skin glowed in the moonlight as she cackled wickedly at him from across the roof. "We've been waiting for you."

The door slammed shut behind him just as his eyes found the figure slumped at the witch's feet. It was Bell.

Chapter Sixteen

NARCISSE'S WHOLE WORLD FELT as though it was crumbling around him. The feeling of invisible walls closing in sucked all the air from his lungs and caused him to sway dangerously on his feet. His wife was lying prone on her side on the cold roof, her face contorted in pain or fear he couldn't tell.

"B-Bell?" he cried, his voice cracking as he lunged at her.

"I don't think so," the enchantress chuckled, holding up her hand. She grinned widely, her teeth snapping as she spoke, much like the wolves that had attacked him all that time ago. "She can't hear you."

Narcisse growled, edging forward, his gaze flicking between the witch and his recumbent wife. "What have you done to her?"

The enchantress tutted, waggling a finger at him. "Nothing that can't be undone—unless you keep moving forward, that is."

Narcisse stopped short, still a lifetime away from reaching Bell. "If you have done nothing, why is she not moving?" he hissed, seeing nothing but his wife, lying prone before the witch.

The enchantress said nothing, her eyes sparking with amusement as she watched Narcisse squirm. Shadows played in her hands, twisted through her hair, only seeming to grow and reach toward Bell the longer he stared.

"No!" he cried, attempting to lunge again.

"Uh, uh, uh," the enchantress grinned, pulling in her shadows only slightly. "Come any closer and see what my shadows can really do."

"What have you done to her?!" he bellowed once more. Tears formed in his eyes, but he blinked them away, furious at himself for showing any sign of weakness.

"There is no spell on her, if that is what worries you," the enchantress chuckled. "She is simply unconscious."

Narcisse narrowed his eyes, both relieved and enraged. *How* dare *she put her hands on my wife!* His hands twitched at his sides as he fought the urge to attack the hag. She stood over Bell, her face a twisted mask of contempt, marring any beauty she had.

"What do you want?" Narcisse's eyes didn't leave Bell as white-hot anger seared through him.

"For you to pay!" she spat. "For you *all* to pay!"

"I have money, I can pay you if that is what you want," he snarled, snapping his head to the enchantress.

The sorceress chortled, a hollow noise, her eyes flashing. "I don't want your *money*. I want you to pay with your lives. And you will. Starting with this one."

"Please, no," he gasped, stumbling towards his wife. Had Narcisse made the wrong decision to come here? He hadn't expected to pull Bell into this mess with him. She was meant to be home with her father, safe from all of this. "Why did you go after Bell? She has nothing to do with this!"

"I did not drag her here, you fool. She came after *you*. Your sweet wife arrived not long after you and your fellow heathens did."

"No," Narcisse whispered. He had asked her to stay home. Her father was meant to keep her there so she'd be safe. *Why did you come after me?*

"Oh, but she did!" The enchantress seemed to find some sort of amusement from the utter fear he felt for his wife. "With no care for their lives, she came inside holding a tiny knife as if *that* could stop me."

Narcisse's ears pricked. *Their?* "Where is her father?" *There is no way she would have been able to convince him to let her go. Surely she sneaked off without him ever knowing she'd left.*

The witch confirmed as much. "She did not come with a man, but rather, a babe."

Narcisse frowned, his brows knitting. "A babe?"

"Yes, it seems congratulations are in order!" she clapped once, mockingly. "A pity you won't live long enough to see your bundle of joy born."

An overwhelming buzzing began in the back of Narcisse's head, his eyes struggling to focus. He'd had no idea. Had Bell known? Would she be just as surprised as he was? "Please," he whispered again. "Please let her go."

"You had your chance to leave. In fact, I warned you all before you came after me. I gave you *many* chances to leave this alone. To leave *me* alone. You and half the town decided to come here and challenge me. I will not stand by and allow you to terrorize me and not pay the consequences."

"Terrorize *you*? We have terrorized *you*?! People came to you for help, and you willingly agreed!"

She shrugged, examining her pointed black nails, as if the conversation were boring her.

"You and your magic have terrorized *us*. You're a plague on this town, one that has to be stopped before it ruins us all."

A loud, incredulous laugh burst from her. She dropped her hand, staring down at Narcisse for having the audacity to speak. "You are unbelievable, you know that. All you humans. All you do it take, take, take, and expect to give nothing in return. When a price is handed out, you act like this." She waved her hand between them. "You have become a thorn in my side, Narcisse, and it is time you are stopped. I am getting quite bored of this."

He didn't know what else to do, except plead for his wife's life. "Please, let her go."

"And why should I listen to you when no one has listened to what I want?" The enchantress crouched by Bell, stroking his wife's hair as her lips twitched in a malicious smile. Narcisse's entire body screamed to lunge at her, to get her hands off his wife. He knew if he moved though he would only make things worse.

"You said you weren't a bad person, that you can be just and merciful. Please allow her to go. I don't care what you do to me; just let her and my babe go home. *Unharmed*," he added with severity.

"You see, Narcisse. . . I have had enough of being kind and merciful when it is taken advantage of. Why must I be the only one to give, when you do not give back?"

"I'm sorry," he cried. "I'm sorry that we thought the doctor deserved better. I should have let you take him and stopped all from coming after you. I knew better, but I was thinking only of his life, instead of justice. I'm sorry."

He took a step back as the enchantress's laughter turned hysterical. Her face contorted then, transforming right before his eyes. He gasped, his hands shaking at his sides. The corners of her mouth turned upwards, lifting high on her cheeks, as pointed teeth extended from her gums and protruded past her lips.

Her voice was strained by the fangs, but amplified as she growled, "They're always sorry when their time comes. But they are sorry that they are to die, not that they have wronged me." She bent down once more, leaning over Bell, strings of saliva falling from her maw to land in his wife's skin.

"Please, *don't do this.*" Narcisse dropped to his knees. Holding his hands before him, he begged.

"Take me, do what you want to me, but don't hurt her."

"You all expect mercy, but it is all an act," she shrilled. "I am not just or merciful, however. I don't care for others, and I don't care for upholding bargains. I will take what I want when I want it."

"But you said—"

The wind picked up, whipping her hair around her face. She bared her pointed teeth at Narcisse, saliva foaming at the corners of her mouth. "I tried to be dignified, but it is a front. I do it so that I can stay here, and nothing like *this*," she motioned between them, "happens. But alas, here we are. It has happened anyway." She ran a hand over Bell's hair. "So why act merciful and kind for the sake of a reputation, so I am left alone, if it was going to come to this?"

"Please!" Narcisse didn't know what to say, what to do - he would do anything to keep her from harming his wife.

"*Please, please, please!*" the sorceress mimicked, before lashing out, kicking Bell in the chin. An audible crack sounded as her foot connected, the sickening sound echoing in the open expanse.

The sound was truly nauseating. Narcisse held a hand to his mouth, swallowing the bile rising in his throat. "Don't touch her! Don't you *dare* touch her, or I'll—"

"You'll what? Bore me to death?" The enchantress held her hand over her elongated mouth in a mock yawn.

He gave little warning as he pulled his rifle from his back and fired. The crack of the firing bullet filled the air as the whoosh of rustling skirts surrounded him. For a moment, they were face to face as she evaded his shot. He scrambled for another bullet in his breast pocket as she disappeared from the roof into the darkness beyond. Narcisse didn't know where she had gone, didn't care. He threw himself at his wife, his hands examining her body. "Bell?" He shook her gently, eliciting a small groan from her bloodied lips. "My dear sweet Bell, please wake up."

Bell's eyelids fluttered, but her eyes didn't open. "Narcisse," she rasped. She remained slumped on the ground, her lips parting in unconsciousness once more.

"She will wake to your own lifeless body," the sorceress leered, appearing from the shadows once more. "She will find you dead and will have to raise your baby alone and poor."

"No," Narcisse cried.

He barely had time to face her before a sudden gust of wind, powerful enough to send even a man as large as himself flying, knocked him to his knees. The force of the wind held such power that he could not get his feet back under him. The wind was cold as ice, and it locked around him, keeping him shackled to the spot. His heart threatened to burst as he tried in vain to stand. He couldn't bear to remain on his knees, to watch as the enchantress looked down at his wife with a terrifying hunger in her eyes. He struggled against the invisible shackles, growling as he fought to free himself. But all he could do was glower at the hag as she sauntered towards him.

"I do enjoy seeing you on your knees before me." She ran her tongue across her jagged teeth.

"Go to hell!"

"I'm sure I will when my time comes, but that is still a millennia away, I am sure." She laughed at her own wit, a hollow, mocking noise.

Narcisse realized that even if she did take his life as payment, she would be around for a long time to come and would continue to torment the village long after she took his life. *She could kill my friends, my family, all without me knowing.*

"Can't you just leave, find somewhere else to live? The town has had enough of your magic, you wretched creature."

"Hmmm. I don't think they have. They may forget me for a time, but they will continue to come to me and offer me their lives in exchange for my magic. It has happened before, and it will happen again."

"They didn't forget," Narcisse said. "At least, not everyone forgot. There are those who remembered before we discovered your lair."

"My lair," she chuckled, shaking her head. "I guess that only befits my current appearance."

Narcisse didn't wish to acknowledge her sharp teeth or the way the corners of her mouth almost stretched to her ears. *Grotesque.*

"Let Bell go, and I will let you live," he said.

Her chuckle turned into a shriek of amusement, and the wind holding him down became almost crushingly heavy. Narcisse's chest contracted, the muscles in his legs and back screaming as he tried to stay on his knees.

"You will *let* me live? How thoughtful of you!" The delight in her expression died, only to be replaced by a feral hunger he had never seen before. "I will enjoy sucking away your life bit by bit, until you are screaming for me to finish you quickly. And when I am done with you, I will murder your wife and child."

Bile rose in his throat like acid, burning a trail up his esophagus until it rested on the back of his tongue. Narcisse swallowed once, twice, but it continued to rise until his eyes watered. His voice was nothing but a rasped plea as he begged over and over again for his wife and unborn child to be spared.

The enchantress ignored his cries, scoffing at him the more he begged. "I am getting tired of this, brute." Her eyes flicked from him to the slight movement beside him.

Bell groaned; the sound laced with pain as she regained consciousness. She lifted a shaking hand to her face, rubbing at aches on her face that he could not see. "What. . .?" Bell groaned, struggling to sit up. Fear flashed in her eyes, finding the enchantress towering over her.

"Welcome to the land of the living," she chortled. "You're just in time to witness me draining the life from your husband."

"What? No!" Bell tried to stand, but her legs trembled as she struggled to find her footing. "You can't do that to him."

"I can't, is that so? Just watch me!" Her words reached Narcisse as if they were spoken under water, obscured by the invisible wind that continued to hold him in place.

"Please, don't!" Bell found her footing though she shook uncontrollably, and she faced the witch. She held her hands before her, as if she could stop her.

The wall of wind closed around Narcisse, suffocating him. He couldn't move, nor could he scream for his wife to stop, to run, to do anything but what she was about to do.

He watched in fear as his wife lunged at the hag, her hands going for her hair. The sorceress shrieked in surprise, but his small, enfeebled wife wasn't nearly strong enough to stop her. She was thrown to the ground as though she weighed as little as a sack of potatoes, and he could see, rather than hear, her head hit the stone floor.

"Stop!" he tried to scream, but the air rushed down his throat the moment he opened his mouth and tore the words straight from him. The air thickened, stealing his very breath. His eyes watered as he tried in vain to steal even the slightest of breaths so that he could stay conscious for Bell.

Cold pricks needled his skin as the sorceress knocked Bell to the ground again, never even giving her a chance to stand. Bell groaned, annoyance laced with pain clear on her face as the witch leaned over her, not giving her any leverage to get onto her feet.

"Let him go!" Her lips formed the demand, but he could not hear her.

The enchantress bared her teeth in a snarl he could feel down to his bones, spittle flying between her jagged teeth. The movement was distraction enough for her to relax her wind, enough for him to catch his breath and hear the world around him again, although very faintly.

Narcisse blinked at his wife, her voice reaching his ears through the onslaught of wind. "Fine," she yelled. "You leave me no choice."

"Ha!" the sorceress sneered. "What do you plan to do, imp? Your strength is merely a drop compared to my mag — ahhhh!" She darted away from Bell, her hand held to her stomach in pain.

There, in his wife's hand, was a small dagger. She had buried it into the hag's stomach, right to the hilt, where he had stabbed her previously. Narcisse didn't know whether it was the pain or surprise, but it was enough for her to let her guard down. The magical wind that held him in a vice-like grip suddenly disappeared. The world rushed at him as he fell to the ground, dust around him.

He sucked in air hungrily, chasing away the shadows that had begun to blur his vision. The world swayed around him as he stood on shaky legs, turning to face the enchantress.

"You will pay for this! I will rip that babe right from you!"

She stalked toward Bell, her pointed teeth dripping with tar-like saliva. His wife backed up, grimacing in pain with each step she took away from the witch. With a hiss of contempt, she rushed at Bell, her taloned hand held before her in a claw-like motion.

No. No. No. "NO!" Narcisse roared at the hag. With no time to think, he rushed at her, colliding with her like a battering ram. The witch screamed again, and she dug her nails into his forearms, trying to break free of his grip. Narcisse held on to her like a vice, ignoring the magic whipping at him and her talons scratching at his skin. He held her through the pain, as he tumbled over the side of the castle with the sorceress in his arms.

Chapter Seventeen

THE ENCHANTRESS DIDN'T SCREAM.

She did, however, claw at his face, screeching as they tumbled through air. Narcisse fought to keep her in his arms, holding her tight against his chest, to keep her from using her cursed magic to escape.

But it was all in vain.

Her torn dress was balled in his fists as he held her, and the next moment his hands were empty. She was gone, and he was falling. Narcisse had no time to scream his frustration or horror as the wind tore at his face.

"*Oof*". Pain lanced through him as he met the slant of the roofing below. First his face, then his arms. He began sliding down the sloped roof toward the hard ground that mocked him below. The shingles were rough and dirty, and caught on his clothes and exposed skin.

With all the will he could muster, his hands dug into the roof, his nails bending back as he tried to find purchase. He swore under his breath when he went over the side of the roof, his trembling hands gathering enough strength to keep him from falling any further. The force of the tumble caused him to swing wildly into the grey stone castle wall, his knees taking much of the brunt. His hands tore on the shingles, but he held on.

As he struggled to hold on, he swore he saw a flash of fabric in the darkness, careening past him into the void of the night.

"Narcisse!" came a shriek from above him.

Narcisse squinted up at his wife, dots blurring his vision. She leaned over the side of the roof, and he thought her eyes welling with tears. His heart was in his throat, his hands were on fire, and his knees and shoulders ached. But he was alive. For now. *I have to get myself back up there.*

"Hold on! I'm coming down." Bell cried out, her voice raw with emotion.

"No! Stay there," he coughed, straining to hold himself up But it was too late; she was already vanished from sight, whisked off into the night.

Would it be easier for him to let go and fall to his death? It seemed a much better solution than Bell risking her life once again for him. It also seemed a better alternative than the pain he was currently experiencing. He stared down at the ground, all those levels below, and he teetered closer without meaning to.

If he weren't holding on for dear life he would have shrugged. "Why not just give up? I can't face the witch again," he whispered to himself pathetically.

"Don't be silly," a voice scoffed in the darkness. Narcisse flinched as Louis' head poked over the side wall where Bell had only just been. He hadn't expected anyone to answer him. "She's gone."

Narcisse's arms screamed at him, his fingers threatening to slip with each breath. His voice quivered with exertion as he asked, "She fled?" He had expected her to kill them all before even thinking about leaving.

"Not gone as in *fled*. Gone as in *dead*." Louis grinned down at him, evidently delighted with his singsong rhyme as he threw a rope over the ledge. "You did it."

I did it? I killed the witch?

He couldn't believe it. Stunned, Narcisse stared at the rope that hung by his face. He was sure he had no strength left; definitely not enough to pull himself up. Louis seemed to have read his mind. "I've knotted a loop on the end, try to link your arm through it and we'll pull you up."

I can't do it. He looked to the side of the roof, movement catching his eye. Bell leaned over the lowest part of the barrier, seeming to assess if she could jump down. He panicked at the thought, knowing she would do it without hesitation. *I have to get up.* If Narcisse waited too long, then he and his wife and his small unborn child would fall to their deaths together. He had to climb back up. For her.

The rope was coarse against his face as it whipped at him in the wind. *Fine.* He bared his teeth, grunting loudly as he released the roof with one hand. The muscles in his other arm pulled so taut that he was sure his tendons would snap. His elbow locked from his weight. Narcisse could feel his fingers slipping from the shingles, one by one. The sweat that coated his hand became a lubricant and he could do nothing as he slipped ever so slowly from the roof.

"Grab hold!" Louis yelled.

He was still grunting— or screaming, he wasn't sure— as he flung out his free hand and lunged at the rope. His fingers slid from the shingles, and he fell a short distance, until the rope snapped tight and repelled him into the side of the castle once more. His shoulder bone cracked from the impact, and he was swung back out to hang precariously in thin air.

"Pull me up!" Narcisse yelled, the ground below taunting him.

"Pull him up!" Louis echoed.

Finally the ground grew further and further away as he was pulled back up the side of the castle. He could hear the rope fray slightly as it slid over the shingles, ever teasing the possibility of it snapping. But it didn't break.

Suddenly there were strong hands on his arms, tugging him up and over the side of the roof and back onto solid ground. He sucked in air through his teeth when his body finally hit the cold stone of the upper roof level. He was safe. He wouldn't be falling to his death as he had been imagining the past few minutes.

Minutes? It felt as though he had been dangling over the side of the castle for an eternity, rather than minutes. His head swam as he rested against the soothing chill of the stonework,

"Narcisse!" Bell was at his side in an instant, her hands running over his face, his hair, his arms, assessing him for any further damage. His shoulder ached, his knees throbbed, and his hands felt like he had peeled the skin from his bones, but he was whole, and he was alive.

"Bluebell," he whispered, pulling his wife onto the ground with him, refusing to let go. He stroked her hair, feeling her fluttering heartbeat against his own. "My Bluebell."

"I can't believe you did it," Louis murmured as he stood over the pair, blinking in wonderment at his friend.

"And you were going to sacrifice your life to rid us of that evil." The mayor crouched down and slapped Narcisse on his shoulder, gesturing for him to stand.

Gingerly, Bell slid from Narcisse, climbing to her feet as Louis and the mayor pulled him up. Red hot anger bubbled within him at the sight of a bruise beginning to form on Bell's chin. He took a tenuous step towards her, but she waved him off with a slight smile. As if to say; *I'm okay, don't worry about it.* He made to ask her if she was sure when the mayor spoke, interrupting him before he got a single word out.

"You would have given up everything to ensure the safety of our village. For that I commend you." Narcisse rubbed the back of his neck, his cheeks heating slightly as he watched Bell nod in agreement with the mayor. Only her thoughts mattered to him now.

"It was nothing."

"Don't be daft, you saved us all." The mayor snorted, as if he couldn't believe Narcisse could be modest.

"And you're sure she's dead?" Narcisse asked. He thought of the way she'd stood over his wife, goosebumps breaking out over his flesh. "You have found a body?"

"What's left of her body," Louis gagged, covering his mouth. "I saw her fall on my way back in, and it was enough to turn my stomach."

Louis and the mayor spoke over one another as they continued to talk at Narcisse. He heard nothing, though, his mind miles away. His feet moved without thought, taking him right back to the roof edge. He leaned on the side of the small fence surrounding the roof and looked down. The ground warped again, as if his fall had suddenly made him afraid of heights. Narcisse tried to ignore his desire to step back, instead searching the area below for the enchantress.

There.

Even in the darkness, with the smattering of torches around him and the starlight above, he could see that Louis was right. What was left of her, indeed. He shivered. At the base of the castle, right by the front entry was a crimson splatter, and in the center lay a disfigured body. He couldn't make out details from this high up, but he could see that she was broken, and could never be pieced back together again.

Bile rose in the back of his throat, causing his eyes to water. He blinked furiously to clear them, but the world continued to blur and all he could do was rush backwards, falling onto his rear. Narcisse pulled his knees to his chest, ignoring the aches of his body, gulping down air as Bell appeared at his side.

"It's okay," she crooned. "You're okay. You never have to see her again. Someone else will deal with it."

She held his head against her chest, gently stroking him. He closed his eyes and leaned against her. He would never see her body, none of them had to. It served no purpose —

He started, interrupting his own thoughts. They did have to go to her still. Trepidation raced down his spine at the idea of touching her corpse. Bell pulled back, kneeling so they were eye to eye. "What is it, Narcisse?"

"The key," he gulped, shaking his head.

Bell held his face in her hands, searching his eyes. "What key?"

"The key to free the other prisoners. It was on her body."

The mayor swore loudly behind him. He turned to see him storm back inside of castle.

"Do you think he'll search for it himself?" Louis stared after him.

"He will no doubt find someone else to do it for him," Bell frowned. "And for once, I cannot say I blame the man."

Narcisse stumbled to his feet in a flurry of motion, almost knocking Bell to the ground in the process. "I should do it."

"No, Narcisse, don't be silly. You should rest!"

But he ignored her, ignored the pain in his knees and the way the ground swayed under his feet. "I did this, I should find the key."

He didn't stop to see if Bell or Louis followed as he rushed down the stairs, disregarding the pain that hugged him. His whole body shook as the darkness enveloped him.

He shook his head to clear the shadows. He trailed down the stairs, keeping an unsteady hand to the wall as he felt his way to the bottom. *Just regular shadows.*

"Mayor!" Narcisse called after him.

"Yes?"

Narcisse almost ran into him as he emerged in the front entry of the castle. The room was abuzz with villagers who had newly arrived to assist with the witch. Her body had not gone unnoticed, it seemed.

"I should do it," Narcisse said as the murmurs quieted, and they turned towards him. "I will look for the key."

The mayor looked Narcisse over, his eyes stopping at his raw hands. Could he see the way his body trembled, or the way his heart pounded? "No, I think you have done enough. I will find someone else to do it."

The mayor took a single step before someone moved forward. "Why don't you do it, then?" the man said, his eyes sharp and demanding as all heads turned their way.

"Excuse me?" the mayor glowered.

"You seem quick to have others do the dirty work, but you are yet to volunteer yourself." The man stepped closer to them, and that was when Narcisse realized who he was.

The mayor hadn't worked it out yet, his eyes full of anger as the villagers grunted in agreement. "How dare you?" he spat.

"Mayor," Narcisse hissed.

"Who do you think you are?"

Narcisse ignored the pain in his hand as he grabbed a hold of the mayor's jacket. "*Mayor*!" Narcisse growled softly. If only he could get the dunce to shut up.

"*What*?!" he barked. "Fine, if you wish to do it, suit yourself."

Narcisse's eyes bore into the mayor's, trying to convey his thoughts to the mayor before he spoke again. *But how do I address the man who stood before us*? Narcisse pondered it.

"Your Majesty, I am delighted to see that killing the enchantress has freed you from her spell."

The mayor started, taking an involuntary step back.

"As am I," the prince said. "I was fearful, but I had hoped."

"You were trapped in your body for all these years?" Bell breathed, appearing beside them.

"Yes. For many, many years, I watched the world move forward without me. We—" he gestured to a man and woman who stood amongst the townspeople, "—have been here, made to watch, to help, the enchantress harm others for all this time, and there was nothing we could do about it."

Bell sighed through her nose. "That sounds dreadful. To want to help, but being unable to must have been hard. To witness all that she has done. . . to see her taking advantage and not being able to warn people away. I am sorry you had to endure that."

The prince nodded, his eyes full of a darkness and sadness that Narcisse wished to never experience himself. "Thank you," he said to Narcisse, grabbing a hold of his hand and squeezing gently, unaware of the sting it caused. "Thank you, for all that you have done. Not only have you killed the beast, but you have freed my parents from this torture. You have freed me."

Narcisse nodded in return, unsure of what to say. Killing the witch the way he had was a fluke. He hadn't expected it to work. He'd expected her to push away at that last moment. Plan B was to stab her just as Bell had, which would have saved him all the pain he was now enduring. He wasn't sure if he had caught her off guard, or whether it was the threat to his wife's and unborn child's life that had given him the added bit of strength he needed. Whatever it was, he was grateful, nonetheless.

"Adam." A woman in her mid-forties hurried over to the prince, her hand resting on his shoulder.

"This is my mother," he said, smiling lovingly at the older woman.

"We thank you," the queen said, her eyes glistening with unshed tears. "Thank you so very much."

Narcisse's chest tightened as she stepped forward and flung her arms over his shoulders. When she stepped back the tears had finally fallen. His own eyes welled in response, for the way she looked at him, her eyes full of such kindness and love, was something he hadn't seen since his own mother.

"I did what I had to do," he said, lifting a shoulder, an attempt to be nonchalant.

"No, you didn't have to do any of it. You could have gone on living, knowing there were people trapped here, knowing that the enchantress would keep taking people for her own cruel and vain reasons. But you didn't. You risked your life to save us all."

"We all did," Narcisse smiled softly, pulling Louis to his side, Bell to the other.

"Indeed," the queen said. "because of your diligent bravery and selflessness, my son, Prince Adam, will reward you greatly." She walked back toward her husband and Narcisse heard her tell him, "We have some restoration to do."

"Wait," the mayor sputtered. "This surely doesn't mean you will resume rule?" He stared at Prince Adam, his mouth hanging open.

"Yes," Prince Adam said. "We will resume our rule. We will pick up where we left off, ruling the surrounding towns and villages just as our family has done for hundreds of years."

"But-but it has been so long, surely you don't expect the villagers to accept you as rulers when they are so used to having none."

"Having none?" Louis said under his breath. "He's so used to the town falling to their knees for him that he can't imagine giving that up."

"I have put so much into this town the past few years; I can't be thrown away like I am nothing." The mayor snipped.

The prince was quiet for some time and Narcisse expected to see him have the mayor thrown away for being so bold, but instead he smiled slightly. "You did a marvelous job, I can see. We thank you for that. Your skills and hard work won't be forgotten. You will be rewarded generously for your time in office. Does that sound sufficient to you?"

"Oh, I, ah. . . yes, that will be quite alright. I thank you." He bowed, backing away.

"And your reward will also be large," Prince Adam said to Narcisse and Louis. "Do you have any requests?"

Louis's eyes bugged. "Anything you deem appropriate would be wonderful, thank you Your Majesty."

"And you. Narcisse, was it?"

Narcisse smiled sweetly at his wife, his eyes softening as he remembered that she was carrying his child. "I wish for nothing but to go home with my wife and forget any of this ever happened."

Bell slid her hand into his, squeezing tightly. *Did she know? If she didn't, did she hear what the sorceress had said? What if the sorceress was lying to get to me?*

"But first, I must search the enchantress's remains for the key so that I can free those who remain locked up." Narcisse made to walk outside, but to his surprise it was the prince who grabbed a hold of his arm to stop his progression.

"There is no need," Adam said. "I had someone free them the moment we awoke from our daze. They are free and resting in the infirmary."

"You have medical staff here?" Bell asked.

"Oh, yes. All of our former staff are here. They were under the same enchantment as us. They too were awoken when the enchantress was killed and are already performing their previous jobs."

Narcisse couldn't imagine being trapped in his own head for all those years just to be freed and to have to go back to being a cook or a maid. Perhaps they enjoyed their jobs enough to return, no questions asked.

"You have done more than enough, Narcisse. Your bravery has saved us, and so all I ask of you now is to take your beautiful wife home and rest."

Narcisse nodded his thanks, sighing in relief. He was alive, his wife and babe were safe, and he was free to leave and never deal with such horrors again.

"Goodbye, Narcisse," Prince Adam waved. "I will call upon you in the coming days to bestow on you your rewards."

Narcisse could do nothing but nod once more. He remained silent as he tightened his grip on Bell's hand and walked with her out of the castle. He ignored the cheers and shouts of those he past. Hand in hand, he and his wife walked through the castle grounds, departing through the front gate. They began the short journey by way of the woods.

To home.

Chapter Eighteen

S *EVEN MONTHS LATER ~*

Narcisse had never felt such fear.

After all he had been through the last year, he had never expected to feel so afraid again, and yet this was worse. It was a strange feeling, to be fearful over something so exciting. But it was a life changing moment – life changing for both him and his wife – and that was what terrified him so much.

It was in the very early hours of the morning when Narcisse was woken by Bluebell shrieking beside him. Her water had broken, soaking the whole bed, and the pain started soon thereafter. Bell was able to remain calm, despite the obvious agony, but Narcisse felt like he was losing his mind.

"What do I do?" he cried, rushing to Bell's side as she stood from the bed and frowned down at the dampness she had left.

"Fetch the doctor," she panted, pulling off her nightgown and wrapping Narcisse's robe around herself. "Get him fast." She doubled over, using the bed to hold herself up.

Narcisse rushed from the house, fumbling with his boots as he shut the front door and dashed off into the dark morning. He found Doctor Salvatore at his house. Despite rousing him, it had taken Narcisse several shakes of the older man's shoulders to convey what was happening.

"When did her waters break?" he asked Narcisse through a stifled yawn, rubbing at his sleep-creased eyes.

"I don't know — not long now. I rushed to dress before coming for you."

The doctor nodded slowly but didn't seem at all ready to rush back to the house with Narcisse. "If her waters have only just broken, then it'll still be some hours before the babe arrives."

"How can you know?" A cold sweat had covered Narcisse, and he fought a sudden rising panic — what if the baby had in fact arrived while he was gone?

Doctor Salvatore narrowed his eyes. "I have delivered countless babes over my time as a physician. I think I can say I am more than qualified and experienced to advise you in the manner. I suggest you fetch the girl's father so that he may be present for the ordeal, and I will prepare and meet you within the hour."

Within the hour. "And what should we do for the hour while we wait?" Narcisse ground out, fists clenched. An *hour!*

"Just keep her comfortable and preoccupied so that she may forget the pain." The doctor paused for a moment, a single brow raised. "You seem a bit green, are you sure you're able to do that?"

"Yes. Yes, of course. I can do it."

"Go now. You don't want to leave her alone during this."

Narcisse nodded, more to clear his head than in actual agreement. He rushed from Salvatore's, running up the muddied path and right to Jacques's front door. He could feel the dried mud crunch under his boots as he pounded on the front door so hard he expected the old man to open the door with a pistol.

"Who's there!" Jacques yelled from behind the door.

Narcisse squinted through the glass window, just making out the outline of his father-in-law and the small candle he held in his hands.

"It's me, Narcisse!"

Jacques swung the door open, peering out to see if it truly was his son-in-law. His brows furrowed slightly as he said, "Is everything okay?"

"Bell is in labor." His throat tightened as the words tumbled out. "I thought you would like to be there."

"Bell is in labor?" Jacques's fingers tightened on the door, but he didn't move. "She's in labor," he repeated, eyes glazed over.

"Yes!" Narcisse growled. "And I would like to be there for her, so if you'd please *hurry up.*"

As if it just registered, Jacques' head snapped up, a fire lit in his eyes. "What are we waiting for?" He almost knocked Narcisse from his feet as he rushed outside. Pivoting, Narcisse raced after his father-in-law into the dim light of the dawn, towards home. Towards Bell.

It surprised him to find that he struggled to keep up with Jacques. Narcisse was eager to return to his wife's side, but he was slow and awkward over the muddy ground. His father-in-law on the other hand acted as if he was simply running through a field. There was an urgency to the way he ran, to the way he looked over his shoulder at Narcisse, to ensure he was keeping up. Narcisse's heart constricted at the terror that shone in his father-in-law's eyes. He was afraid, just as Narcisse was. But this was a different fear altogether. That was when it struck him. Jacques was scared that he would lose his only child, afraid that she would join mother. He was afraid she would die during childbirth. That brought a new sense of dread, hitting him square in the chest as if someone had chucked a rock at him.

When he spied the candlelight coming from his windows in the distance he sped up, his feet navigating over the familiar terrain like it was nothing. He beat Jacques to the door and rushed inside, wanting to get to Bell's side before him. *How petty of me.* Narcisse flinched slightly as he fell to his knees beside Bell. She had come out to the living room, and was now doubled over on the sitting chair, her hands gripping the arm rests.

"Bluebell, love, are you okay?" Narcisse brushed back the hair on her face with a shaking hand. "I'm sorry I was gone so long, but I brought your father."

When Bell's eyes met his, they were full of pain, but behind that pain there was a love that shone that she seemed to hold only for him, no matter the situation. "And the doctor?" she panted.

"He will be here within the hour."

"Within the *hour*?" she snapped as a shudder of pain gripped her.

Jacques had come inside, shutting the door behind him. He glared at Narcisse, as if chastising him for acting like such a child, racing inside to beat him to his daughter.

"Yes, he said the babe will not be here for some hours yet. He was getting his medical equipment together then coming."

"*Hours*!" Bell's eyes were wide with fear, hands tightening on the arms of the chair as she moaned. "I don't know if I can put up with the pain for hours."

"You can do it just fine," Jacques said, crouching by the chair and taking his daughter's hand. "You are strong, just as your mother was, and you can get through this."

A single tear fell from Bell's eyes, balancing on her lashes. Narcisse caught it before it began its trail down her cheek, and then rested his palm against her face.

"Think of what happens after all this pain." He stroked his thumb against her temple. "Imagine our small son in your arms."

Bell laughed slightly, her face contorted with amusement and pain. "A son," she grinned. "No daughters for Narcisse."

Narcisse couldn't help but laugh with her. "There is no way we are having a daughter — not with my strong genes." He waggled his brows.

His wife's wane smile vanished her face contorted with agony as she doubled over. Her arms went to her stomach, and she cried out, gritting her teeth. Narcisse felt useless then. He could do nothing but watch his wife as she screamed.

His eyes welled, but he blinked the tears away. He needed to be strong for his wife. With a shaking, clammy hand, he rubbed circles over her back, murmuring into her ear.

"You're doing great," he said. "You are the strongest woman I know, and you are going to be fine."

There was a loud knock at the door just as she screamed in pain once more. It was Jacques who got up to answer it, leaving Narcisse to stay at his wife's side.

"Doctor Salvatore, thank God you're here." Jacques led the doctor through the kitchen and back into the living room. "She is in a lot of pain; we weren't sure you'd get here in time."

"How far apart are the contractions?" the doctor asked as he dropped his bag onto the side table.

"The *what*?" the other two men asked in unison, glancing at one another in confusion.

"When she screams in pain— how far apart are her screams?"

Narcisse hadn't thought to time them. Was he *meant* to time them? "More than seven minutes, I think?" he answered.

"Good. It is not time yet." He surveyed the room, frowning at what he seemed to find there. "Bell, dear, let's get you to your bed and make you will more comfortable."

"But the bed is wet," she cried, averting her eyes.

"I'll lay down some fresh blankets." Narcisse didn't wait before rushing to do it, feeling like he needed to busy himself. He had just spread out the last blanket when Doctor Salvatore and Jacques helped Bell onto the bed.

"What should we do now?" he asked.

The doctor held his hand against Bell's forehead. "Bring me a bowl of water and some towels."

Narcisse made fast work of this request, not wanting to leave Bell's side for even a minute. Once he had handed the items to the doctor, he stretched out on the bed beside his wife, his hand resting on her stomach.

He waited beside her for hours, growing more impatient as time went on. He felt useless, like he could do nothing at all to help. But his presence beside Bell seemed to ease her slightly, and he murmured his encouragement into her ear so that the other two in the room would not hear.

"How long?" she cried after some time. It was the first time she had spoken in a while, the only noises she had made mostly screams and cries of pain. "I don't think I can handle much more if this."

Salvatore lifted the sheet they had laid across her legs and disappeared underneath for a moment.

"Jacques," he said when he rose again. "If you would please wait outside of the room."

Jacques looked as though he would protest but nodded. The next time he saw his daughter he would be a grandfather.

"Bell, it is time. Would you like Narcisse to wait outside?"

Narcisse glowered at Doctor Salvatore as his wife shook her head. "I need him with me."

"Very well. Narcisse, if you would hold this damp cloth to her head?"

Narcisse clambered from the bed, hurrying to the side of the bed closest to Bell, holding her hand in his, using the other to press a cool, damp cloth to her forehead.

Her hand was clammy, just as his was, but he held her tightly, breathing through her painful grasp.

When the doctor removed the sheet from his wife's legs, Narcisse thought he might faint. There was so much blood. *Was that normal?* His head swam as he stared. Then the real screaming began.

The fear he had felt when his wife had first gone into labor was nothing like what he felt now. The pain his wife had experienced seemed to intensify, and Narcisse felt as though he would be sick at any moment.

I take it back, he thought. *I would rather be childless than see Bell in such pain.* But as the final crescendo of screams eased and were replaced by the startled cries of a newly born babe, he knew it wasn't true. He would go through everything again if it meant experiencing such a miracle once more. And when he saw the tears of utter joy and relief that his wife shed when the baby was placed in her arms, he knew that she would do it all over again.

"Congratulations," Doctor Salvatore said. "A very healthy girl."

Narcisse's ears rang. "What did you say?"

"You have a daughter, Narcisse. A beautiful, healthy daughter." Doctor Salvatore squeezed Narcisse's shoulder before exiting the room.

"A daughter." Narcisse tested the words in his mouth. "I have a daughter."

Bell looked at up him with such pure happiness in her eyes that it floored him. He dropped to his knees beside her, his hands reaching for the small bundle. "May I?"

She looked up at him through hooded eyes as she handed over the babe. She was so small in his large arms, her head small enough to fit in his palm. "I have a daughter."

"We'll just have to try for a son in a year of two," Bell smiled.

It was a struggle to lift his eyes from the plump pink face that stared up at him. "After all that pain, you would do it again?"

"I would endure the world if it meant seeing you so in love."

Was he in love? As he stared down at his tiny daughter once more, there was a pang in his chest that he had never felt before. A new kind of love — one of adoration — flooded his entire body and he realized then that he would do anything for this baby. He would move heaven and hell for this tiny being who had only just been brought into existence.

Not only did his heart grow big enough to fit this new love — Narcisse looked up at his sweat-soaked wife and realized that he loved her more than he ever thought possible. She bore his child, birthed his child and he loved her more for that than anything she had ever done for him.

"Hattie." Narcisse blinked away his tears, looking up at his wife. "We will name her Hattie, after your mother."

THE END

Acknowledgments

FIRSTLY, I WOULD LIKE to thank my favorite person in the whole universe – my husband, Sean – for emotionally and financially supporting me while I spent time writing and procrastinating, and at times living in a depressive slump. You continue to pull me out of those dark days and keep me pursuing my dreams. I love you.

Secondly, I thank my family – particularly, my mum, Lynda – for realizing my dreams as a writer and believing in me from such a young age. Having a loving support system only fueled my dreams.

Thirdly, thank you to Joanna, Brianna, and Jen for editing Brute on such short notice. I know I threw Joanna and Brianna into the deep end, but your hard work was invaluable, and I would still be sitting on Brute now if it weren't for you.

Fourthly, Emma – my friend, critique partner, business partner, and cheerleader – thank you for reading my terrible first drafts, editing when I needed the help, and pushing me when I couldn't bring myself to work. Without you, I really wouldn't have finished my first novel during NaNoWriMo all those years ago, and I certainly wouldn't have published Brute. I can't wait to see what our writing journeys have in store for us in the coming years.

Lastly, I thank you, the reader, for picking up Brute and giving it a chance. I hope you love it as much as I loved writing it.

About the Author

L AUREN ROSE, A ROMANCE author from South Australia, resides in the suburbs with her husband and cat. She's been writing since early primary school, entertaining teachers with strange little fairytales. These days you can still find her writing strange little fairytales, as well as watching horror movies, and playing video games and RPGs. Find out more about Lauren Rose at laurenros ewriter.com

Keep up with Lauren Rose at:

Instagram

@laurenrosewriter

Facebook

@laurenrosewriter

Twitter

@lrosewriter

Goodreads

@laurenrosewriter

If you enjoyed this book, please take a few moments to write a review of it on Goodreads and Amazon.

Thank you!